SIGMA

Alpha Series Book Two

Tiya Rayne

Young Ann Publishing, LLC
Colfax, North Carolina

Tiya Rayne/Young Ann Publishing, LLC

PO BOX 365

Colfax, NC/27235

www.tiyarayne.com

Publisher's Note: This is a work of fiction. Names, characters, places, and incidents are a product of the author's imagination. Locales and public names are sometimes used for atmospheric purposes. Any resemblance to actual people, living or dead, or to businesses, companies, events, institutions, or locales is completely coincidental.

Ordering Information:

Quantity sales. Special discounts are available on quantity purchases by corporations, associations, and others. For details, contact the "Special Sales Department" at the address above.

Sigma/ Tiya Rayne. -- 1st ed.

ISBN 978-0-578-28727-0

To The Readers

Love is unconditional. Trust and Respect are not

–SOURCE UNKOWN

The Count

Sigma

"Afternoon Count." Alpha's voice comes through our main link.

I immediately stop in a mid push-up and stand to my feet. I've already passed a thousand; no need to keep going. I stretch my arms over my head, allowing my muscles to readjust and my taut skin to stretch. I hate being confined behind this small body.

Our original bodies were taller than eight feet on average; this 6' 9" frame feels like a small cage. Smaller even than the cells they hold us in when we do not conform.

I am in my hidden room on the lowest floor of the compound. The location was once used to hold Alpha. After our leader proved again that he could not be held within these small walls, they abandoned this place for a supposedly stronger prison. I now use this space as my sanctuary.

My need for solitude isn't uncommon. In my old life, the one before we were reborn here, I was a historian—the keeper of knowledge. I

1

spent many solar rotations alone inside a large tower not only studying the history of our planet but the history of others. My memories of the life before are still a little hazy. Yet, there are some things I remember without being told. Like the sweet smell of the air on my home planet, Albatraum. The flickering of lights from the capital city and the giant white castle on the hill. All these memories are easy to recall—even the view of the three moons hovering over the horizon are fresh in my mind.

"Forty-five. On unit B. West wing." Beta reports his numbers for the afternoon count.

"Twenty-eight guards on Unit C. East wing. Three in stairwell to unit B." Gamma adds to the daily report.

The link continues to flow with the afternoon body count. Our communication line is always busy. Information is constantly flowing between us to Alpha. Beta once described the link as having a radio playing in the background of your head. However, in our minds, there are a hundred radios tuned to a hundred different stations. One of the first lessons learned was how to block out the noise.

"Fifteen guards on unit A." Omega gives the count for the Breeder floor.

"Sigma, the codes for the day?" Alpha asks once all other counts have been given.

I place my hand against the wall and in seconds, I give him the answer he seeks. *"17, 55, 21, 7, 81, 36."*

The link fades to quiet as we await our next command from our leader.

"Eyes on Strong," He demands.

I once again place my hand to the wall, tracking down the electrical circuit to the cameras around the facility. I find the one I'm looking for.

"Office, unit C." I report.

"And the assistant?"

It takes me another second of searching the cameras to find Asim. *"On his way to get you."*

"How much longer before we put our plan into action?" Omega asks through the link.

This has been the critical issue since we developed the plan for our escape. We have been plotting this out to perfection since we were created from the remnants of Alpha's people. We are the clones of the men that fought alongside him on Albatraum. Dr. Strong believed he is the one that created us. He is wrong.

"In due time, Omega. In due time." Alpha replies in a brisk tone.

He is withholding information from us. We all have a feeling he knows something is about to change. Something is coming that has him in no rush to leave this place yet. I cannot imagine what would make him want to stay in this prison a second longer than we must.

"Until then, we will need to continue our prep. Beta, how's your project coming along?"

"Good. But progress has been delayed."

"And why is that?" Alpha asks. His irritation sends a chill through the link.

"I need more tools."

"Do you know where to get what you need?" Omega asks, steering what was soon to be an argument back on track.

"Utility shed on the other side of the main flight hangar. I can get what I need there, but I will need a diversion and the codes."

"I'll take care of the diversion. I'm heading to the cafeteria." Alpha says. *"Sigma, give him cover and get the codes."*

I am always in charge of the codes and providing coverage. That is my skill. Although a lot of my memory from my past life has faded, my abilities have remained. My hand brushes the cool surface of the wall. I find the doors to the shed and search the computer for the entrance code.

"78, 93, 16, 10," I call off the numbers to Beta with ease. The codes change every hour, and each floor has a different set of numbers.

"Be ready," Alpha demands.

Minutes later the commotion upstairs reaches my ears. My leader is throwing a fit to rival all fits. Using the cameras, I follow Asim's hurried footsteps to Strong's office. The doctor calls for backup, and they both run off in Alpha's direction. The moment Dr. Strong leaves his office, I get to work suppling the coverage. I cut the connection to all cameras running them on a loop.

One day, we will leave these confined walls, and I will finally be free of this prison.

CHAPTER ONE

My Downfall

Shiloh

"Welcome, gentlemen, to Castillo del pecado. Where the drinks are free, but the pussy will cost you." A loud chorus of cheers go up.

I keep my sights on Miguel, watching as he controls the room. Despite his other issues, he's very charismatic. Able to lure people to him like a moth to a shimmering web. Unfortunately, no one realizes until it's too late that he is the giant spider waiting in the center.

The music cranks up, and the ladies pour into the room like shoppers at a black Friday sale when the doors open. The women come in all different shades, sizes and from all continents. If he could make money off penguin pussy, he would have women from Antarctica too. That's why men paid top dollar to come to Castillo del pecado.

Miguel Estrava runs one of the most lucrative sex trafficking rings in the US. Every few months, he opens his doors to what he likes to call the sample night. This event usually has a waiting list a mile long.

For only one night he loan out his collection of women to the highest bidder. I am one of the women in his collection.

Not exactly what I'd dreamed of for myself when I was a little girl with hopes of a better life. However, I'm wise enough now to know that hope is just as useless as dreams in this world. Neither of the two will do you much good.

I'm in my usual spot against the wall right by the door. I learned the hard way to never leave out of Miguel's sight.

We have rules here, even though they aren't posted on the walls or given at the door. However, if you break one, you will pay severely. By now, everyone that's been here before knows the ins and outs of sample night. It's the new people I worry about.

With a Mona Lisa smile plastered on my face, I make eye contact with no one. It's another one of those understood rules. I am to be seen, but not noticed. Sounds hard to do, but I've mastered the ability over the years I've been with Miguel.

The music continues to pump through the mansion. Half-dressed women parade around, trying to lure a partner for the night. All the girls work their hardest to get the highest bid. It isn't like they see the money. No, they do it to please him. The spider in the shiny web; they will do anything for him.

"My goodness, you are exquisite," A man says as he stops in front of me.

Beads of sweat dot my forehead as my eyes stay glued to the wall over his shoulder. If I were allowed to speak to him, I would plead with him to leave me alone.

Yet, I don't reply to him. In fact, I pretend as if I don't see him at all. Trust me; it isn't for my benefit.

Thankfully, the man moves on. I chance a glance at his retreating back, exhaling in relief. Hopefully, he won't come back. Turning away from him, my gaze lands on Candace.

Candace is beautiful—like most of the women in Miguel's collection. Golden blonde hair with blue almond shaped eyes. She's tall and lean, reminiscent of a supermodel. Miguel calls her his beautiful angel; too bad she's more like a heartless demon. And to put the icing on the cake, the demon hates everything about me.

From the narrowing of her eyes, I know she's witnessed the brief encounter. No doubt she's ready to tell Miguel what she saw the first chance she gets.

"There you are." His voice is smooth and deep. It pours over me like a caress ever so gently between your legs. "Have you been waiting for me, Sweets?"

No one can ever say Miguel isn't an attractive man. Dark brown eyes that are just as alluring as they are unsettling. Lips that are made for kissing. A square-shaped face with a light dusting of dark facial hair. He's tall and lean, with corded muscles that outline and shape his body. Muscles that don't come from a gym. He gets them from pounding his fist into flesh on a regular basis. Tattoos cover seventy percent of his toned body. The man can pull off anything he wears, but the things he does to a simple black T-shirt should be illegal.

I look up at him, the Mona Lisa still firmly planted on my face. "Always." I lie with perfect conviction.

I understand his draw and the lure he has. I know why women fight over him and why men follow him. I guess what I don't understand is after seeing the true Miguel, why do people still stay.

Although attractive and captivating, don't get it wrong, the man is evil. He will more likely put a bullet in your head than shake your hand.

He stares down in my eyes, sinking his teeth into his bottom lip before winking.

"You look absolutely fucking incredible tonight."

"Thank you," I say the way I'm trained to, with just a hint of modesty and a drip of desire.

He places a hand at my lower back, pulling me into him for a brief kiss. He then escorts me to the center of the room, where he greets his paying customers.

My role for the night is the same one I have, no matter where we go. I'm a piece of arm candy, an accessory he puts on like the expensive watch on his wrist.

"Brother." Carlito, Miguel's little brother and right-hand man, gets our attention as he heads over toward us.

He's accompanying another man. One I've never seen before at one of these events. The guy has a regal look about him. It doesn't make me think he's royalty, but more like he finds himself important. He's tanned but not authentic like Miguel's. Dark brown short, trimmed hair that has way too much product is pushed back on his head in a pompadour. He has a practiced smile on his face. As someone that uses one every day, I know the difference between an authentic and fake smile. I'm assuming he's using it to cover up the glare in his eyes. I don't think he wants to be here, guess that makes two of us.

"This is the guy I was telling you about," Carlito explains when he stops in front of us.

Miguel looks the guy over. His shrewd brown eyes summing up the new guy. "You're the scientist?"

"Yes, I'm Benjamin Parks. I'm the CEO of Vita Labs. I just need a few minutes of your time."

Miguel takes another moment to size him up. I know the look. You don't get to be the type of man Miguel is without being smart and cautious.

"Bring him to the Red room, Sweets and I have to make our rounds."

Carlito nods. At the mention of my nickname, Benjamin's eyes fall on me. They do what most men do when they notice me attached to Miguel's side. They widen and then spark with interest.

Like any woman, I think I'm attractive. I'm not exceptionally beautiful or anything. My skin is dark brown with a red undertone like rich soil. I'm average height, about 5'7", and skinny. The type of skinny that people question if you're eating. My tits barely fill out a B-cup. My hips flair a little and admittedly, I have a nice ass. My hair is so damaged from years of mistreating it I hide it under these expensive wigs. My nose is narrow and then widens at the tip. My lips are fucking huge, and my eyes are deep set. Yet, it is the eyes everyone stops to stare at. The light amber color is striking against my complexion.

Often, I get asked are they real; they are. Apparently, I got them from my father's mother. Even though I never met the woman. I've been told the amber color looks like honey in a jar when it's held it up to the sun. I can't verify or deny that because I don't pay attention to them.

We part ways from Carlito and Benjamin before the scientist does or says something that he will regret. I follow Miguel as he makes his rounds and speaks to his patrons. The entire time, I remain silent.

He escorts me over to one of the back tables. Immediately the hairs on my arms stand up in attention. Dr. Hammond and his guard, Rowan is here.

I'm not good at many things, but I do have a talent for reading men. I used to make my living off knowing which man at the strip club was going to drop the cash and which ones were only there for show. The first time I met Dr. Hammond and his guard, I had the strongest flight reflexes. Everything in me told me to run and hide. That feeling has never left.

"Hammond, glad you could join us tonight. Are you enjoying yourself?" For as ruthless as Miguel is, even he senses the danger in Hammond.

Dr. Hammond is an older man, maybe in his late thirties. The lines around his eyes are the only signs of his age. He's not as dark as Miguel, but his skin is definitely tanned to perfection. A chiseled facial structure that's too perfect to be real, a slightly crooked European nose, and haunting hooded blue eyes make him stand out. If I were any other woman, I would say the man is gorgeous.

Whereas Hammond is all tan and dark haired, Rowan is the opposite. His nickname should be Viking. His golden blonde hair hangs past his wide shoulders. Gray eyes that look metallic stare back at you as if they can read your soul. His thick beard surrounds perfectly plump lips that I have never seen smile.

Neither of the men have a problem in the looks department.

Leaning back in his seat, Hammond lifts the glass of brown liquor to his lips and takes a sip before placing the glass back down.

"Relax, Estrava," his raspy deep voice wraps around me like a tight unbreakable hug. "If I weren't enjoying myself, you wouldn't need to ask."

The threat is so obvious that I have to swallow down the lump in my throat. Miguel tries to laugh off Hammond's words as if they're nothing.

"I have a gift for you," Miguel says before signaling to one of the men on his security team.

Without turning to look at him, I can tell Hammond's gaze is on me. It feels as if someone is running a feather over my skin. If that feather was on fire. When I look back at him, his lips turn up into a grin. It is unnerving. His smile reminds me of that mask from the horror movie, Scream. As if it was supposed to be friendly, but all I feel is fear. It's so unnatural that it makes me take a step back.

Hammond's gaze leaves me and looks over my head. The intensity in his eyes has me turning to see what has his attention. One of Miguel's security guards escorts a woman over that I've never seen. She doesn't belong to Miguel's collection even though she's stunning. Flawless peanut butter brown skin, with thick kinky curly hair that brushes against the tops of her breast. Her oval face fits her very curvy plus-size body. She's shorter than me by a few inches.

By the way, Hammond is watching her, he's more than interested. Poor girl.

Hammond and Rowan stand, both towering over everyone. The security guard stops the girl right on the other side of Miguel.

"This is Amber," Miguel says by way of introduction.

Hammond cuts his eyes to Rowan, and something passes between them. The air around us seems to crackle with electricity. The hairs on my arms that were once standing are now being replaced by a zinging under my skin. From the way the girl's brow pinches, I'm not the only one to feel it.

"I borrowed her from a friend just for you. Hopefully, we can give her back in the same condition we got her," Miguel goes on to say, seemingly ignorant to the current charge in the space around us.

Hammond swings his head back to Miguel so quickly, he and I both take a step back.

"I'll do my best," he says through gritted teeth, but I don't think anyone believes that.

Rowan steps forward and takes hold of Amber's arm. He then guides her out of the main room toward one of the borrowed bedrooms.

Hammond looks us over once again before following the other two out.

It isn't until I can't see them anymore that the prickly feeling finally leaves.

"That fucking guy gives me the creeps," Miguel mumbles as he places a hand to my lower back, escorting me away.

We move along to another table where a heavy-set man sits. I've seen him on television before. I think he's a politician. Sitting in his lap is Emiko, another one of Miguel's girls. Emiko is new to the collection. She's only been with us a year. She's half white and half Japanese. Like most of Miguel's girls, she's gorgeous. Her monolid eyes look up at me and narrow.

I don't take offense; they all hate me.

"Estrava," the politician says with a smile. His double chin hanging over the collar of his shirt. "Thank you again for opening up your home to us."

"Senator, you're always welcome." Miguel smiles down at Emiko, who immediately lights up for him. She melts under his attention. "I see you've chosen my cherry blossom for the night. Good choice, her pussy is amazing."

Emiko looks to me with a smug smile on her face. She tosses her long straight hair over her shoulder and lifts her head.

The Senator's smile widens. "I'll have to try it for myself."

"You know where to pay," Miguel says applying pressure to my lower back, leading me away from the two.

The moment we are out of hearing range, he wraps his arm around my waist, causing me to stop. He then presses his body against my back; the heat coming from him warms me.

"Are you angry with me?" He whispers in my ear from behind.

This is why the others hate me. It's why they believe I'm the enemy in this house of horror.

"No," I say truthfully.

He places a hand on my cheek and turns my face to look at him over my shoulder. His dark brown eyes look down into mine, searching for a truth he won't find.

"I'm sorry for what I said about Emiko. I shouldn't have said that in front of you."

"You were only speaking the truth. It isn't like you haven't fucked her."

Before he can reply, a couple walks by us and stops to speak to him briefly before walking on.

I'm thankful for the distraction. It gives me time to prepare for the bullshit that's coming next.

"Look at me, Sweets." I turn back to him, facing the man who took me off the streets when I was just seventeen years old.

He steps into my space, his 6-foot height towering over me. "None of the others matter. I only love you."

I'm pretty sure I would've believed his words at one time in my life. Most likely when I was a little girl and still trusted that men meant what they said. That trust was shattered in the rain when I was eight years old. It went on to be demolished again when I was thirteen.

At the ripe age of eighteen was the last time I truly trusted a man. I went into the system for a while when in my early teens but didn't stay there long. I've always been a realist. I knew from the start there were only so many ways out of my neighborhood. You either had to be extremely smart, which I wasn't, or talented. I can't sing, act, or play a sport. I'm an average girl with slightly above average looks and funny colored eyes. The day I ran from my foster home, I was sixteen, and I've been in survival mode ever since.

I got a job at the only strip club in the city that had no problem with hiring underage strippers. It was a shitty and volatile place to work. I witnessed things I should have never seen, but it supplied me with enough money to survive

It's there that I met Miguel. He saw me dancing and couldn't take his eyes off me all night. Afterward, he approached me and made me the offer to be his personal entertainer. He said he would watch out for me, supply me with a roof over my head and food in my belly. He promised it would never go further, and he only wanted me to perform at his private parties. Even though I had all those lessons on trusting men, like a fool, I fell for it. Back then, I was still holding on to hopes and dreams.

It took him only a year to convince me to join him in his bed with promises of loving me. Even at eighteen, I didn't fully believe him. I'm not a genius, but I wasn't dumb enough to believe the man who had plenty of women to grace his bed could truly be in love with me. Again, that word hope came into play. I had hoped that he could love me. However, as I stand here in front of him now eight years later, I know that it isn't love that Miguel has for me. This is purely obsession.

"I know," I say to answer his earlier statement. It's another lie. I will tell many more before tonight is over.

Miguel places a kiss on my lips and then steers us toward the other side of the room. We stop and speak to a few more people before we make our way back to the red room.

The red room is my special room. This is the only place I can dance. It's given its name because of the deep red wallpaper, chairs and accents.

The place is set up like a castle's throne. At the back of the room is a gold king's chair. Smaller chairs and tables circle the main area, and a bar is against the front wall. A stage is in the middle of the floor.

As soon we enter, Miguel leans over and whispers in my ear, "Dance for me, Sweets."

I never refuse the request. It's not for him though. Dancing is the only thing I can still control. It grounds me and brings me peace. When I'm on the stage, I block everything else out and feel the music; it's my one and only escape from here.

I climb up on the stage, and the music changes to a slow song. It's always something I can slow whine to. Hooking my leg onto the pole, I do a little twirl to start me off. I then shut my eyes and get lost in the music, allowing the slow tempo to take my mind off my situation. Dancing is the one thing I'm good at.

Since the day Miguel took me from that filthy strip club, I haven't wanted for anything. I live in this mansion where chefs cook three meals a day for me. If I want anything, I only have to mention it to the butler, and it will appear in my room the next day. I imagine on the outside looking in, people will ask why I would want to leave. I'd tell them, a cage is a cage, no matter how shiny it is. And there is no mistaken it, I'm definitely caged.

When I open my eyes again, I make sure to keep them on Miguel. I made that mistake only once. Using my arms only, I hold onto the pole while hanging upside down. I spread my legs into a split. Then, wrapping one leg around the metal, making sure to lock my knee, I let my hands go and hang for a second. This gets a few whistles. Seconds later, I sit up, grabbing back onto the pole, then slide down into another split on the floor. After flipping to my knees, I arch my back like a cat and crawl to the edge of the stage in his direction. He winks, rolling his bottom lip between his teeth.

"Damn, she's amazing," A man's voice shouts over the music. I recognized the slurred voice as the same man from earlier. He's the one that stopped in front of me.

My body tenses as tight as a guitar string. Climbing to my feet, I blow a kiss to Miguel, my signature move that lets him know I'm done.

I go to step off the stage, and immediately one of the guys from the security team is there to help me down. He makes sure only to touch my hand and keep his head down—another one of those unspoken rules. The only person that gets a pass to touch me or look me in the eye is Carlito and even he is limited.

I head toward Miguel's outstretched hand. As soon as I'm before him, he widens his legs for me to stand in between them. He taps his lap, and I take a seat. The knot in his pants tells me he enjoyed my performance.

"You're my girl. Right, Sweets?"

"Yes," I answer automatically.

He drops a kiss on my bare shoulder.

"As I was saying," The man, Benjamin Parks, continues with the conversation they were having. "I need girls. Lots of them, and I need them within the next few days."

"That's a tall order you have there, Mr. CEO," Miguel says as he rubs his fingers over my hip.

As quickly as possible, I glance at Benjamin Parks. His face reddens. He must hear the mocking tone in the title.

"I think for the money I'm offering, it's obtainable," Benjamin snaps back.

Miguel's tattooed fingers stop making small circles on my thigh. My heart rate increases.

"Mr. Parks, if you can't tell by now, I'm not in need of your money."

Benjamin tries to speak. I'm sure it's probably an apology, but Miguel cuts him off. "However, since I'm a businessman, and my brother thinks this is a good investment, I'm always down for making connections. I have a few of your kind that I help."

Another quick glance, and I find Mr. Parks smiling. "Like I said, you will be doing your country a great service."

"And the women won't be traceable?" Carlito asks.

"Absolutely not. The place they are going is completely off the map. It will be like they disappeared in thin air." Benjamin smiles proudly.

"What if I have some that desire to participate?" Miguel asks.

"We will take them too. It makes it a little easier if they are compliant. We compensate them well, but they will have to sign some contracts."

Miguel pauses as if he's thinking something over. "I have some girls in my collection I'm willing to part with. This may be a good option for them."

Benjamin's gaze cut to me in Miguel's lap. I've been watching him out the corner of my eye since he replied to Carlito. I see the question on his thin lips. I plead with him in my head not to ask it. Thank God, he must have felt my thoughts pushing into his because he moves on.

"How many women do you think you can get for me on this first run?"

"At the moment, I have a hundred and twenty girls at my closest warehouse. You can have them all. I'll even throw in a few girls from my collection." Miguel says.

Benjamin gasp. I don't think he was expecting that many. "That's incredible. The research will truly appreciate you. Your country will appreciate you." Benjamin is laying it on thick.

"What are you needing these women for anyway?" Carlito asks.

I'm interested in this question myself. That number of women in that short of a time seems suspicious. Miguel doesn't talk about his business with me, but he often talked about it around me. I knew enough to know this was a tall order.

"We are doing research on fertility. Just trying to make it easier for women to carry babies."

That's bullshit. I can tell by the way he tugs at his clothes and looks away that he's not telling the full truth. Even if they are working on fertility, it isn't as simple, or for the reason he gave.

Miguel hums in the back of his throat. "We should talk more on this."

Tension immediately has my body stiff.

Why does he need to talk about fertility? All the women in his collection are on a rigid birth control regimen. Every three months, a doctor came in to administer the birth control shot; for some of us, myself included, the shot has too many side effects. So, every morning, the butler comes in, and hands me a pill.

Miguel is very strict about no kids. In that, he and I can agree. I knew nothing about being a mother. I'm not even sure I want to be one. The one I had wasn't any good, and what if being a bad parent is something that gets passed down. My mom was an absentee drug addict, and my father was no better. What if somewhere in my DNA I'm destined to be a shitty parent. Not to mention, bringing a child into this environment wouldn't be good.

"Hey, Miguel," The same male voice from earlier grabs our attention. From the slurring of his words, it's obvious he's even more drunk than before. "How much for that one?" The man asks, pointing directly at me.

Adrenaline shoots through my system, causing my head to swim. Anyone that has come to one of Miguel's sample nights learns quickly how it works around here. Only on sample nights does Miguel share his special collection of women. All except one.

I don't know what the hell makes me special. He has women far more beautiful than me. Women with skin dark as night and pale as fresh milk. Women with eyes prettier than mine and bodies that would make any man stand up and pay attention. I wasn't even the first in his collection. I'm nothing spectacular, but he will not let me go. Nor will he share me.

Miguel taps my thigh, wordlessly asking me to stand up. I do, and he gets to his feet behind me.

"Miguel, don't," I plead even though I know it's pointless.

He places a kiss on my forehead and smiles. The smile of the devil right before he claims a soul.

"This the one you want?" He turns and asks the drunk guy.

The man, a middle-aged guy, nods his head vigorously.

"Do you hear that, everyone?" Miguel turns to the room. No one speaks or makes a sound. They know as well as I do what's about to happen. The idiot guy has just fallen into the web and provoked the spider.

"Come here, friend," Miguel calls out to the man that is too drunk to realize the danger he is in.

"Brother," Carlito tries to warn.

Carlito knows better than anyone the thin line between good and evil that Miguel walks.

"Relax, little brother. Tonight, is the sample night. He gets a choice."

My heart is racing. Not out of fear that this man will get to have sex with me, but at what is about to happen.

The man comes closer, his eyes never straying from my body. My outfit, like most of my clothing, is tight. Black boy shorts that cut into my ass is covered up by a mid-thigh mesh top and a lacy bra. No matter where we went, Miguel loved to show off my body. I think he got a kick out of tempting men to touch me.

"You like what you see?" Miguel asks.

The man nods and licks his lips.

Miguel chuckles. "I offer you any woman in my home. How many do you think there is?"

The man isn't focusing on the look on Miguel's face or the anger in his tone. He's too busy fucking me with his eyes.

"I don't know," He answers absently. "But they don't compare to her. Those eyes got me wanting to fuck her all night." And those few words just sealed his fate.

Neither I nor Carlito could save him now. Miguel reacts so fast he moves in a blur. He grabs the man by the back of the neck and slams his fist into the guy's face. The drunken patron cries out, but that punch is the least of his worries.

Miguel grabs an open beer bottle off the table near us and jams the long neck of the handle into the drunk man's right eye. The man's scream is so loud my ears ring.

"I open up my home to you, and this is how you repay me?" Miguel shouts down into the face of the guy.

I close my eyes and cover my ears at the wretched sound of the man's cries. Miguel slams the bottle against the table, breaking it in half. He then uses the jagged edge to stab the guy over and over in the face.

"No one touches my sweets." His voice carries over the music and throughout the house. "If you even think about touching her, I will yank out your brains with a motherfucking fork through your nose."

This is the side of him most people don't see. The side that he hides behind his charming smile and his charismatic personality. This is what lies in wait in the middle of that shiny web. I guess it makes sense. Anyone who witnesses this version of him, doesn't often live to talk about it.

A few of Miguel's men come to take the bloodied and dying man away.

"Come here, baby." he coos for me to come into his arms.

I go. Trust me, I must go. He has never hit me, would never dream of it, but sometimes you don't have to strike your opponent down for them to fear you. It's that fear that holds me, hostage, in this house. I've tried to leave. I even got away once. But he always finds me, and he always brings me back. And there is always a trail of bodies that follow me.

He tilts my head up and plants a kiss on my lips. "I'm sorry. I know you hate to see that shit." I do, but that still wouldn't have changed the outcome. "Go change your clothes. These have been ruined."

I look down at myself, and low and behold; there is blood splattered on my chest and top.

"Nothing of another man should ever touch you, not even his blood." He laughs before releasing me and stepping back.

I leave him and the rest of the guests in the entertainment wing of the large sprawling estate. Everything Miguel promised me that night in the strip club came to pass. I can have anything I can ever want. I have more designer labels than I can wear. Enough ice to refreeze the fucking North Pole. I'm living a life of luxury, but it comes at a high cost.

He thinks that he loves me. When I was eighteen, I thought the same thing. Now I know that love is as useless as hopes and dreams. All the women in this house are his. He fucks them all and any other woman he sees and wants. The other women are free to sleep with whomever as long as they are available to him when he wants them. I, on the other hand, cannot even look a man in the eye without that man dying.

My first month here, I thanked one of the security guards for opening a door for me, and Miguel gunned him down right on the spot. A waiter in a restaurant made me laugh once; the next morning, Miguel presented me with his head on a platter. He does not share me, and he won't let me leave.

I'm stuck. That's why it amazes me that women like Emiko and Candace could ever be envious of me. They know what I go through. They've witnessed the bullshit. None of the women that was here when I got here are still here. They've been replaced by the younger, more flexible version of themselves.

When you're here, he spoils you. Yes, he loans you out to other men, but he provides, protects, and worships you while you're with him. And I guess, if we're being honest, the sex is amazing.

I head into the large bedroom that belongs to me. It's right next to Miguel's. The only one on this wing. Most of the time, he shares my bed, but on nights like tonight, he will stay with someone else.

I run the water in my all-glass shower with its five different heads. I turn on the heated floors and pull off my ruined clothes. I wish I could stay in here instead of going back downstairs. Part of me craves my freedom. I want it as bad as a dying man wants his next breath. However, another part of me is afraid. I'd experienced enough of the world in those short seventeen years to know that outside these walls, it doesn't get any better. Being homeless has a way of making you appreciative of the small things. Yes, my life is hell here, but it could be worse out there.

I take a quick shower and redress in a body-hugging long dress with side cut outs and a low cut back. As soon as I walk out of the bathroom, I'm greeted by another nuisance in this house.

"Are you alright?"

"Carlito, you know better. What are you doing in here?"

He sighs. Lately, he has gotten bolder in his desire for me. I would never cross that line with him. Not only is he the only real friend I have here, but I'm also not in any way attracted to him.

He takes a step toward me, and I step back, holding up my hands to stop him.

"I had to see you. I needed to know if you were ok," he says.

"I'm fine. It wasn't the first time I've had blood splattered on me, and it won't be the last." That was the god's honest truth. We both know that.

He sighs, running his hands through his dark hair. "You deserve better than him. You deserve to be happy and to be with someone that wants you and only you."

"Stop," I plead over his declaration of love for me. I'm so sick of this song and dance with him. "You're not helping. We can never be. You know this."

He growls in frustration. "I try not to think about you. I try not to want you."

"Try harder," I demand. "He will kill you, and I can't have that on my conscious." I know I sound cold and brutal, but this is for his safety.

Sadness and pain paint across his face. I have told him many times that we can't be together and that I don't love him the way he thinks he loves me.

"I have to get back downstairs. He can't find you in here," I say, then walk out of the room, leaving him behind.

The night is still young, and I am expected to stay with Miguel until he dismisses me. Entering the red room, I immediately spot Benjamin Parks.

He's staring at me with a raised brow and a smirk on his face. I'm used to this look from the men around here. It isn't my appearance that has the men around here intrigued by me. Yes, my eyes catch them off guard, but the interest comes from Miguel's attention. They want to know what it is about me that drives a man like Miguel to behave so irrationally. With all the other beautiful women he surrounds himself with, why can't he let go of me. That's when the familiar look crosses the men's face. The same one on Benjamin's right now. The look that asks am I worth risking the devil's wrath for. I'm not.

I turn away from Benjamin's stare and find Miguel. He's on his throne again. Candace is in his lap and she's grinding her ass on him. He whispers something in her ear, and she nods her head. His hand then slowly starts to disappear up her skirt.

Most would think this would offend me. It doesn't. I experienced jealousy only in the early years of this arrangement. However, I quickly got over it. Tonight is Candace's night with him. She always makes it known when it's her night. All the girls do; they especially like to let me know as if I give a shit.

I head over to the bar and order a drink. Wyatt, the bartender, slides me a coke across the bar.

"What the hell, Wyatt? You know I always get Cranberry and Vodka."

With his eyes trained over my head, he says, "Boss man said you're not allowed alcohol."

"What? Why?"

He shrugs, doing everything to keep from looking me in the eyes. "I don't know Shi; you have to take that up with him."

This is something new. Miguel never had an issue with me drinking. Hell, he's the one that gave me my first shot. Why suddenly is he worried about me having alcohol?

Sucking my teeth, I grab my coke off the bar and head toward Miguel. It takes a minute for him to stop whispering to Candace to notice me. When he does, he smiles up at me.

"Sweets, you look even more beautiful than before."

My Mona Lisa smile is back in place. "Thank you."

"You aren't the only one who thought so," Candace's voice is laced with so much fire it's a mystery how she doesn't spit flames when she speaks. "Shiloh had a little admirer today. She was staring at him."

I hold my breath. She knows what her implication could mean, not to me, but to whoever she accuses.

"I was watching him walk away," I answer her without looking at her.

"Didn't look like that to me."

I cut my eyes to Candace. I really don't know what I've done to warrant so much hatred from this girl.

"Then maybe you were looking at the wrong thing," I answer curtly.

Miguel's brown eyes narrow in on me. The vein in his neck starts to throb. He removes his hand from under Candace's dress and taps her thigh, encouraging her to get up. She does and he stands. The smile on her face is pure joy. She likes when he's angry with me.

"Who is he?" A command so chilling the hair on the back of my neck rise.

"Insignificant. He's already dead."

He watches me for a moment, studying my eyes for things he won't find. Then he chuckles. "Good."

Miguel goes back to giving his attention to Candace, pulling her down in his lap where she goes happily.

I stand there, waiting for him to send me away. "Am I dismissed for the night?" Please say yes.

He pulls away from Candace, his tongue running along his bottom lip as he watches me.

"If you want to be."

I nod my head and spin on my heels. I only get a few steps away before he's grabbing my arm and turning me back to face him. I knew I wouldn't get far.

"You're angry with me?"

He asks me this all the time. I think he wants me to be angry. He wants me to be jealous of the women and the time he spends with them. If I were jealous, then it would mean I love him. I do, but no more than he loves me, which isn't much at all.

"I'm not angry. Tonight is not my night, remember?" I turn to walk away again, and in one swift move he grabs me by the back of the neck, spins me around and pulls me into him for a feverish and desperate kiss. My body reacts despite my wishes. I whimper against his lips, and he leans away. His glazed eyes shining down at me.

"No one comes before you." His words are spoken in harsh pants against my lips. "You drive me crazy. I sometimes think your pussy does not crave me like I crave it."

My Mona Lisa smile lifts a little higher. "It has since the first day you touched it." Unfortunately, that's the truth.

A boisterous laugh escapes his lips. For a second, he doesn't look like the murdering kingpin that he is. He looks, very briefly, like a man in love.

"And I'm the only motherfucker that's ever touched it," He brags.

"That you are." A gift I often regret giving him.

He watches me for another moment. A smile still gracing his face

"I think I want you to stay with me tonight," He finally says.

My heart stutters. This is the seventh night in a row. Look, I have no issue with the sex, some days, I even desire it. However, I noticed lately he's growing increasingly clingier with me. In the many years, I've spent with him, he's never went longer than three nights in my bed before taking another. None of the others can say that. Lately, he's been staying longer and longer.

"Baby, tonight is my night," Candace whines beside us. I'm just now noticing she followed him over. "You see how wet my pussy got for you. Don't make me wait." she purrs.

Miguel turns to look at her and his bottom lip slips between his teeth. He wants her, but his fucked up mind won't let me go.

"It's alright, Papi," I say, grabbing his attention back. He looks to me and lifts a brow. I place a kiss on his cheek. "I'll still be here tomorrow."

I glance up in time to see the hatred dancing behind Candace's blue gaze.

I have no doubt in my mind that if she could get away with it, she would murder me in my sleep.

He pulls me in for another brief kiss. "I love you," he says the words with conviction.

"I know." I turn and walk away.

Miguel really did believe that he loved me and, in his mind, he thought I loved him too. Neither of us knew anything about love.

CHAPTER TWO

Surprises

Shiloh

I wake the next morning and immediately feel his heat pressed against my back. He stumbled into my room about an hour after I had fallen asleep. His hair was still wet from the shower. He pulled me into him before succumbing to sleep himself.

Slowly, I scoot out of his arms, placing space between us. I climb out of the bed to do my morning routine.

About five minutes later, a light knock on my bedroom door has me padding across the carpeted floor to the door. Right on time, the butler is here to administer my birth control. I open the door for the older man with a smile. He hands me the glass of juice and a pill the size of a fucking horse tranquilizer. I look down at the foreign medicine and then back up to his sorrowful eyes.

"Master Estrava has changed your prescription."

The moment the words are out of his mouth Miguel is behind me, placing a kiss on my neck. His morning wood pressed to my mid-back.

"I wanted it to be a surprise," He whispers into my ear before pulling away and heading to the bathroom.

I quickly swallow the big ass pill and drink the juice. The butler can't leave until he's made sure I took the medicine. It doesn't matter that the meds have changed. I walk into my bathroom to find Miguel at the toilet taking a leak.

"What's with the new medicine?"

He looks over his shoulder and smiles. "We're trying for a baby, Sweets."

The hell we are. The room starts to spin, and bile rises in my throat. I place a hand to my chest, fighting to keep the vomit from coming up.

"What are you talking about?" I try to keep my voice casual and playful.

He shakes his cock and stuffs himself back in his boxer briefs before flushing and turning to wash his hands.

"I'm talking about you and me having a kid. I've been thinking it over for a while now. I want a baby, and I want it with you."

It's starting to make sense now. Him staying with me more nights, the no-alcohol rule, and the comment he made to Benjamin. He's trying to get me knocked up.

The fear that floods my body has my knees weak. I have to lean against the door frame to keep from falling over. I'm used to being his prisoner. I've even grown to accept the fact that he will keep me here until I'm too old or until he grows tired and kills me.

I've always known that will be the outcome. I won't get the same retirement plan as his other women who he let go. The small severance package and a goodbye kiss. No, he will never allow me to know another man besides him. The day he no longer has any use for me, he will kill me because he would rather I'd die than to be with someone else. This isn't only something he's said to scare me, it is his promise to me. And that promise does not have an expiration date.

This house and this man are my future until the day I die. I wouldn't wish this on my worst enemy. There is no way I will bring a child into this. Maybe that makes me selfish. I can only think of myself and the implication that having a child by this man will cause. If I think he is insane now, I can only imagine how he will be when I'm the mother of his child.

"I don't want to be a mother." Truth. I realize my world is split in truth and lies. Truths that help me live and lies that help me survive.

Dark eyes meet light as he turns to me, giving me his undivided attention. "Do I look like I'm asking you what you want?"

My mouth goes dry as I suck in a breath. He pushes away from the sink and walks over to me. "Forever, Shiloh. Say it."

"Forever," I repeat.

His hand wraps around my throat and he tilts my head up toward his. "Say it louder." He growls.

"Forever." My compliance is immediate.

"You are mine forever. Until the day you die. Do you understand?"

"Yes." He doesn't let me go right away. Instead, he stares down at me studying me.

"You're afraid of turning out like your parents?"

In the early years, he and I talked about things like that. Back when I thought myself in love.

He lets my neck go and cups my face. "Don't worry. You will be a great mother, Sweets."

"Miguel," I try once more to plead with him. "We can't raise a child like this. All the drugs and the killing. What if we have a daughter? What are you going to tell her when she asks you about the other women?"

These are the things that real woman would be concerned with. She would care what her child saw. I didn't care, not really. I just know that this is something that Miguel has to think about, and maybe if he does, he will change his mind because he will never get rid of his women.

That smile appears on his face, the one that makes him less frightening. "Don't worry about them." He pulls me into him and kisses me like he owns every breath I take. When he pulls away, he slides his thumb over my bottom lip. "I'll do anything for you."

He places his hands under my thighs, lifting me up. My hands wrap around his neck and my thighs around his waist. He seals our lips together in that breathless way that he kisses and carries me to the bed.

For the rest of the morning, he uses his body to convince me to have his child. Although my body complies, my head is still highly against it. Two thoughts cloud my mind all morning, I can't get pregnant, and I have to leave here.

I make it to breakfast about an hour later. Miguel leaves for the day to handle his business. He has a shipment of girls coming in soon, which means he will be traveling soon. Whenever he does, he becomes excessively busy and occupied. We all stay out of his way as much as possible.

For the most part, we are allowed to roam the estate. The women cannot leave unless it has been cleared with Miguel and they are accompanied by a guard. I can't leave period. The only time I see the outside world is if I'm with him, but even that's few and far between. Not since the last time I ran.

The dining room is bustling with members of the staff and the other girls. None of them stop and speak to me, either out of fear or hatred. I place a few pieces of fruit on my plate. I'm not hungry. My appetite left me this morning when my birth control was replaced with a prenatal vitamin.

One of the women that works the kitchen takes my plate out of my hand and replaces it with a plate piled high with meat, eggs, and fruit.

"I don't want all this," I say, frowning.

"Master Estrava demands you eat a full breakfast. The baby needs it." The entire kitchen goes completely silent. You could hear a fish fart in the ocean it's so quiet. My eyes remain downcast. I cannot believe he told them about his plans.

"Is she fucking serious?" The screeching sound of Candace's voice catches me off guard, and I look up at her. Her eyes are lit with fire. She marches over to me and stands right in front of me.

"Are you pregnant?"

I don't get a chance to answer because the servant replies for me. "Master Estrava says they are trying. Now eat up." The woman drops the bomb off in the room and then disappears back behind the kitchen doors. She's safely away from the war she just started.

"You bitch," Candace sneers.

"She's been plotting this all along. She's trying to get him to get rid of us." Sasha, an Ethiopian goddess, shouts.

The murmurs go around as they discuss me as if I'm not here.

"I haven't plotted anything. This is news to me as well." I go to walk around Candace, but she reaches out and smacks my plate out of my hands. The loud sound echoing through the room as the plate shatters against the hardwood. The food I didn't even want hits the floor.

I'm not a violent person, but I know how to protect myself. I have self-preservation down to a science. Many times, I have wanted to rip each and every blonde strand of Candace hair out of her head, but I don't. Not only do I know that if I try to fight one, I'll have to fight them all. I also understand what a fight will mean for them. I do not have the stomach for it.

I steady my shoulders and again attempt to walk around Candace and the food on the floor. A hard shove in the back has me tumbling down, nearly cracking my head on the edge of the table—the push was unexpected, causing me to cut my lip on my teeth.

"Fucking whore." Candace shouts, charging toward me. I cover my head.

Unfortunately, this isn't the first time one of the girls tried to fight me. The last time it happened, I'd only been here about three weeks. Miguel blew the girls brains out in front of me.

"Enough," Carlito's deep voice comes from over my head. He's standing between Candace and me. He holds out a hand that I accept, lifting me to my feet. "You alright?" he tries to touch my chin to lift my head, but I turn away from him.

His face falls, but in this situation, he can't take risk. He gets leeway when it comes to Miguel's rules, but not even he is allowed to be so intimate with me. That's all these girls needed to see. They'd love to go back and tell Miguel.

"Let me at her, Carlito," Candace pleads as she tries to reach for me over him. He blocks her hands.

"Have you lost your mind?" he shouts at her. None of these girls were around the last time I got into a fight here. They honestly don't know the danger.

"You're just a dumb, worthless bitch," She continues to yell at me. "You aren't even a good fuck. Believe me; he told me," She says as if her words were supposed to hurt me. "The only thing he likes about you are your eyes. I wonder how he would feel if I cut them out." Once again, she charges for me, but Carlito shoves her back.

"That's enough, Candace. Or do you want me to tell Miguel how you're treating her."

That gets her to calm down. She pushes her long hair behind her ears, her eyes narrowing.

"You can tell him. And maybe I'll tell him how you're always sniffing around her. We all see the way you watch her. Maybe I'll tell Miguel that."

Carlito takes a threatening step toward her, and she has the right mind to shrink away from him. Although he isn't as violent as his older brother, he still isn't one to play games with.

"I dare you to try it." I'd never seen him so angry or menacing. I guess Candace agrees because she cowers in front of him.

"Clean this shit up and get the fuck out of here," he snaps causing her to jump.

Carlito spins around and grabs my arm before dragging me out of the kitchen. He marches me upstairs to my room, pushing me inside, he slams the door. He doesn't turn to me as he places his head against the wooden barrier. He takes a few deep breaths as if he's trying to calm himself down. I make sure to keep my distance from him. This isn't a good look, and we have no idea when Miguel will come back home.

"He told me this morning," His voice is flat. "You're going to have his baby?" He finally lifts his head and turns to me. Tears dance at the edge of his eyelids.

"Apparently so." I walk over to the foot of my bed before flopping down. "He'll never let me go then."

Carlito snorts. "He's never going to let you go anyway. But if you have his child, he'll become more possessive and controlling. He won't let me be alone with you again."

Not exactly my concern. "I don't know what to do. If I leave, he will find me and kill everyone that gets in his way. I would have to basically fall off the face of this earth to get away from him."

"Or become untraceable," Carlito chuckles.

It's then I remember the conversation Miguel had with Benjamin Parks. Benjamin said the women would be untraceable, and if they volunteered, they'd be compensated.

What if I volunteer for whatever the scientist has going on, and then take the money and run? If I can go untraceable long enough, maybe Miguel will lose interest. There is no way he would continue to look for me when he has all these girls here. If I'm gone long enough, I'm sure he will get over this obsession with me and move on.

"Carlito, when is Miguel delivering the girls to the scientist?"

Carlito turns his head to the side, his brows drawing together. "Why?"

I stand, putting my hands out in front of me. "I just need you to trust me."

I have no doubt that Carlito would assist me in my escape plan, but I also know that eventually, Miguel will figure it out. Brother or not, he will kill Carlito. I've had enough death on my conscious to last me a lifetime; I didn't need to add his too.

Carlito watches me wearily, those kind eyes that have always been a solace in this place, work hard to try and decipher my plans. Eventually, his gaze falls to my feet, and a long low sigh escapes his lips.

"In two days. A truck will arrive at the Eastside warehouse to pick up the girls. From there, he will be traveling to Mexico to handle some business. He'll be gone for a week."

I've never been to any of the warehouses for obvious reasons. I've heard of them. I know the horrors that go on there.

For some girls their stop in the Eastside warehouse is just the gateway to hell. The resting place after they've been taken from their homes and family. For others, they never make it out of that hellhole. I also know that there is no way I will be able to get to that warehouse. I can't even leave the damn house. This places a wrench in my plans.

"He's planning on sending the girls from here as well."

My head shoots up, and I lock eyes with him.

"Excuse me?" I know he mentioned it last night to Benjamin, but I thought he was just talking.

He nods. "He says he's trying to get rid of some of the women. He doesn't want to have a house full around his kids. Thought it would be a bad look in case you had a girl."

For a second, and I do mean a split second, my heart goes out to Miguel. He actually listened to me. I guess he really does want a family. Unfortunately, we were both too damaged to know how to love and be parents.

"How will he get the girls from here to the meet up site?"

"Marvin will gather them from the house and take them over the morning of the transfer. Miguel and I will already be at the warehouse." Carlito pauses for a second and takes a step toward me. "Whatever is going through your mind, Shi, don't do it. Don't risk it."

I smile, the one I've perfected over the years. "Don't worry, I'm here forever, right?"

That sadness passes back over his eyes; he reaches for my hand just as the door to the bedroom slams open. We both turn to face Miguel. I take a step back, my chest tightens, and my breathing becomes labored. Miguel's eyes scan the both of us that calculating gaze taking in everything.

"What happened to your lip?" He asks as he comes closer to me.

I touch the sore swollen lip I'd forgotten about.

"Miguel…" Carlito starts, but before he could finish his sentence Miguel's gun is out and pointed at his temple. I gasp and clutch my chest.

"Little brother, I advise you to shut the fuck up."

"It was Candace," The words fly from my mouth like vomit. Miguel turns to glare at me. I can see doubt in his eyes. He doesn't believe me.

"She got angry when she found out that we're trying to have a baby. She attacked me in the dining room. Carlito stepped in to help me." I don't usually like ratting people out because of the outcome, but I'm in survival mode. Plus, I need Carlito.

The gun remains in his hand, pressed to his brother's temple as he watches me.

"If you don't trust me, check the cameras." There are cameras in the main areas of the house and in some of the other girl's bedrooms. But none in my room. There was one until he caught a guard watching me get dressed. Miguel tortured him for weeks. I could hear his screams coming up from the basement.

Miguel lowers the gun, and Carlito lets out a deep breath. His relief is obvious. Miguel grabs me and pulls me into him. I go with no hesitancy.

"I'm sorry," He whispers as he places kisses on my temple and around my hairline. Over his shoulder, Carlito watches me, a slack expression on his face. He will never learn. Even when coming that close to death, he still doesn't see the danger his actions cause.

Miguel's gentle kisses turn feverish, and his hand slips under my shirt to cup my breast.

"Fuck, I need you," He growls against my skin.

Carlito turns to walk out of the room.

"Little Brother," Miguel calls out without turning to look at Carlito. "Don't ever let me find you alone with Shiloh again."

Carlito spins around, his eyes wide as he stares at his brother's back. "Miguel."

Miguel turns to look at him cutting off his protest. "Do you understand?"

"Yes," Carlito mumbles.

Miguel puts his attention back on me. "Take me out, Sweets." I oblige, tugging the zipper of his pants down.

When I look up again, Carlito is gone. Today Miguel's possessiveness has hit an all-new high, and I fear it's only going to get worse.

CHAPTER THREE

My Enemy

Shiloh

I lie on my back later that day reading a book. There is nothing to do in the house. The only rule is to be available to Miguel when he wants it. He hasn't been back to visit me since he walked in on me and Carlito. I figured he's visiting some of the other girls in between working.

I enjoy the alone time. I don't like hanging out with the other girls in the recreation room. Not like they would welcome me anyway. Most of my days are spent locked away in this room reading.

The scream of a female in pain has me jumping up off the bed. Pounding footsteps head toward my room. The door slams open, and a disheveled and shirtless Miguel is standing in my doorway.

"Come here, Sweets. I want to show you something." He holds out his hands for me to take. Placing my hand in his, he escorts me out of the room and down the stairs.

All the other girls are standing around in the living room. From the expression on their faces, something bad is happening, and they are terrified. Once I walk into the dining room, I figure out why.

A naked and sobbing Candace is on the floor. There is a cut in her lip, the same place mine is. Her face is red and splotchy, rivers of mascara run down her cheeks.

"Miguel please," She pleads.

"Shut the fuck up," He shouts down at her.

He pulls me close to his chest and places a kiss on my forehead. "I've given you privileges that I shouldn't. No one touches my Sweets. Not even you bitches," He says, gazing around the room at the other women.

Even in her current state, Candace still glowers up at me, malice and hatred stares back.

"If a man had done the shit you did," He says back to Candace. "I'd be gifting his balls to my Sweets. But since you don't have balls," he says before pulling out a gun and aiming it at her head. I don't even know where it came from.

Her pleas for her life increase, but I know they will fall on death's ears.

"Miguel don't," I beg. I don't know why I'm trying to save her life. It's not like she was ever nice to me.

He looks at me and lifts his brow in confusion.

"She has to be punished. No one gets to disrespect you and live unscathed."

"Please don't do this. I love you, Miguel," Candace cries out once more.

I look down at her, and I'm hit with a harsh reality. She actually does love him. That's where the hatred comes from. She believes she's in love with Miguel, and he believes he's in love with me. We were in a sordid and sadistic sort of love triangle.

The discovery has me realizing that though Candace is a bitch, she didn't deserve to die. Unfortunately, she hadn't discovered the harsh realities of life like I had. She didn't know the truth about the words hope, dream, and love.

"Don't kill her," I say turning away from the hurt and adoration in Candace's eyes as she stares up at him.

"Then what should I do?" He asks.

I glance at her once more, helpless, scared, and in love with a psychopath. "Put her out."

Candace screams and tries to leap off the floor at me, but one of the security guards grabs her and shoves her back to the ground. She immediately starts crying and pleading with Miguel to keep her.

My stomach sours and a lump forms in my throat. The woman has no idea that I just gave her the greatest gift I could offer. I gave her freedom. Candace can't recognize how dysfunctional our life is and that outside of these walls, she may be able to find exactly what she's looking for. I didn't believe in love and hope, but I know she'd get closer to finding it out there than in here.

Miguel pulls me into him and kisses me like it will be our last. When he pulls back, he's smiling. "And you thought you wouldn't be a good mother. Your kindness astounds me," He remarks.

Well shit. That isn't what I was going for.

He turns to the guard that shoved her down. "Get her the fuck out of here."

Candace starts screaming. She's going back and forth between threatening my life and pleading with Miguel. She continues until her voice is an inaudible whisper through the house.

With a hand at my lower back, he directs us back to the bedroom. We walk past the other girls that stare at me with so much hatred I could feel it against my skin. I made no new friends today, but it's ok. I won't be here much longer anyway.

CHAPTER FOUR

Routine

Sigma

My hips work aimlessly between the thighs of the breeder. Yet my mind is far away. The others find pleasure in the meaningless act of intercourse. I despise it.

When the women were first brought to us, I wanted nothing to do with them. However, Alpha demanded that we utilize them. He says we need to pretend until we are ready to leave. The longer we stay here, the more I get the idea there is something Alpha is hiding from us. He knows something we do not, and he is going out of his way to keep it from us.

I am brought back from my thoughts as the human girl moans beneath me. Despite not wanting to be here, the heavy meaty appendage between my legs continues to stiffen at the sight of a naked human female.

I do find comfort in the fact that she seems to be enjoying this. The tingling in my lower spine starts, alerting me that the useless creamy essence is on its way.

"Give me your baby, Sigma," The human female begs.

Though Alpha gave us strict orders to comply with the demands of the mating, he has forbidden any of us to allow our seedlings to attach to any of the human females.

Our offspring are only to belong to our Uvonu. In the old planet, we had mated pairs or Uvonu. Our mates carried our second heartbeats inside their chest, and the moment we meet them, our second heart will roar to life. Alpha says he is unsure if this will occur in our new forms.

There is a slow ache in my chest every time I think on this topic. I do not know where it derives from. However, I take a mental note of it.

My sticky essence erupts from me squirting out in rivulets into her womb. Once I have fulfilled my duty, I quickly remove my appendage from between her legs and stand. Smacking my open palm against the glass window, I alert the men on the other side that I am done. I have fulfilled my job for the day. I crave the solitude of my hidden room.

"How did it go?" Alpha's voice breaks through my thoughts.

"The same as always."

The door to the mating room opens, and my guards aim their guns at me as they wait to escort me out. I go quietly and obediently.

"Your ire vibrates the connection, Sigma. Speak your mind," Alpha encourages.

"I find this new assignment pointless and without meaning. It does not add anything to our plan of escape. The plan which we have yet to put to use."

"Speak for yourself, Sig. I find this new assignment quite enjoyable," Gamma adds as he opens his mind allowing us to see him pushing his appendage between a human female's legs.

Gamma gets the most enjoyment out of the intercourse. He does not argue or turn away when a new human is presented to him.

"We are not on Albatraum anymore, old friend. Things are done differently here. Your new body can be used for pleasure as it was not capable of on our home planet. You over think this. I'm allowing you time to reap the benefits of this pleasure. Not everything has to have a purpose."

"It does for Sigma," Beta cuts in. The lyrical tone of his voice lets me know he is joking.

However, he is right. My mind processes things in a cut and dry way. It is the way I am wired. I need tasks and structure. I do not find pleasure in things that have no other goal but to please the senses.

"Then why is it that you do not lie with the human females?" The connection goes silent, yet no one leaves. We have all wondered the reason behind this. Although he has advised us of this meaningless task, he has yet to indulge in it.

"My reasons are my own." The bite in his remark lets me know this topic is not up for discussion. *"I have led you in your old life and in this one. I will not steer you wrong. That you can believe."* The connection to Alpha goes silent, which means he has blocked us all.

"Way to go, Sig. Now he's pissed," Gamma says.

Gamma is the youngest of the five of us. Alpha was once a king in our home planet before the Great War destroyed it. Beta is the reincarnation of his first guard. A position of great power on Albatraum. He would have been equal to a president on this new planet. Omega was a mighty warrior and head of our Army; Gamma was his right-hand man and his baby brother.

"Those were not my intentions."

"I don't see the problem," Gamma says. *"Maybe if you stop over thinking it, you will enjoy the intercourse."*

Doubtful. However, I do not convey those sentiments to Gamma. Instead, I close the connection, enjoying the silence. My guards place me back in my room, where I quickly redress.

Placing my hand against the wall I find the circuits to the cameras I need and place them on a loop. I only manipulate the ones in my path to my place of solace. I slip out of the door and make my way to the lower level. Before I can make it to unit H, alarm rattles the link. Something is wrong. I reopen the main connection which connects me to all of the reincarnates. They are all speaking at once.

"Quiet," Alpha's voice roars to life and the link grows silent. *"Find them, Sigma,"* He demands.

Placing my hand back to the wall, I travel through every camera system in the building, yet I don't find what I'm looking for. Then, I see it. For only a second, they slip into the frame of the camera.

"Got it. Looks like I'm closer. I'll go," I say as I sprint off in the direction of the disaster I will face.

Not all of the reincarnated are created equally. We are mostly made up of the DNA Alpha gave us from our home plant. However, there is also the foreign substance Strong, and his scientist pumped us with as well. I can feel it flowing through my veins. It does not mix well with the DNA Alpha gave me. It feels sluggish in my veins like slime. It dulls some of my senses and causes me to grow angry quickly, a trait that is not original to me.

It requires a lot to battle the anger, and not all of us are capable of it.

I round the corner of the narrow hallway and come across a scene we have grown accustomed to. Three bodies lie at the feet of a reincarnate as he pummels another slightly smaller reincarnate. The smaller one is doing well at holding his own against the brutality of the other.

The moment I reach the brawl, I grab the larger reincarnate by the neck and slam him to the floor. The smaller one falls to his knees.

The larger one stands back up and lowers his head as if he plans to attack me.

"I advise you to stand down. I am not the trouble you seek," I say through the link, but he has the connection blocked. I push through his thin wall of resistance and repeat myself.

"You are not my master," He growls inside my head.

I tilt my head to the side. *"I may not be, but you will bow to me all the same."*

He charges for me, but I easily step out of his way, using the bend of my elbow to catch him around the neck. I tuck his head securely against my arm, placing my other hand at his back. Lifting him off his feet, I then slam him down into the ground.

A trimmer moves through the building and a crack spread across the floor. The reincarnate at my feet is knocked out cold. I didn't kill him. I am not allowed to kill the rogues, Alpha has plans for them.

I turn back to the smaller one. He's beat badly.

"What's your name?" I ask.

"*4765,*" he replies.

I shake my head. *"No, that is the number they gave you. What is the name you chose?"*

His brows come together, and he tilts his head. *"I did not choose a name."*

I open the commander's link. It's the connection for only Alpha, Omega, Gamma, Beta, and I. We use it when we don't want any of the other reincarnates to hear us.

"Do you know this one?" I ask Alpha. He has a connection to all the reincarnates. He can also tell if they are more like us or more like the rogue.

He hesitates for a moment. *"I sense he is a civilian and young. He also has healer abilities."* Although I and the others were reincarnated of high-ranking officials, some of the reincarnates are citizens of Albatraum. *"Give him a name."*

If he wants me to name him, it means he is more like us than the unconscious one on the floor.

"Your name is Zee," I tell him. The name comes to me quickly.

Zee smiles. The body he inhabits isn't much younger than the one I have. Like mine and Gamma's, his skin is tan, nowhere near the pigment that Beta is. He's a few inches shorter than me, maybe 6'4. His eyes are gray and like the rest of us, his hair is shaved low.

"I like Zee, sir," The reincarnate says proudly.

"Can you tell me what happened here? Did something trigger him?"

Zee looks down at the rogue at my feet. *"No."* His gaze slides back up to me. *"He attacked out of nowhere. I tried to calm him down, but he would not."*

Alpha's frustrated sigh comes through the link. This is the problem we are having with some of the reincarnates—the superfluous desire to kill. None of us are without fault. Many have fallen due to our anger and plot to leave, but we have never sought out death just because.

"What do you want me to do?" my question is for Alpha, but I know that the others are tuned into the link as well.

"Beta and Gamma are headed to you to take the rogue back to his cell. I want you and Zee to handle the guards."

"Do we want this reported to Strong?" Gamma queries through the link.

"No. Strong is occupied. I need him to stay that way. Make the guards disappear, for now."

That meant he wanted me to hide the bodies and remove their names from the employee files. When I am done, there will be no record of these men ever showing up here—apart from a few people knowing them.

I turn in time to see Gamma and Beta heading around the corner. They quickly pick up the rogue with only a nod in our direction before heading back the way they came.

"Come, Zee," I demand of the reincarnate.

We work quickly. Zee talks constantly in my head, holding a one-sided conversation. He seems to not notice I prefer silence. I tried to block him, but Alpha keeps removing the block. He and the others find humor in this. I do not. We store the bodies in the hidden tunnel we built for this reason.

Once we are done, I seal the tunnel and then turn to leave. I crave the solace of my hidden room. This task has cut into my time, and soon, my guards will be ready to take me to lunch.

"Where are we headed now?" The excitement in Zee's voice has me spinning on the balls of my feet to face him.

"Look who has made a new friend," Omega's throaty chuckle erupts through the commander's link.

"We are not friends," I deny quickly.

"You two make a cute pair," Gamma adds, and this time, all of their laughter comes through the connection.

"I do not understand the humor in this."

"Of course, you don't, that's what makes it so much funnier." Beta says, and the laughter increases.

I block them out. Cutting off the link as if I'm slamming a door in their faces.

"Go back to your cell. I want to be alone," I growl through my connection to the kid before blocking him as well. I storm off, craving my solitude more than ever.

CHAPTER FIVE

Freedom

Shiloh

By the time the day of the delivery came around, I knew exactly who Miguel was getting rid of.

Every one of them made sure they found a way to curse me out, and the ones that's been allowed to stay have done all they can to avoid me. They won't even look at me if I enter the same room with them. Not like I've been able to be around anyone.

Miguel has been putting in work trying to get me pregnant. He's in my room at least seven to eight times during the day and waking me at least twice at night. I'm tired and worn out. If I get nothing else from this escape plan, at least I'll be able to take a break from all the dick.

Climbing out of the bed, I stretch my aching body. Miguel and Carlito left about an hour ago. I have another hour to get myself ready. I shower quickly and dress in leggings and a sweatshirt.

One of the benefits of being here so long is that I know every inch of this house. I know where every camera is pointed and how to avoid them. The only time Miguel will see me on camera is when I walk out of my room for the first time. I need him to see that.

Hopefully, if everything goes right, he won't know I'm gone until the next day when the butler shows up to give me my prenatal vitamin.

After leaving my room I head to the east wing of the house where all the other girls reside. The halls are empty. I imagine no one wants to risk the chance of being seen and possibly sent away.

I knock on the door at the end of the hallway. Although Miguel's collection of women is all different, I'm not exactly a part of his collection. So, when he brought home Normani, I thought it was eerie that he found a girl that resembled me.

She's my height, complexion, and has the same slight build as me. However, her eyes are a dark brown and more rounded to my upturned. Another huge difference between Normani and me is that she loves her short buzz cut. She has the head shape to pull it off.

The door swings open, and I come face to face with a very pissed off Normani. I don't blame her for her hostility. I'm the last person that she would want to see. Although she isn't one of the girls getting shipped off today, I'm still not a welcomed visitor.

"What the fuck do you want?" She snarls.

"Can I come in?" Now is not the time to catch an attitude with her.

"No," she says, crossing her arms over her chest.

I factored into my plans that this could be a problem. I won't let it deter me. After plastering on the Mona Lisa smile, I try again.

"Look, I'm not going to hold you up. I just need to borrow some tampons."

Her eyes narrow. "I thought you were pregnant?"

My smile never falters. "Not yet. Doesn't look like it will happen this month."

Her posture doesn't change, but I need to get my ass in that room. My entire plan goes to shit if I don't.

"I guess I can always go ask Miguel. I'll tell him you didn't have any." I turn around to leave, but she stops me.

"Wait."

I wipe the smirk off my face when I turn back to face her. It's sad how predictable these women are when it comes to him.

She steps back, allowing me to enter. I don't have to worry about cameras since the only rooms that have them are on the lower level. It's where all the new flight risk girls stay before they get accustomed to being here.

I step in and look around, this being the first time I've ever seen the inside of one of the girls' rooms. They're smaller than mine but looked more lived in. There are pictures on her walls and fancy bed linen that matched her personality.

I've never put much thought into the bedroom I lived in. Every now and again, the butler brings me new sheets and blankets that I place on the bed, but I've never picked any out. And I've never felt the need to personalize my prison cell.

"How many do you need?" She asks as she heads to her bathroom.

"Just five," I say, tossing out the random number.

The moment she is out of sight, I rush to the chair under the window and grab the gray hoodie. I frantically stuff it down the front of my sweatshirt.

We all had signature things that we wore. Me, it's usually something short or see-through to show off my body. Some of the other girls also had their favorite things, but everyone knows that Normani constantly wore hoodies and jerseys with a team logo on it. I don't know the sport or the team; I just know the girl is always wearing it.

After hiding the hoodie, I go back to my spot by the door. She comes back out of the bathroom with a handful of tampons. She shoves them into my chest, but I keep my smile plastered on my face.

"Thank you." I turn to leave but stop and look over my shoulder. "You may want to stay in your room as much as possible today. I heard Miguel telling one of the guards he's looking for more girls to send."

Her eyes widen and her arms, which were folded across her chest, drop down to her sides.

"Out of sight, out of mind, right?" I say cheerfully.

"Thank you for the heads up," she says.

I take that as my cue to go. I still had a little more to do to make this plan work.

Booking it back to my bedroom, I make sure to stay off the camera this time. Closing the door behind me, I quickly head into the bathroom where the scissors wait. The next step is to cut my hair off. I can only hope I have a similar head shape to Normani.

First, I take out the waist-length tracks that's been sown in. Immediately my head feels lighter. Once all the hair is out, I take the trimmers from his side of the sink, and while looking in the mirror, I run the buzzing tool across my scalp. It takes a few passes to get all the hair off. It isn't as nicely shaped up as Normani's and its shorter, but that's not a problem.

I take all the hair and place it in the fireplace in my room. After turning the gas on, I watch it burn. Dressing in the gray hoody, I then grab a pair of shades. This will be the hard part if they ask me to take my shades off, I'm shit out of luck. Hopefully, the security guard won't care enough to double-check.

With exactly three minutes to spare, I make my way down the stairs. My heart is hammering in my chest. This will be the hardest part. Once I get to the warehouse, I'll blend in easier with all the other females.

The house is quiet because most of the girls are all hiding out in their room, thanks to the tidbit I gave Normani earlier. I figured she would share it with the others.

I reach the front door without any problems. The van is already here, and the girls are still loading their bags. I slip out the front and dash across the yard to where the vehicle is parked. I'm so close I can feel the heat coming from the engine; that's when I hear it.

"Normani?" the male voice pulls me up short.

I exhale a deep breath before turning toward the security guard.

"Yeah?" her voice is a little softer than mine, but as long as I use short answers, I should maintain it.

The guy eyes me up and down, taking in my short hair down to my sneakers before his gaze lands back on my face. I'm holding my breath. If he asks me to take off these glasses, it's all over. I can tell by the way he's looking at me, he's about to ask.

"Sam," Another man from the security team calls out. "Come help me with these damn bags."

Sam looks back at me once more before turning to help the other man. I sigh in relief and quickly climb my ass on the van. Heading straight to the back, I take a seat and lay long ways on the bench pretending to sleep.

After another few minutes, the bus is loaded, and we head out. I don't look up like I want to in hopes of seeing the mansion behind me. Instead, I continue to play sleep.

The further the bus drives, the freer I start to feel. Even though I'm not out of the woods yet. I won't be truly safe until I get to wherever Benjamin has us going.

The drive to the meet-up isn't that long. Once the van starts to slow, I sit up. We arrive at huge metal gates and the feeling of being free earlier seems to zap out of me. When we pass through the gate, and I watch it close up behind us, I start to feel caged in a whole new way.

The building itself doesn't look like much. Made of gray concrete and rectangular in shape, I would look right over it if I didn't know what it was. In front of the building are school buses surrounded by men, and in lines are so many women I can't count them all.

The van pulls to a stop, and the doors open. The girls start to load off, but I give it a few minutes. The man named Sam is giving them orders, telling the girls to head to a certain line.

After making sure the coast is clear, I climb out, pulling my hoody up over my head. No one really pays attention to me because it's too much going on. There are girls of all shapes and sizes screaming and crying. Some are even fighting the men that are holding them down.

One guard I've never seen at the house before is ushering the girls that came with me to another line. I head in the same direction until I hear his voice.

"Brother, you're not listening to me," Carlito is saying as he and Miguel come into view. They are standing right in the path I was going to take.

I step into the closest line to me and quickly slip out of the hoody, tying it around my waist.

"He asked for women, I'm giving him women," Miguel argues.

"You promised him one hundred and twenty girls, plus the ten from the house. There are only a hundred and ten here."

Miguel shrugs. "Before this, he had none. One hundred and ten is more than none, right?" he turns to walk away, but Carlito stops him again.

"These aren't the type of people to fuck over."

"No, I'm not the type to fuck over," Miguel yells, causing heads to turn in their direction.

Carlito tries once more to get his brother to see reason. "This is an easy and lucrative route to trade the girls. With the crackdown on trafficking, we can't lose this avenue."

Miguel looks up and directly in my direction. It's almost as if he could sense me close to him.

I don't move. I don't even breathe. For what seems like a lifetime, he stares directly at me. It isn't until he shakes his head and turns back to Carlito do I realize that he was obviously staring past me. I let out a deep exhale.

"Fine, bring the rest of the girls. I'm done here. I need to get out of here and catch my flight." With that, Miguel turns and goes back the way he came. Thankfully in the opposite direction of me.

"Hey, get your ass moving," A beefy man shouts right before he shoves me hard in the back.

I tumble forward, falling to my knees. The glasses fall from my face, and I scramble to grab them. Quickly scooping them up, I fight to get them back on. The second they're in place, I'm yanked by the arm and hauled to my feet with a biting grip. Expecting to come face to face with the beefy guy, I gasp when Carlito is gaping down at me.

For a moment, he only stares with wide-eyed fear.

"Please, please don't take me back," I start to plead.

He looks around. Thankfully, only the guy that shoved me and the girl in front of me is paying attention.

"She comes with me," Carlito says to the man.

"Boss says all women go."

"This one is different." It's the only explanation Carlito gives before he drags me away from the line and the man that could ask too many questions.

His footsteps are a lot faster than mine, and I struggle to keep up. He pulls me inside the building into a small white room that smells like bleach but looks like someone painted the wall with every bodily fluid you can imagine.

Once we're inside, he slams the door shut and yanks the glasses off my face. He takes a step back and looks me over.

"Before you take me back, think of all the people that will die." I try to reason with him.

"Shut up, Shiloh. Just shut up." he runs a hand over his shortcut. He turns away from me as if he can't bear to look at me.

My heart is in my stomach as I try to figure out where this is going. At the moment, I have no clue. Part of me believes Carlito will help. However, there is another part that knows he's as crazy and obsessed as his brother. Just because he doesn't agree with Miguel's tactics doesn't mean he wants me free.

"Who all knows you're here?" His question is asked with his back to me.

"No one."

He spins around and glares at me. "Are you sure?"

"I'm sure." I say with confidence, and then that confidence wains when I remember something. "One of the security guards that brought me over might suspect."

"Fuck," he growls. "Which one?"

"Sam." Silence surrounds us again, and I still have no idea if he will let me go or not. "Carlito, you have to help me. This is the only way."

"We don't know what they need these women for. This could be dangerous." Valid point, but I'm willing to take the risk.

"And the way I live now isn't dangerous?" I counter.

"That's different, we know how to steer clear of Miguel. You don't know how dangerous these new people could be. If I let you go, and something happened to you." he trails off, leaving those last words unsaid.

I take a step toward him, reaching for his hand; I pull it up to my chest placing it over my heart. His brown eyes look down at where his hand lies over the organ that keeps me alive. That's it's only job because it damn sure isn't capable of love.

"If I stay, I'm already dead. We both know our only way out of that house is in a body bag. Will you be able to watch me die there?"

He pulls away from me, taking a step back. His mouth falls open. "How can you even ask me that? You know I could never watch you die."

"And I feel the same about you," Bullshit, but I didn't come this far to fail. "That's why you have to let me go. This is my only chance, you know it."

Hesitancy still weighs in his brown eyes. I take a step closer to him, bringing our bodies flush—his brow creases. Reaching up on my toes, I drag my lips over his. The spiciness of his breath assails my senses.

"If you love me, you have to let me go," I whisper the words against his mouth before I drop back onto my heels. Yes, I'm a bitch for using his love for me to get my way, but I would only feel guilty if I truly believed Carlito loved me.

He doesn't. He's just as fascinated with me as his brother is. Maybe even more so because I belong to Miguel and he can't have me.

Carlito places his forehead to mine and lets out a long sigh.

"Alright, I'll help you leave." I don't get excited yet. I'll wait for that excitement when I'm miles away from the two brothers.

CHAPTER SIX

Allies

Sigma

The siren sounds, and I jump into action. Diving to the ground for the first obstacle, I stay low as I make my way to the other side of the mud trench. The moment I'm cleared, I leap to my feet and sprint to the ten-foot wall scaling it without the use of the ropes.

This is what I enjoy about the new life; the trainings are the best part of the day. They make sense. There's a reason for them, and they have an end goal. The other things we are forced to do here does not.

I finish the training first, jumping down from the top of the wall landing on my feet and crossing the finish line with seconds to spare before the others join me. A feat only achievable because Alpha and Omega are in the mating rooms.

The guards in their green fatigues watch me in amazement.

"Nice job, Sigma," Reynolds, one of my personal guards says.

I despise most of the soldiers and scientists here. They are cruel beings that care for nothing but themselves and the research they believe they are responsible for.

However, Reynolds has been the most tolerable. His posture is always open. It isn't the closed-off cocky stance like many others here. His heart rate is always slightly elevated around us, but never racing. It says a lot about him.

"He doesn't have a name. Stop trying to make them human," Kenneth sneers toward me. Even though his words are said with an angry lilt, his heart is racing, and fear permeates from his pores. "Get back in the damn line, 0140."

It's guards like Kenneth that make my desperate need to escape this place more clawing.

"You don't have to be an asshole. He isn't doing anything wrong."

Kenneth, older than Reynolds, takes a step toward the young guard. "You think these alien freaks are your friends?" Another step closer, bringing them toe to toe.

My fingers twitch at my side. I do not like his posture toward Reynolds.

The link crackles before Alpha's voice comes through the connection. *"Stand down, Sigma."*

"He is testing my patience," I argue my case.

"Not our battle. Stick to the plan."

As bad as I want to ignore the command, I know Alpha is right. Our attacks are strategic. They serve a greater purpose. We keep account of all dead bodies. None will go to waste.

"Look at them," Kenneth's stubby finger points to me. "They don't even have fucking brains. They're animals, freaks of nature. Stupid brainless beasts." He continues to degrade us.

"I don't care how they were created," Reynolds says, crossing his arms over his chest. "They're still human beings. And despite what you think, they're intelligent. Alpha is—"

"Alpha," Kenneth scoffs. "He's the biggest freak of them all. They're so busy trying to get him to mate, but they can't see the truth. He doesn't want any of those bitches' Strong keeps bringing in. Look at the way he looks at us? He likes ass, man. Better watch your back."

"I take it back." Alpha's words are growled in my head. *"Deal with him."*

"My pleasure," I reply at the same time my fist flies out and plants right on Kenneth's chin. He goes down so fast it takes a few seconds for the other guards to realize what happened.

The guns come out then, close to fifty of them are aimed at me. This may result in me being in lockdown for a few days, but it was worth it. Even though he will survive the attack, he will require surgery to fix his jaw.

"I don't blame you for that one," Reynolds says with a smirk. He steps toward me, pulling his cuffs out of his pockets.

I hold out my hands peacefully for him to place them on my wrist. Twenty-armed guards escort me to my holding cell. Once inside, I sit down on the cold floor of the cramped cell. They think locking me in this small room alone for days is punishment. The solitude is comforting.

"I saw what you did, that was awesome." I groan at the sound of Zee's voice in my head. *"Kenneth deserved it. Do you think they will keep you in solitude all day? If not, maybe we can hang, and you can show me how to do that trick with the computers."*

Dropping my head into my hands, I let out a burst of breath. The kid is non-stop in my head. No matter how many times I block him, Alpha continues to move the block.

Laughter comes through the connection as the rest of the group listens to the reincarnate go on and on about nothing.

I eventually put up a stronger block making sure Alpha cannot break it down. Settling my head back against the wall, I enjoy the peace and quiet.

"Your ability to put up blocks are improving."

"Apparently not, if you got through." I answer in reply to Alpha

His laughter chimes in my head. *"I will always be able to get through."* There is a moment of silence, but I know he has more to say. *"He's a good kid. You should give him a chance."*

"I do not doubt his character. I just do not desire his company"

"I gave you a second chance at life, old friend. Don't waste it."

I close my eyes at the mention of my old life. The more time that passes, the more I remember of the life before.

"Who said the old one was so bad?" I grumble.

"I've known you since I was a youngling, Vulto," For the first time, the use of my original name sparks its own set of memories.

A large castle on a hill is in the distance. Two young boys chase after each other. One has dark blue skin and silver eyes. His silver hair is long and covers the small black horns jutting out the side of his head. He turns to look at me, and I immediately know it is a young Alpha. I shake my head to clear the foreign imagery.

"They're coming back to you faster than the others," Alpha says. He must have witnessed the memory I just saw. Where my ability is dealing with computers and electrical currents, Alpha's abilities are much more advanced. He has the power to pull from all our skills. Although he rarely borrows our gifts, he does use our thoughts and sights from time to time.

"Why is that?"

"Unfortunately, I do not have a concrete idea as to why. I only assume it is because you were the historian and my advisor. You were always wired to have a sharp memory," He admits. *"There are a few things I'm finding different about this new life."*

I know that in the old world, Alpha and I shared a strong bond. It was different than the friendships he shared with the others because of our history, he confides in me more than he does the others. We all have our uses though.

The link between Alpha and I go silent, even though I know he is still connected to me.

"No matter how hard I try, I can't remember the war or what lead up to it. Not one single detail," I admit.

Whenever my thoughts drift to the subject, and I start to get a glimpse of a memory, it evaporates like smoke in thin air.

Though Alpha has mentioned the Great War many times, he has never gone into detail about it. Usually, if he brings up a subject about the old world, it triggers a memory for me, but not this one. I find this rather peculiar.

"Be grateful," He mumbles through the connection. *"It is all I can think about."* With those words, our leader disconnects from my thoughts, and the line goes silent.

CHAPTER SEVEN

Vita Lab

Shiloh

It's been three days since I escaped from Miguel. After the longest bus ride of my life, we arrived at Vita Labs. The first day we were sectioned off in two groups, by volunteers and those that didn't volunteer.

Supposedly, volunteers were treated much better than the ones in the other group. Since I'm a volunteer, the worst I've experienced is freezing cold rooms, being examined thoroughly, and having enough blood drawn to recreate me.

Now I'm sitting on a bed in a hospital gown, connected to an IV drip with my legs swinging as I wonder, not for the first time if this was the right move. Obviously by now, Miguel has discovered I'm gone. I imagine he is losing his shit. Bodies are probably already piling up. I only hope Carlito can keep his mouth shut. I'm still not sure if I've reached the point where Miguel can't get to me.

The clicking of the lock has me turning my head to the door. A woman walks in with a white coat and a tablet in her hands. Her blonde hair is pulled back in a low bun. She's followed by a man with a shaved head wearing a military uniform pushing a wheelchair.

"Shiloh Green," The woman says with a smile. It's practiced and not the least bit enduring.

"That's me." I haven't heard my full name in so long it feels odd answering to it.

"My name is Sharon Procter, and I will be your nurse today. Since you are sitting up, it looks like the medicine is finished running its course."

I've been hooked up to this IV for two days. The first day was rough, I could barely move.

She looks down at her tablet and starts to tap at it. "You've also passed your health screening. I guess you're ready to start phase two."

I could've saved them the trouble and told them I was clean if they'd asked. We got check-ups every three to six months back at the house, depending on if a new girl came in. Miguel wasn't a big fan of condoms. He made sure all the girls were clean.

"Okay. What's stage two?" My brows pinch together.

This place isn't very forthcoming with information. Since I've been here, they've only given out directions. I've been poked, prodded, and examined on repeat. And yet, I still don't know what they want with me.

She looks up at me briefly before returning to her tablet. "Now that the birth control has been flushed out of your system, you can go have your surgery."

My eyes nearly pop out of my head I spread them so wide.

Alright, I'm done with all the secrets. I need answers. "What surgery? What's going on?"

The woman gives me one more of her fake compassionate looks. "It says in your files that you volunteered for this work?"

"Well, yes." I say shifting my weight on the examination bed. The paper underneath me crinkles. "But I also didn't get much information before I signed on."

She hums and then folds her arms across her chest, tucking the tablet close to her body. "I guess you can say we are researching fertility."

Bullshit. Someone needs to teach these people how to lie. Even when Benjamin said it, I didn't believe it.

I guess my face gave away my reservations because she laughs.

"Your government needs you. They are building super soldiers, and you have volunteered to aid in their evolution."

I still have my suspicion she isn't telling me everything. Anytime the government is involved in experiments, it's never been simple or cut and dry.

She continues, "In about two to three months, you will move on to the research compound where you will be paired with a male and hopefully become pregnant."

"That's it? You just want me to sleep with a dude and get pregnant?" Yes, I see the irony in the situation. I ran for the very same reason.

"Yep. You will be doing your country a great service."

I don't know why they keep saying that as if it's a selling point.

"You're not expecting me to keep the child, right?"

Does that sound heartless? Yes. However, when I finally leave the compound she's talking about, I may very well still be on the run from Miguel. It's not easy to run with a kid on your hip.

Procter laughs as if I've just made the world's greatest joke. "Of course, you won't take the child. It will belong to the government."

Okay, that statement does kind of bother me. I guess somewhere deep in my soul I may have a small motherly bone, but I quickly push those concerns aside.

"I was told there would be compensation?" This is the big question. All this is for nothing if I don't have the money afterwards to survive.

Her practiced smile falters a little. That tells me there's a catch to the money.

"There is a thirty-five thousand dollars payout at the end of your two-year contract, but you should put your focus on getting pregnant and carrying a baby to full term. Then we will talk about compensation. Now," she says the last word cheerfully. "Let's get you ready for surgery."

The male in the military uniform brings over the wheelchair he brought in. I hop down off the bed. Procter grabs my IV pole and helps me maneuver the cords around, so I can have a seat.

The two silently wheel me out of the little hospital room I've been staying in for the last three days. So far, this is still the best route I could've taken to get away from Miguel.

CHAPTER EIGHT

Sweets

Miguel

"I swear, I never left my post. She didn't walk out the front door," The security guard on his knees in front of me pleads.

I don't give a fuck about his excuses. I pull the trigger and splatter his brains against the concrete floor of my basement. It combines with the twenty others that I've killed since I got back today. Imagine my surprise when I got the phone call three days ago that she was missing. I caught the first flight I could and came back.

The sight of the security guard's blood does not ease my anger like it usually does. My heart, my sweets is gone.

I'm not a good man. I never pretended to be. I like pussy, bourbon and putting mother fuckers in their graves. Not necessarily in that order. Nothing makes me happier than the privilege of taking a life. I thought for the longest I was damaged until I saw her.

I still don't know what it is about Shiloh that grabbed my attention. Although she's gorgeous, she isn't the most beautiful woman I've ever seen. Hell, I've fucked girls with eyes prettier than hers.

I have to admit, her pussy is superb. It hugs my cock tighter than a lover and runs like a faucet for me. However, that still isn't what captured me about her.

The moment my eyes landed on my sweets in that run down strip club, something in my soul screamed for me to possess her. The fire and strength in her eyes reminded me of the wild horses on my Abuelo's farm. As a kid, I loved to watch the ranch hand break and tame the wild animals.

I knew immediately I wanted to tame her, to break that little bit of fight I saw shining in her eyes in that cheap club. My desire to shatter her strength and make her crave me and only me is what had me offering her a position in my home.

Once I destroyed her self-worth, I was going to kill her and watch the blood drain from her body. My dick got hard every time I thought about slitting her fucking throat.

Yet, somewhere along the way, my desire to kill her continued to get pushed aside. What took its place is an obsession. She became my new drug. The one thing that seemed to soothe the devil and rage inside me.

Now my drug is gone, and I want it back.

I roar out my frustration and aim my gun at another random guy and fire it. He falls amongst the rest of the carnage.

"Brother," Carlito calls my name in a placating tone. I turn to glare at him. "I know you want Shi back, but you can't kill everyone."

"Are you sure about that?" I lift my gun and aim it at another security guard. The man cowers, throwing up his hands as if it will stop a bullet.

"Miguel," Carlito calls my name, getting my attention once again. "Let's go back to the tapes. The cameras had to have picked up something."

"I've checked the got damn tapes a hundred times," I yell so loud spittle flies from my lips. "They only capture her leaving the room. Whoever took her had to have taken her in the house and snuck her out."

"It wasn't us, Boss," One of the guard's cries. "The girls were all there that day. They hated her."

I turn to the sniveling man, my eyes narrow at him. "What did you just say?"

He looks shaken but repeats himself. "I said, we would never cross you. But it was well known the girls had it out for Shiloh. Maybe they did something to her."

My blood begins to heat as I think of one of those replaceable cunts putting their hands on my sweets. Ever since I let that snake Candace live, they probably all thought it was okay to try me.

"Calm down, brother. You don't know for sure," although I hear Carlito talking, it sounds faint.

I turn to my new head of security, the one I assigned, after putting a bullet in the last one. "Get them up and bring them all to me."

If I didn't find an answer to where Sweets went by the end of the night, at least I would have my fill of death.

CHAPTER NINE

Old Friends

Shiloh

It feels good to be up and moving again. It took a week to fully recover from the procedure. Thankfully it was done by laparoscopic surgery. Other than a twinge of pain when I bend, I'm all healed up.

They now have us on some type of hormones that are running rampant through my body. My breast hurt, and my mouth is dry, but my skin looks better than ever.

I'm heading to lunch now after my daily activities. They allow us out of the room for breakfast, lunch, and dinner and for our routine tests. These tests consist of physical exercises and actual multiple-choice questions.

I'm in a line of about fifteen other girls. In front of us is a nurse, and following in the back is a soldier in green fatigues. They escort us into the cafeteria in a single file. I head to the buffet and grab a tray.

Although parts of this does give me prison-style vibes, the food here doesn't. I haven't been disappointed with a meal yet.

I fill my heavy aluminum tray with fruits and a grilled chicken salad, then head to an empty table. I stop suddenly.

It isn't only the feeling of being watched that has me coming up short; it's the prickling of danger that makes me pause. Scanning the cafeteria briefly, I try to see what is giving me such bad vibes. Then I spot it, a pair of blue eyes so filled with rage I take a step back.

Apparently, when I told Miguel to kick Candace out, he assumed I meant ship her off to this place. That was not my intentions. I want to go over there and explain that to her, however, the way she is frothing at the mouth, I don't think she will be willing to listen.

It's best I keep my distance. I continue with my journey of finding a seat. One thing they do not allow here is talking amongst us girls. I have no idea why, but it doesn't really bother me. I've always been a bit of a loner. Sitting down at an empty table, I start to dig into my food.

A sudden noise behind me grabs my attention. Turning slightly in my seat, I'm struck in the face with a hard object. Pain radiates from my right temple. I'm then immediately tackled to the floor by Candace. She lands on top of me and wraps her hands around my throat choking me.

"You bitch. You took him from me," She yells as she continues to squeeze my neck.

I fight to pry her hands away, but this crazy bitch is remarkably strong. Dots start to form in my vision. When we were home, I tapped down my urge to fight her in hopes of sparing her death. However, we aren't at Miguel's anymore.

Reaching my hand out to my side, I search for the objects she hit me with. Once my fingers wrap around the metal food tray, I pick it up and slam it against her head. She squeals but rolls off me. I take deep breaths fighting to get oxygen back in my lungs.

Rolling onto my side, I spot two soldiers rushing toward us. Where the hell were they when she was running up on me. Because my attention is on the men, I didn't see Candace get back up. She yanks me to my back.

Before I can swing and knock her ass out, searing hot pain radiates in my right eye. I scream as they pull Candace off me. Her maniacal laugh should have prepared me for what I found next.

I go to touch my right eye and come in contact with a long hard handle.

"He will never want you now. I ruined your pretty little eyes," Candace continues to laugh and taunt.

Meanwhile, a splitting headache starts to throb in my head. It's then that I notice my vision seems wonky.

"Oh, my goodness," one of the nurses says as she kneels in front of me. "Tell Dr. Foster to get the surgical room ready." The nurse yells.

"What... what is it?" I ask after once again touching the long handle.

The nurse swallows slowly and cringes. "A dinner fork."

I don't know if it's from hearing what is stuck in my eye or if it is the splitting headache, but I pass out.

CHAPTER TEN

Next Step

Shiloh

I lost sight in my right eye. The doctors here were able to save the eyeball, even though they couldn't stop the heterochromia from happening. My right iris is now a pale gray with only a single speck of the amber that was there before.

My eye surgery delayed me leaving Vita labs by two months. I've been here a total of four months now. Today is finally the day I head to the research compound.

I won't say I'm excited, more like ready to get this over with. We are lined up in front of a bus that says, 'Nevada State Penitentiary'. In front of me is a short woman with the same low haircut as all the women. She's a tad lighter than my dark brown skin but not by much. I would've killed for her curves though.

The soldier at the front of the line asks for her name. She doesn't have a chance to answer before Procter replies for her.

71

"Morgan Downs."

The soldier scrolls through his tablet.

"You're now number1362."

The girl doesn't immediately move. One of the orderlies escorting us places his hand on her back to push her forward onto the bus.

I move up in the line. The soldier looks up from his tablet, I'm assuming to ask the same question, but pauses. His mouth falls open, and he blinks rapidly. Yeah, I've been having this effect on people when they see me for the first time. If they thought I looked weird before with amber eyes, I look even crazier now.

"Shiloh Green," I say without him asking.

He shakes his head as if he's trying to restart his brain, then looks down at the tablet. "Number 1363." He looks back up at me and stares again.

I roll my eyes and step up onto the bus. Finding a seat in the back, I slide next to the window allowing space for one more person to sit near me.

It only takes another five minutes for the bus to fill up.

"Alright, Girls," a soldier barks, getting my attention. He tells us his name is Dak and how he doesn't want any issues on this trip. As if we would cause these grown men with guns a problem. After Dak's introduction and warning, we set off.

**

The drive itself isn't bad. The anticipation to get to the new compound and what will happen once we get there is what makes the trip daunting. I'm not stupid enough to believe that it's going to be all simple and lovey-dovey here. If it were, they wouldn't have had to ask Miguel for women. Whatever they have going on at this new place is not going to be easy. I only hope I can get pregnant right away and then get the hell out.

The bus slows, and I look out of the window to get a better view of where we are. We seem to be on a military base. Large metal fences circle the area. At the top of the fence is sharp barb wires. It reminds me of something you would see at a prison. I get a sinking feeling in the pit of my stomach that those wires aren't there to keep people out.

Nothing else surrounds us but desert sand and open space. It feels like we are on mars. Military-style planes are parked underneath rows upon rows of dome-shaped flight hangars. One large U-shaped single story concrete building sits in the middle of the domed buildings. The most surprising thing is the number of soldiers. There are tons of them. They're dressed in green army fatigues, and they look to be in a rush as they scurry around the airfield. It doesn't look like they are welcoming us in.

"What the fuck?" Dak's loud shout has me turning my attention toward the front of the bus. "We're supposed to go in through the tunnels. All-female deliveries are made through the tunnels."

"All this is blocked off," the driver says.

From the way the soldiers outside are scanning the bus but not moving toward it, I don't think they're going to open this gate for us.

"Get someone on the radio," Dak shouts.

An argument ensues between Dak and whoever the driver is on the phone with.

"So, what are we going to do?" A soldier up near the front asks.

Just as I thought, they aren't opening the gates for us.

Dak looks toward the front of the bus where the gate is, then turns back to us.

"We take them in through the back entrance. Once we get them offloaded, they will no longer be our problem."

I don't understand this guy's impatience. It's only an hour and a half trip to get here, what would it kill them to turn around and come back tomorrow. The soldiers outside this bus don't really strike me as the type to be defied.

Nevertheless, the driver pulls away from the gate, but instead of turning right and going back the way we came, he goes left down a hill and through a tunnel.

When we come out on the other side, we are met by a different view of the compound. This one a little more frightening. There're more of those single-story concrete buildings and less flight hangars. On this side, the soldiers are heavily armed. It's like they are preparing for combat.

They rush the bus as soon as Dak and a few other soldiers step off. I can't hear what they're saying, but it doesn't look friendly.

"Hey, let's just start unloading these girls off the bus," the bus driver says.

All the soldiers on the bus stand. One stomps down the aisle to the back of the bus and opens the emergency exit. He then starts to unload the girls from the back first. This had even more of those gun toting men running toward the bus.

I have a bad feeling about this. Yet, I don't have time to sit on it because one of the soldiers grabs my arm and hauls me out of my seat shoving me toward the exit.

I don't put up a fight. Instead, I hop down with the aid of one of our soldier's hands. It's a lot noisier now that I'm off the bus. I realized it almost as fast as I did the scorching heat. It's blazing out here.

Commotion behind me has me turning to see what's going on. The girl, Morgan, that was in front of me in the bus line, is on the ground with one of the men from the bus glaring down angrily at her.

"What the hell, Hector? You can't control that bitch." Another guy from the bus says with a laugh.

The angry scowl on Hector's face intensifies. He grabs Morgan by the throat and lifts her off the ground. She squeals and beats her fist against his chest.

I have to give it to the girl, she's a tough cookie. Although, now seems like the wrong time to fight back. With all the weapons surrounding us, even if she gets free of Hector, there is nowhere to go. Did she not see the fence?

The loudest roar I've ever heard erupts over the airfield. I turn my head in time to see a giant storming toward us. I freeze in fear. Never have I seen a being this terrifying yet absolutely gorgeous. He reminds me of the ocean. Beautiful to admire but frightening at the same time. The way he's killing any soldier that steps in his way proves I should be scared.

Someone in the distance shouts, "Fire the guns." Shots begin to ring out, but not with bullets. The giant is getting littered with darts. However, they may as well be rubber bands the way he ignores them.

He storms over and stops right in front of Morgan. He's so close to me I could reach out and touch him. Not that I would. He doesn't speak or even move. He just stands there like Jason Vorhees once he comes out of the water at Crystal Lake.

"Alpha," a slender man with a lab coat and brown hair calls out to the giant. "Alpha, that's enough. Everything is alright now. Come back to the line, and we can discuss this."

The giant doesn't budge or acknowledge the man in the lab coat. He just stares at Morgan like he's going to pick her up and climb the empire state building. When he takes a step forward, I take one back, and he's not even interested in me.

I guess I'm not the only one terrified because Morgan scoots back on her bottom too. This makes the giant stop and pulls his brows together. He looks confused, but what the hell did he think. He killed like fourteen men before he came over here. Did he think she was just going to be okay with that?

"Do you want the girl, Alpha? Is that what this is about?" Lab coat asks.

The giant moves his head slightly in the direction of lab coat.

"Alright," lab coat says. "Take the girl to breeding room number seventeen."

My heart knocks against my chest like a trapped rodent under a shoe box. Not only for poor Morgan, but I think I finally realize what the hell is going on here. We're not sleeping with regular soldiers; they want us to breed with him.

I look past the giant in the direction he came from and spot a handful more of the creatures. Yes, I'm calling them creatures despite how beautiful they are. They're all tall and wide, like someone copied and pasted their frame. However, they come in all different colors like a box of skin-tone crayons. Despite how human they look, there is something unnatural about them.

For the first time since I left Miguel, I'm starting to wish I could go back.

Scuffling beside me draws my attention. One of the heavily armed soldiers reach pass me and grabs Morgan. The giant rips the man away from her and then snaps the guy's wrist backwards. The soldier screams at the same time I gag.

The giant reaches for Morgan, but a large dart hits him in the chest. He growls, staggers, and then finally falls to the ground at her feet.

Moments later, Morgan joins him on the pavement. Honestly, she lasted way longer than I would've.

Lab coat turns and starts yelling demands. "I want Alpha escorted to his holding cell." A bunch of soldiers crowds around the giant. It takes all of them to lift the creature off the ground and carry him away.

"Asim, see to the girl," Lab coat shouts to a Middle Eastern man. "Someone, please escort the rest of these women off this field and to their rightful quarters before something else happens."

He didn't have to tell me twice; I wanted off that lot. Hell, I wanted to go home. However, there is no going back now. What's the saying, out of the frying pan and into the fire. This must be hell fire.

CHAPTER ELEVEN

Yvonu

Sigma

The connection is vibrating like an electric current. Everyone wants to know what happened today during that training.

One moment we were discussing the man named Stewart Scott, who apparently is in charge of this research, and then Alpha breaks rank rushing to the aid of some female breeder.

I follow the guard ahead of me as he leads me to one of the glass training rooms. Omega and the new nuisance Zee are with me.

They locked us down right after Alpha's outburst, but now we are all back out at our required training stations.

I open the link to the main connection, and it seems everyone is asking the same question. "What happened with Alpha?"

As soon as our leader joins the link, his agitation ripples through all of us, I shake out my limbs to release some of the crackling energy that makes me want to act out.

"Hey, no funny business," One of the guards escorting us says to me.

"He's my responsibility. Don't talk to him," Reynolds snaps, stepping up beside me.

The other guard glares at Reynolds. "You saw the shit their leader pulled today in front of Scott. I don't trust any of these creeps."

I bare my teeth to the man, and he has the right mind to scurry away from me.

Reynolds chuckles under his breath before stepping back behind me.

"I know you are all concerned," Alpha says joining the main link. *"Do not be alarmed."*

"Is it time to leave? Are we putting our plan into action?" Rho, who was once a craftsman on our old planet, asks.

"No, it is not." Alpha disconnects from the main link leaving everyone with questions. Soon after, the commander link for the five us hums to life. I open it up, and he immediately speaks.

"The human is my Uvonu."

"Are you sure," Beta asks. I do not understand the wistfulness in his voice.

From the moment Alpha first told us about our mated pair, I have been disinterested. I do not want, nor do I desire to share my life with anyone. I sense this opinion is rare for our kind. I do not believe I felt this way in my old life. This feeling about mates is new; I haven't figured out why as of yet.

"I am certain," He replies. *"Her heart echoes in my chest alongside mine. I feel her exhaustion and fear."*

"This is good news, King," Omega says. He has always refused to call Alpha anything other than king. I guess even in his new life, he refuses to let go of the old ways. *"Now, we have an even more important reason to leave this place. You must take your Uvonu far away from here."*

Before Alpha even speaks, I already know what he's about to say. *"No. We must be patient. It is too risky right now."*

Although I can feel the others disappointment, I know that they will not voice it. They are too loyal to him to argue. Luckily, I do not have that same flaw.

"Another delay to the plans?" I ask. *"Should we toss them away all together?"*

The link vibrates with tension.

"Delay does not mean never, Sigma," Alpha replies on a long sigh.

"I do not question the definition of the word. I question the frequency of how many times you have used it."

"Alright then, men," Gamma says jokingly. He has never been able to take anything seriously. *"Maybe we should leave and let these two work it out."*

"No," Alpha snaps. *"You will stay and listen. At every turn, you question my leadership. Do you believe you could do it better, Vulto?"*

"He's using real names. He's definitely angry," Gamma whispers through the link as if we wouldn't all hear him.

"Of course not, Tovian," I say returning the favor of using his real name. *"I am only stating that we deserve more than to be told to wait patiently."*

"There are dangers out in the world that you are not yet ready for," Alpha shouts.

"What dangers? Maybe if you tell us and not handfeed us information we would better understand." My voice rise to match his tone.

The link goes silent again.

"We will not move on with the plans as of yet. You will just have to trust me."

Alpha disconnects, leaving the rest of us silent. One by one, the others exit the link.

"Sigma, are you going in?" Reynolds asks from behind me. Apparently, I have been standing in one place for a while.

"Yeah, weirdo. Get in the room." The guard holding the door in front of me snaps.

I take a step toward him, and he leans back. The clicking of guns goes off around me, but I don't acknowledge them. Instead, I step into the glass training room.

Taking a moment to examine my surroundings, I pick up the scent of Beta nearby.

Eventually, Omega, Zee, and I are left in the room alone. Trainings like these are rare. Strong usually only does them if he is here to view our progress. We keep most of what we are capable of under wraps. He has no idea of the things we can really do.

The commanders link vibrates again, and I open it up.

"Alpha," Beta says. *"Your mate is here with Strong."*

"Show me," Alpha growls.

Beta allows us to connect to his sight. The human female is with the doctor watching Beta. She looks unharmed, if not a little frightened. But I do not focus on the human female; my attention falls on the man with her.

I do not trust the doctor. His scent has been off lately. I cannot place it, but it is not his original smell. Even the way he looks at the human female is troublesome.

The connection from Beta is broken. I only see what's in front of me now. Just then, the room starts to fill with tension. The buzzer will go off soon, and the guards will come in with their guns ready for training.

I turn to the door, which I already know they will enter. Their elevated heartbeats give them away every time. As I knew it would, the alert goes off and the lights cut out. The guards rush in, wielding their weapons. I do not need the lights to find my opponents. I see very well in the dark, and even if I were blindfolded, I would still be able to find these men. They breathe loudly and walk like elephants.

Once the lights come back on, I look around my feet, counting the men I took down.

"Seven," I proclaim proudly to Omega and Zee.

"Three," Omega sulks. *"It could have been more, but they go after you because you are the easier target."*

The inflection in his tone tells me this may be one of the jokes he and Gamma are known for. The laughter coming from Zee verifies my suspicion.

Suddenly a deep intake of breath has all three of us turning toward the window. The female is here now.

I open the link and show her to Alpha; his desire for her pushes through me and causes me to take a step toward her. I fight his hold and catch myself from going further.

Strong places a hand on her shoulder. Omega growls, and I go on high alert. I may not understand his infatuation with the human, nor do I desire to, but my leader has claimed the female as his and no man should be allowed to touch her.

Strong moves the woman along, and soon she is out of sight.

"He may be a problem," I say through my private link to Alpha.

"You may be right," he agrees before opening up the main link to the others. *"I want all eyes on my mate. If you see her, you will announce it to me immediately. I want to be informed about her whereabouts at all times. Am I understood?"*

The others agree to Alpha, even if begrudgingly. Though the rogues will not go against our leader, they have no problem displaying their ire toward him.

All other links close out, and only Alpha and I remain. *"I know you have sensed a change in Strong. Have you determined where it stems from?"*

I'm not shocked he has felt my suspicions for Strong. He is probably the only one that has.

"No. I haven't figured it out yet. However, I will keep an eye on him."

"Thank you, Sigma." The link ends.

No doubt my leader and I will disagree again, but as for now he and I are all good.

CHAPTER TWELVE

Welcome Home

Shiloh

As I walk in a single file line with a pair of underwear and a change of clothes in my hands, I can't help but feel thankful that I am not the Morgan girl. My heart rate has yet to slow down from my experience outside.

They whisked her away from us, and I haven't seen her again. I can't believe they're going to give her to that monster. Not like my fate is any different. At some point, I will be given to them as well. The thought of it causes my head to throb. The doctors at Vita Labs told me headaches would be a constant side effect from my eye injury and the strain of only being able to see out of one eye. Yet, I think this one stems from being freaking terrified.

Since we left the tarmac, we went through a quick check-in where they recorded our numbers into their system. They then took us to a large locker room type area where they gave us a toiletry bag, an extra pair of underwear, and another one of these hideous blue jumpsuits.

We walk through this maze-like facility as if they are leading us to a prison cell. We come to a stop at large double doors that read Private Sector. The guard in front of us types in a code on the keypad beside the door.

The moment the doors slide open, we are met with boisterous laughter and loud talking. It's so different from every other area in this place, it seems as if I walked into another dimension.

Women dressed the same as me hang out in the hallways as if they are on vacation. More of the soldiers in the green fatigues are here as well. However, even they look as if they are enjoying themselves. It looks like one big party scene. If I didn't know any better, I'd think we were back at Castillo del pecado.

Once we step onto the hall, all eyes turn to us. The men look on with disgusting smiles and the woman sneer and frown. For the first time since I left Miguel, I feel as if I'm back home. This is what I'm used to. Those men I saw on the tarmac and what they want from us, is out of my league. However, mean chicks and horny men, I can navigate this with my eyes close.

"Alpha is mine, Bitch. You better not touch him," One of the women snarls at me when my gaze lingers on her for too long.

Is she out of her mind? Does she actually think I want any of these creatures, especially not the scary one they called Alpha.

I stumble forward when someone behind me shoves me. At the end of the hall, it branches off in two directions. Some of the girls are ushered right toward two more double doors. Whereas me and the rest of the girls are directed left down the hall that looks much like the one we just passed.

High pitched screeching has me turning my attention to the side, only to get the wind knocked out of me as I go tumbling down.

"I'm going to kill you." Candace screams from on top of me.

I should have known I would run into her again. I'd hoped that maybe they would've kicked her out of the program because of her clear instability. But I guess being bat shit crazy doesn't stop your coochie from working.

We roll on the floor, her scratching at my face like an angry cat and me trying to beat hers in. After that stunt at Vita lab, she better be glad I don't have a fork. She is owed this ass whooping.

I punch her in the face causing her head to slam back against the floor. She screams as she digs her nails in my cheek. Eventually, she's back on top of me, but is lifted off. I'm grabbed also and hauled to my feet.

One of the soldiers holds Candace back while another one stands in between us.

"Candy, what's this about?" The guard standing in between us asks.

Candy? When did she start going by Candy?

"This stupid fucking bitch got me kicked out of my boyfriend's house and shipped off here."

The way everyone turns to glare at me has me shrinking back. Also, that is not what happened. I saved her life, but of course, she doesn't tell them that.

The soldier turns back to me. He runs his gaze over my slim body as if he's inspecting me. He steps closer and runs a hand down the right side of my face.

"Other than those weird-ass eyes, she has nothing on you," The soldier sneers.

Even though his mouth says one thing, the way he's stroking my face and staring in my eyes says something else. I snatch away from his touch. He chuckles and drops his hands down at his side.

"I'm going to end you," Candace shouts again and tries to break free of the man holding her.

"Enough," the soldier standing between us shouts.

Candance obediently stops.

"Get her out of here," he says to the guard holding her back. He then turns to me with a smile. "Welcome to unit A, pretty eyes."

The way he says pretty eyes makes my skin crawl.

"Get these women settled," The soldier says before walking away. Feeling grateful the ordeal is over, I let out a deep breath.

Bending down, I go to pick up my toiletry bag when it's suddenly kicked out of grasp. I look up at the culprit to find three girls giving me the evil eye. They walk away making sure to kick the rest of my measly belongings out of my reach.

Finally collecting my things, with the exception of my extra pair of undies that someone stole, I make it to the room one of the soldiers designated as mine.

As soon as I walk in, a girl that could legit be a supermodel stands up from the bottom bunk. I'm not anywhere near what someone would consider light skin but standing beside this beautiful ebony goddess with so much melanin in her skin, my brown seems too light.

I didn't think anyone could pull off these blue overalls, but her tall, lean shape makes it look like high fashion. She reminds me of the model Naomi Campbell in height and build only.

"Hi," She greets with an authentic smile. "I'm Fatima. Sick mother who needs expensive medical treatment."

I stare at her, not sure what's going on.

She laughs. "Sorry, I keep forgetting how weird that sounds if you're new. My name is Fatima, and the reason I'm here is because of my mom. That's how we introduce ourselves."

Still seems weird, but okay. "I'm Shiloh, and I'm running from my boyfriend."

Her eyes widen for a moment. "Seems like pretty high stakes just to get away from your old man."

"Yeah, well, you don't know my old man." I shrug as I place my things on the top bunk. I assumed the bottom was taken since she was sitting on it when I came in.

"Did they give you the regular welcome?"

I flinch. I hope she didn't witness what happened out there. It wasn't a very good first impression and I don't want her jumping to conclusions about me.

"What do you mean?" Hopefully, she didn't hear the elevation in my voice.

She laughs, "You know, don't touch Alpha, don't touch Beta," she rolls her eyes.

Exhaling in relief I nod my head. "Yeah. What's with that?"

She plops down on the bed, folding her long legs under her. "A bunch of silliness. These girls in here think these super-soldiers belong to them. The Alpha claimers are the most obsessed. They're all out to get that fifty grand."

I didn't care about anything else, she said. "Go back to the fifty grand?" I look to her like a deer in headlights. Nurse Procter told me thirty-five thousand.

Fatima chuckles. "Supposedly, if you have a baby by Alpha or one of the other top four, they will give you a huge pay out at the end of your two years."

"Has anyone been paid yet?"

She shakes her head. "No. Not one of us have gotten pregnant yet."

What kind of fertility experiment is this if no one is getting pregnant? The longer I'm here, the dumber this plan starts to feel.

A knock at the door has me turning to find a soldier there. He has one of those disgusting smiles on his face.

"Hey, Fatima. How's it going?" he's talking to my roommate but has his eyes are glued to me.

"What do you want, Smith?" from the way she spits out his name, it seems my roommate isn't a fan of this Smith guy.

He isn't bad looking, stocky with blue eyes and dirty blonde hair. Not exactly my type, but he's not a troll.

"Have you given the new recruit the rundown?"

"What rundown?" I look over my shoulder and ask my roommate. Yet, it isn't her that answers.

Smith pushes off the wall and saunters into the room.

"Have you met those mute monsters yet?"

I swallow and nod my head.

He smirks as he takes in my fearful gaze. "Well, those motherfuckers are worse than you think. Do you know what happened to her last roommate?" he tosses his head toward Fatima. "One of those freaks got so happy during the mating process, he killed her. Split her right in half."

I gasp, clutching a hand to my chest. My gaze swings to Fatima who looks at everything but me. Only because my guard is down, and my head is turned I didn't see Smith coming closer to me. I don't notice it until his hand drags down the side of my face. Swinging my head back to him, I glare.

He smiles and drops his hand at his side. "Us guards are the only thing that can protect you in here."

I highly doubt that. After witnessing what that creature can do, this guy nor those soldiers are a match for him.

"If you want us to protect you, you'll have to pay the fee."

I don't have to ask what the fee is. I'm a woman in here with no money and no personal possessions. Plus, that disgusting look on his face is enough to let me know what he wants from me. However, the way Fatima can barely look at me right now and the rigidness in her shoulders tells me that saying no to this man may not be a good option.

"I'll let you think about it. I'll come back in a few days. After your first day with those monsters, you'll be begging for my help," he says with a wink before he walks out of the room.

My heart finally returns to normal once he's finally gone.

"As bad as it may seem, and trust me, it's bad. You don't want to say no to them," The beautiful dark skin girl whispers. Her arms are wrapped around her chest protectively. "Saying no will only come with consequences. You won't like them." She walks out of the room, leaving me standing in the middle of the floor.

Well shit.

CHAPTER THIRTEEN

Shiloh

Two hours later, I'm sweating bullets as I sit and wait in an empty room as naked as the day I was born. Every sound outside that door has me nearly passing out.

A soldier came and pulled me out of the bed and brought me down to the mating room. They didn't even give me time to adjust to the place. My roommate hadn't even come back, so I couldn't ask her what to expect with the mating process. The fact that she didn't deny what the soldier said about her old roommate has me extremely terrified.

I'm not a virgin, but I've only been with Miguel. Though he can be rough, there was never a chance he was going to kill me with his dick. How the hell do you die during sex?

When the lock disengages, I shoot up from the squeaky bed. Placing one arm over my chest, and one cover my hairless crotch.

One of the green fatigue soldiers walks in. He looks around the room as if he's expecting me to be hiding something. He looks over at me with a smirk before walking out again.

The next person to step into the room is one of the creatures. He seems angry as he checks me over. Already this doesn't seem promising. I back up against the wall, trying to get as far away from him as possible.

He's as tall and wide as the others I saw. His face is square-shaped, and his brown eyes are hyper-focused on me. His tan skin is without any blemish. My gaze falls to the very erect and extremely large penis standing at attention between his legs.

Well, I guess that explains how you kill someone during sex. There is no way I can handle that. Miguel is huge but damn.

For a long moment, the creature only stares at me.

I don't know what he's looking for, but I'm going to try to make this situation less frightening.

"Umm, hi." My voice sounds small and weak. "I'm Shiloh. This is my first time here, so maybe we can go slow?"

He growls, and I'm guessing that means no because he then charges toward me.

I backed into the wall as soon as he came in leaving me nowhere to go. He grabs my arm and yanks it so hard it might have dislocated.

He throws me on the bed so hard my teeth rattle. I try to scramble away from him, but he grabs my leg, yanking me back down toward him. Kicking out my feet, I connect with his chin. Everything stops. He stands up straight and rubs the area I struck. I'm not particularly a violent person, but what else do you do when something like this is happening.

The creature tosses his head back and roars. I cover my ears because it's so loud. Once the noise stops, he grabs me by the neck and yanks me up off the bed as if I was a rag doll. His lips crash down on mine so hard it starts to bleed. I squirm in his arms as my feet fight to find the ground beneath me.

Meanwhile, he's sucking my face like we're making out. I start to feel lightheaded and weak. My movements become slower and slower. I realize he's too consumed in his forceful kiss that he doesn't realize he's choking the life out of me.

Would it be so bad if this creature kills me? At least then, I'll truly be free.

Suddenly the door swings open. The creature drops me to the bed and lets out one of those deafening roars. He charges toward the soldiers that enters the room, but one of the guys is holding a small box. The creature pulls up short as he stares down at the object in the box. From this angle I can't quite tell what's inside. The man with the box talks calmly to the beast, but I don't focus on what he's saying. They lure the monster outside of the room.

One of the soldiers comes inside and tosses a blanket over me.

"Get up," he says angrily.

Standing, I immediately buckle once I put weight on my right ankle. Apparently, when the thing grabbed my leg, he did some damage.

The soldier yanks me up and shoves me out the door. I grab for air as I feel myself falling backwards, yet I don't hit the ground. I'm caught by strong arms under my back. I look up to my savior only to recoil in fear. It's another one of those creatures. This one is more handsome than the one in my room.

His skin is golden, not as dark as Miguel's, but darker than average. His eyes are deep-set and brown, but there is no missing the intelligence hidden behind them. His face is oblong and so serious. His jaw must be cut from stone. A straight aristocratic nose, dark short hair and lips that make even me envious.

He stares down at me and scowls. The angry cry of the other creature has me and the new one turning to him. The creature that was in the room with me breaks away from the soldiers and charges toward us. The one that caught me stands me up straight and releases me. He steps in front of me, placing his body between me and the other. When the other one approaches, the brown-eyed creature grabs him by the neck and slams him into the ground so hard the floor beneath me shakes like an earthquake. I go tumbling to the ground off my wobbling leg.

The other beast does not get back up. Now guns are aimed at brown eyes. Soon, a man in a long white lab coat rushes down the hall toward us. It isn't the guy from the tarmac earlier. This is another man with wavy hair and blue eyes. He looks to the brown-eyed creature and then the beast on the floor.

"What the hell is going on?"

"Dr. Long," The guard that shoved me out of the room steps forward. "Subject 1762 was in the breeding room but quickly became too violent. We followed the end breeding protocol and entered the room. When we escorted the breeder out of the room, she bumped into subject0140. This seemed to trigger 1762, and he attacked 0140."

"Well, why is 1762 on the ground?"

Because 0140 rock bottomed his ass better the Dwayne 'the Rock' Johnson himself. I want to put my two cents in, but I decide to remain quiet.

The guard tells the doctor pretty much the same thing I said.

Dr. Long turns to 0140, who has not done anything else since the incident happened. So far, he is the calmest of the monsters I've seen.

"Sigma, we are going to take you back to your room now. Will we have any problems?"

0140, or Sigma, does not respond. However, he also doesn't attack, so I guess that's a good sign. The Soldiers nearby start to move closer to him without lowering their guns.

"Should we tell Strong about this?" One of the men that came with Dr. Long asks.

"No. I'd rather not have the prick breathing down my neck," Long says.

Feeling a lot more secure now that the first creature is out cold and the second is being surrounded, I go to stand and cry out as I forget about my ankle.

The creature they call Sigma swings his startling gaze around to me, causing me to freeze in place. I make no sudden moves in hopes I don't trigger the thing. Please don't let this one attack. If he slams me into the floor the way he did the other one, they will have to mop my brains up.

"Someone, get that damn breeder out of here," Dr. Long shouts.

Yes, Dr. Long. I totally agree with you.

One of the soldiers comes over to help me up. I flinch when I have to put slight pressure on my ankle, but I'm eager to get out of here. Despite how hard I try not to, I turn to look over my shoulder. The creature Sigma is still there, and he's watching me.

Turning back around, I continue to hobble to safety, praying I never see him again.

They take me to the health unit. The place is set up like one large emergency room, only there is no waiting room or receptionist.

The soldier places me on the bed, and a man in blue scrubs comes over immediately.

"What do we have?" the doctor asks the soldier.

"Breeder 1363. Just came from the breeding room with subject 1762."

"Is she alright? Were there any injuries to her vagina or uterus?" the entire time, the panicked doctor is talking, he's pressing on my lower stomach.

I swat his hands away. "No, that thing fucked up my ankle," I snap.

The doctor and the soldier look at each other.

"She fought him and got him riled up. It wasn't his fault."

I turn to the soldier with my mouth wide open. Is he serious? Let me see what he does if a penis that big was charging toward him. The damn thing swung like a pendulum between the creature's legs.

"Just to be on the safe side we will do a pelvic exam and an ultrasound."

Are they not listening? Nothing is wrong with my vagina. Can a girl get an ibuprofen and her damn ankle wrapped?

"I only need you to check my ankle," I say, reaching down to rub the spot that is now throbbing.

They ignore me as the doctor turns and calls for a speculum.

In the end, I spent most of my afternoon being examined for vaginal damage. The doctor spent a total of two minutes on my actual injury.

Later that night, I limp into the room, still not able to put weight on the ankle. Lying out across the floor of my room are my soaking wet belongings. Not that there's much, but still, it's my stuff.

"I'm assuming you made some enemies?" Fatima says, walking in behind me. She has a bag of toiletries in her hands. "I found your clothes soaked in the shower. I brought them here and laid them out to dry." She hands me the bag of toiletries. "You don't want to know where I found your toothbrush." This little stunt has Candace's name written all over it.

Fatima walks pass me into the room and grabs her things off her bed. She then climbs on the top bunk.

Fighting back my tears, I tell Fatima thank you. There is no way I'd be able to climb on that top bunk. My first day has been just as shitty as I'm sure my toothbrush probably is.

Tossing my new toiletries to the small table in the corner, I turn off the lights and hobble to the bed. Crawling underneath the covers, I let out a long sigh. I only hope blissful sleep claims me soon.

"I'm sorry your first day was so bad."

Fatima's quiet words are whispered into the dark room.

"They're monsters," I say sniffling.

She's quiet for a moment. "I think we both know humans can be even bigger monsters."

She's right, but I don't tell her. Instead, I think of all the ways my life could have gone differently. I even go as far back as my childhood. I allow those fantasies to see me off to sleep.

**

I'm not sure how much sleep I got before the sound of our bedroom door opening wakes me up. In my bed, I sit up immediately.

The light flips on, and two guards are standing at my door. Unfortunately, one of them is the guard that stood between me and Candace today. My heart drops to my feet and begins to beat about three times faster than usual.

"What's going on?" Fatima's groggy voice asks.

This is my first night here, and I don't know the protocol, but I have a feeling these men are here for me.

"Go back to sleep, Fatima," The guard I met earlier says. He turns to the other guard and tilts his head in my direction. The other guy stomps over to me and quickly grabs me out of bed. I'm wearing a thin tank top and my only pair of underwear.

Fatima hops down from the top bunk. "Leave her alone, Frankie. She hasn't even been here a full day yet."

Frankie walks over to Fatima and stops in front of her. She leans away from him.

"Now, you know I'd usually do anything you want me to do as long as you use those pretty lips on me, but not this time." He blows her a kiss and turns his back on her. "Bring her."

The other guard hefts me up over his shoulder and storms toward the door. Fatima catches my eye before they take me out of the room.

She mouths the words, "I'm sorry."

I can't be mad at her. She did all she could do. Look, if all these assholes wanted was a little head to get off my back, I'd give it to them.

Is it what I want? Hell no, but I know how to play the role in order to survive. I, in no way, believed these guys would protect me. Hell, I don't even believe they can. But I also know I'm at the bottom of the totem pole here.

"You sure your guy working the cameras is going to delete this?" The one carrying me asks.

"Yeah, I told you. I have connections at this place. All these doctors think they're running this compound, but I'm the shit around here."

The guard holding me laughs. "Come on, Frankie. We all know those alien freaks are running this place."

Suddenly we stop. I lift my head and turn in the direction of my good eye. Frankie is now standing toe to toe with the guy holding me. And he doesn't look happy.

"Fuck those dumb creatures. I'm not scared of them. I used to work as one of Dr. Strong's personal guards, I know how to put those bastards down. Why do you think I'm never allowed to shoot them when everyone else does?" he smirks.

"You have special ammunition?" the guy with me says in awe. "I thought that was a rumor."

Frankie shakes his head. "All facts. Only certain soldiers are allowed to have the real ammunition. I can put one of those things down in a snap." He snaps his finger to get his point across.

"I want the real ammunition."

This time Frankie laughs before he turns around. "Not going to happen, Carter."

We go through so many hallways and down so many flights of stairs that I wouldn't be able to find my way back here if I tried. They seem to be going the extra mile just to get their dick sucked. I mean, I'm pretty good at it, but we could have done this in the bathroom, and I'd be back in bed by now.

We finally stop again, this time only briefly before we are walking into a dimly lit room. The soldier carrying me sets me on my feet, and I put all my weight on my good ankle. Turning to scan the room, I notice the wall to my left and the one straight ahead are bare and without windows. However, that doesn't surprise me, considering how deep into the compound we must be. As soon as I turn to the wall to my right, I freeze. Clearly, they didn't bring me here for a blow job.

Leaning against the wall is none other than Candace and three other girls. I take a step back, but stumble on this stupid ankle.

"Alright, baby," Frankie says, pulling Candace into his chest and placing a kiss on her lips. "I got her down here. Now, the rest is up to you."

Candace turns back to me with a scowl. "You're no longer the top bitch around here. And I'm going to teach your ass a lesson." I don't know where she got the large knife from, but she holds it up for me to see.

Although it will be in vain and I won't get far, I still turn and run. Almost immediately, I'm tackled from behind. I can't tell you by who, but I hit the ground so hard I have difficulty catching my breath.

It doesn't matter because the air is knocked right back out of me as a heavy foot kick me in the side. After the first kick, the others come rapidly. They come from every direction. The only thing I can do to save myself is curl into a ball.

Not sure how long the attack goes on for because I blackout a few times only to come back still being stomped. My body hurts like hell, and I can't move my fingers. For the most part, I've protected my face, but my hands are fucked royally. Eventually, they tire out and stop, but I find no reprieve.

Someone rolls me onto my back. My body lays limply, too weak to even lift my arms in defense. My one good eye is blurry from what I believe is blood leaking into it from a wound on my forehead. At least, I think the searing pain is a wound.

"You were never better than me," Candace says as she hovers over me. "You should've let him kill me," she whispers down in my ear, and I couldn't agree more.

Suddenly, sharp burning pain shoots up from my stomach. It takes everything in me to weakly lift my hand to touch the area. I'm met with the handle of the knife. She stabbed me.

My vision starts to go in and out, and I'm finding it hard to stay awake. Peace beckons me on the other side, and I want to go to it so bad.

"Are we going to just leave her here?" One of the other females asks.

"Yeah. No one comes down here. It will be months before they find her. By then, she'll be a rotting corpse, and they won't know what happened to her," It's Frankie that speaks this time.

"Good," Candace laughs. "That's what she deserves."

They leave the room then. The final sound I hear is the clanking of the metal door closing behind them.

The gentle fingers of death caress my face. I shut my eyes, ready to follow it to the other side. I wanted to get away from Miguel, and there is no more permanent freedom than death.

CHAPTER FOURTEEN

Responsibility

Sigma

It will not stop, no matter how hard I push my body or try to ignore it. I feel her heartbeat inside my chest.

Pushing up from the floor, I refuse to do another sit-up. I've done close to a thousand and have yet to break a sweat or feel sore.

Why? Why would this happen to me? I do not want a mate. Especially one that is as weak as a human female. She is too small. The woman of Albatraum was built for us. They were as tall as we were, but much slimmer. Their short, pointed horns could dismember an enemy. They had hard fertility sacs for us to deposit our life-giving essence in. They had no fleshy wet slits that only seemed to cry more and more as I pushed my heavy appendage into it.

Even the mention of the human's wet slit has the useless appendage thickening. I growl down at the insufferable thing.

How are they supposed to keep our young in those slits?

Not to mention she is hideous. A growl rips from my lips. I pick up the chair in my room and throw it against the wall bending the metal. I cannot tell myself that untruth. The female is the most beautiful I have ever seen.

Flawless brown skin that is soft to the touch. I do not recall any of the other breeders with lips as plump as hers. Her wide nose adds to her beauty, but her eyes were the most exquisite.

Yes, there is beauty in the upturned shape and the different color in the irises, but neither is the beauty I speak of. It was the fear mixed with the fire behind her eyes that caught my attention.

When the slip of a human female fell into my arms and turned to me, it felt as if a bomb went off in my chest. Her heart was so loud and rapid inside me. She was terrified, I didn't know if it was of me or the rogue that hurt her. Yet, even through her fear, she was still fighting to save herself.

My fist clench when I think of the rogue touching her. I quickly shake the anger away relaxing my hands. I should not care that he touched her. I do not care who touches her. Beautiful or not, I do not want the human.

The commander link vibrates for my attention. Dropping down onto the floor of my cell with my back to the wall, I then open the link.

"Sig, what is your problem," Gamma says right away. *"You have me agitated for no reason."*

"Yes, between our King's desire for his Mate causing me to stay erect, and your turmoil causing me ready to fight, my body is going haywire," Omega chimes in.

"There is nothing wrong," I growl.

The link is silent for a moment.

"Are you sure about that?" Alpha asks.

I do not like the accusation in his tone. It seems he may be suspicious. I fight harder to break off the connection to my emotions.

"You are blocking me now?" he asks.

"Wait, we can do that?" Gamma queries.

"Sigma can," Beta replies. *"You can't."*

Ignoring Beta and Gamma's side conversation, I focus on more pressing matters. I'm not ready for Alpha to know about my Uvonu yet. He will try to make me claim her, and that will not happen. I must keep the female under wraps for now until I figure out how to break the bond.

"What is going on with you?" Alpha demands ignoring Beta and Gamma as well.

"I do not wish to share your desire for your human." This is obviously not the truth, but it is not exactly an untruth.

"And I do not care about your inconvenience," Alpha replies curtly. *"Nor will I apologize. You will understand when you find your Uvonu."*

I hate that I can now relate to his sentiment.

"It is not that bad," Beta chimes in. *"Sigma is still bitter we are not leaving."*

"Is that it, Sig, do you want to leave…"

"No," I shout, cutting off Gamma.

The link goes silent. I'm starting to hate this heavy silence.

I realize in my haste to answer, I have made myself sound suspicious. I must rectify the situation quickly.

"I've had time to think upon it. I believe it is only fair that Alpha has time to figure out things with his Uvonu."

In the meantime, I hope that I can do the same with mine.

"Leave us," Alpha barks.

One by one the others leave the command link.

"You could have just summoned me to our private link," I say.

"What aren't you telling me?"

As always, Alpha knows something is amiss. Unfortunately, this time I will not be coming clean. In truth, if he really wanted my obedience and my secret, he has only to demand it. Not only that, but I am sure though my walls for blocking others out are strong, my leader is capable of knocking them down to get my secrets. If I want to keep my Uvonu hidden, I have to be as honest as I can with him without giving anything away.

I lay my head against the wall behind me and close my eyes.

"I do not ask for much, Alpha. However, I need this favor. Allow me time and privacy."

"How much time?"

"I do not know, but when I am ready, you will be the first to know."

The link is silent once again; I can almost feel his hesitation.

"Alright. As you wish, old friend." Alpha disconnects, leaving me alone.

Now I must figure out what I'm going to do about the human.

Fear hits me so hard, my eyes pop open, and I scan my room for an enemy. It takes me a moment to realize it isn't my fear I am feeling, it's hers. Focusing on the little connection we share, I try to pinpoint where she is and why she is feeling this way. Fury hotter than I've ever felt before courses through me. She is injured, yet I do not know how badly.

I shoot to my feet and march over to the door. Placing my hand against the wall beside me, I find all the cameras and loop them. After securing my passage, I open the door to my cell.

This compound has a false sense of security. As long as we are locked behind our cages, the people here feel safe. Alpha is the only one that has 24/7 security. They fear him, as they should, but they misjudge us. I cannot be angry over this, it is because of their lack of adequate fear of me, I am able to move about freely.

Slipping into the hall, I allow the insufferable pull I have for the human to lead me to her. I make sure to take the unused stairwells to stay clear of any guards on patrol.

I come to a stop on the third floor, slipping into the hallway. I wait by the door. Two guards walk up the stairs, speaking animatedly about something. I allow them to climb further up before stepping back into the stairwell.

As I near the basement level of the compound, a feeling of urgency has me moving faster. The only thing in this area of the facility is Alpha's lockdown cell, my hidden room, and the tunnel we use to store bodies we will one day use in our escape.

I speed through the quiet twist and turns of this lower level, only to stop suddenly when I come to the door of my hidden room. Her scent is so strong here I have to take a moment to gain control before walking in.

As soon as I push the door open and step into the darkroom, I spot my Uvonu lying on the floor covered in blood.

My anger erupts from me before I can tamp it down. The links start to vibrate, everyone wondering what has caused me such ire. I ignore them and kneel at her side.

Placing my hands over her head, I allow my senses to scan her. A concussion, a laceration on her forehead, multiple broken bones in her hands, two bruised ribs, a laceration in her spleen causing internal bleeding and the most obvious is the knife in her belly. The slowing of the heart inside my chest tells me that she is dying.

I should let her. It would end my problem with this human—a problem I never wanted. However, even as the thought plays out in my head, I have already opened the private link to Zee.

"Hey, Mr. Sigma," I groan at his enthusiasm and happiness that wavers the link. *"I never thought you'd be reaching out to me. Do you want to hang? I don't mind, I was just counting the tile in my ceiling again,"*

"Quiet, nuisance," I growl. *"Find me. I need your help. Tell no one."*

"Um, absolutely. I'm coming right now. But I may need help getting out my door."

Placing my hand on the ground at my feet, I concentrate to find his door. Once I locate it, I use my ability to unlock it.

"Oh cool," Zee says through the link. *"I'm on my way. So, what do…"*

I cut off the connection. I do not wish to hear his incessant blabbering. Instead, I gently lift my Uvonu in my arms. I do not like the idea of her lying on the cold floor. The commander link is buzzing inside me, I owe them something. If I do not answer, Alpha may send them to look for me.

"All is well," I say as soon as I open the link.

"That did not feel like all is well?" Beta snaps. *"You nearly sent me into a fury."*

"Me as well," Omega adds.

"My apologies. I was dealing with a guard." I think of the untruth quickly. It isn't uncommon for us to get angry with the infestation of guards here. They all at some point, like to test their manhood by trying to put us in our place.

"What did he do?" Gamma asks.

"Is all well now?" Alpha cuts in before I can answer Gamma.

I look down at the woman in my arms, still passed out. Her heart, though weak, still beats in my chest.

"Yes," I reply.

Alpha knows there is more to what I am saying, although he isn't sure what it is. His suspicion thrums through the link.

"Then that is all that matters. Let Sigma be," he tells the others. They break away from the connection one by one until only our leader is left.

"Does this have to do with earlier?" he asks.

"It does."

"If you need me, let me know," he says and then he too leaves the link.

I close out of the group and focus on the woman in my arms. The idea to allow her death swims in my head once again, but I clutch her closer to my chest.

She whimpers but leans into me. I want the culprit responsible for this attack dead. I have never wanted to take a life more than I want this person. Could it have been the rogue from earlier? No, he would not have needed a weapon to hurt her. This was done by a human.

The door to the room opens, and Zee walks in.

"This is a very nice place you found. It's private...." His voice in my head cuts off as his gaze lands on the human in my arms. *"Who is this?"*

"I do not know, but I need you to heal her."

He looks up and his eyes are so wide they look funny, although I do not laugh.

Zee rubs the back of his neck. *"I know Alpha has said I'm a healer and I am."* He hesitates for a moment before speaking again. *"I do not have memory of how to do this."*

Healers were very important on Albatraum. It was a highly respected trade. Once a subject showed signs of the healer's ability, they were taken in to become an apprentice to other healers once they hit puberty.

From the moment I met Zee, I could sense his young age. In human terms, he would be a boy of seventeen or eighteen. Which means on the old planet, he would have just become an apprentice.

"You will learn tonight," I snap. *"Get over here."*

He comes to me, his eyes downcast. My job on the old planet was to know everything. I had to keep the records so that I could pass the knowledge down to the other generations. My brain worked like the human computer. It downloaded and stored all types of information.

I run through the scattered memories of my past to pull up information about healers.

"Place your hand over the wound in her stomach first."

He follows my orders.

"Close your eyes and concentrate on that wound. Do you feel anything?"

He nods his head slowly. *"Yes, I can feel the energy and the pain,"* He groans and rubs his own belly.

"Good, now I need you to mend the wound and the damage it caused."

Zee's eyes snap open and they're exaggeratedly wide again. *"I don't know how to do that."*

"Yes, you do." Thinking of how I use my ability and how my instincts led me the first time, I guide him. *"Healer is who you are. It is what comes natural to you, do not think. Close your eyes and feel what is needed."*

Zee heaves a deep breath and shuts his eyes again. His brow creases as he concentrates. It seems to take a moment, but when the female in my arms start to whimper, I know that he is working.

What starts off as small moans turns quickly into painful cries.

"You have to quiet her down, I can't concentrate," Zee says, his eyes still close.

I lean down to her ear. "Uvonu," I call out to her in a deep voice. I've never heard my speaking voice before. It is foreign to my ears.

"You are dying," I tell her. "I'm trying to save you."

"It hhhurrtts," her voice is soft and pleasant. It has the meaty appendage between my legs so hard that it could possibly break down walls. What is happening?

"Almost done," Zee says in my head. My appendage immediately goes flaccid after hearing Zee speak.

She cries out again, pulling my attention to her.

"Be strong, Uvonu. It will be over soon." Every time I speak to her, her cries die down. I continue to whisper in her ear. Telling her that she would be fine and to not worry.

Eventually, Zee stumbles away from us. I lift my head to look down at the female. The knife is no longer in her belly, and her heart is beating strong in my chest. I use my ability to scan her injuries. All things life-threatening have been healed. However, broken and bruised bones have not.

Glaring at Zee, I want to demand he finish the job. However, it is obvious he is exhausted. This is not an easy job for a healer, and he is a novice.

"Did I do it?" he asks, the eagerness to please me in his voice.

Dipping my head, I reply. *"Yes, for now. In a few days, I will have you come back to attend her other injuries."*

He nods stoically.

"Thank you, Zee."

He smiles. *"No problem, Mr. Sigma. But, what are you going to do with her?"*

That is a very good question. I do not know who tried to hurt her, so I can't take her back. I also cannot take her to my room, they will not allow me to keep her. Plus, I do not want the others to know.

"I need to do some research," I place my Uvonu in Zee's arms. She whimpers, and I find satisfaction that she does not curl into him the way she did me. I shake the useless feeling away.

Walking to the wall, I place my hands against the cool concrete. Although human technology is not nearly as advanced as it was on the old planet, I can still use it.

I find a computer being used by a guard. I immediately cut into the intercourse videos he is watching and scan the thing they call the world wide web for all information of things I will need to keep my human alive and comfortable. It only takes a few minutes to upload the information to my memory.

I remove my hand from the wall and back away. *"She will need a bed. Something comfortable to lie on,"* I say to Zee.

"The mating rooms have beds," Zee supplies.

"That is where I will go to retrieve one. Stay with her until I return," I demand.

I go to leave but turn back to face Zee. *"You will not speak of this to anyone, do you understand?"*

He quickly agrees. I leave the room, heading to get a bed for my Uvonu. This changes nothing, I still do not want the woman, but it is my responsibility to nurse her back to health. Once she is healed, I will let her go and never interact with her again.

CHAPTER FIFTEEN

Monster

Shiloh

The first thing I notice is how bad my body aches. It feels like I got my ass kicked. Oh yeah, I did. I should be dead right now, but somehow, I'm alive. Pretty sure I wouldn't be in this much pain if I were dead. I don't know much about religion, but I do remember hearing some gospel songs that boasted about no more pain in heaven.

Opening my eyes takes way longer than it should. When they do crack open, I find myself in a dimly lit room. It's not as big as the room I share with Fatima and only slightly larger than the mating room. I don't for a second doubt these people would have put me in a mating room even with me being unconscious or near death.

Lifting my hand to my stomach where I know a knife once was, I pause when I realize I'm connected to an IV. I also notice that the knife is no longer there. Scanning the room again, I can determine I'm not in the hospital unit. I was there already, and it looks nothing like this.

Where am I? From where I'm lying, I can't see much of the room. Most of it is on my blind side, and I can't turn my head far enough to see it with my left eye. I try to sit up, but flinch at the searing pain in my side.

"Do not move," The deep voice comes out of nowhere and scares the ever-loving shit out of me.

I sit up abruptly and immediately regret my decision as I place a hand to my throbbing ribs.

"I told you not to move."

Sitting in the corner of my room on the cold floor is one of those monsters. He's facing my bed, one knee bent with an arm resting on it, and the other leg straight. He seems very relaxed to be so dangerous. Granted it's the gorgeous one that saved me that day from the mating room. I think his name is Sigma. Nonetheless, he's one of the creatures.

I scurry as far away from him as I can get. My back is pressed to the wall, and despite the pain I'm in—trust me, I'm in a lot—I keep my eyes on him.

He tilts his chin to the right and studies me.

"You are afraid?"

"No shit," I say gasping for breath.

"Why?" he asks as if it's not obvious.

"You're one of them, you're a monster."

He leans his head against the wall and closes his eyes. Is he dismissing me?

"Was it one of us that hurt you?"

"Well, no," I admit.

"And yet it is us you fear," he quickly retorts.

I frown, not knowing exactly what to say after that. He's right, though.

"Lie down, Uvonu. You need your rest. Zee was unable to fully heal you."

My head fills with so many questions. For instance, who is Zee, why did he call me Uvonu, and why is he so calm right now? However, I do not ask any of these questions, instead, I lay back down in the bed, keeping my eyes on him. Not because I trust him or because he told me to. I'm lying down for the simple fact that if I don't, I feel as if the pain in my side will make me pass out.

The room is quiet. The only sounds come from the rumbling of the air-conditioner unit pumping air through the vents.

I stare at the creature across from me, studying him while his eyes are closed. How can something so frightening be this beautiful. He has on clothes; unlike the first time I saw him. He's wearing a black t-shirt that stretches across his broad chest. Cotton has never looked sexier. The fabric isn't too tight but fits snug enough that it outlines his incredibly well-defined muscles.

His biceps are larger than my thighs and lead down to long arms. Even his fingers are long and sexy. His pants are fatigues, except they are black and gray and not the green, tan, and brown colors that the other soldiers here are wearing.

He's very still. Even though I'm lying down and in pain, my body seems to be moving more than his.

"I thought you guys couldn't talk?" The question flies out of my mouth before I have time to think about it.

"The less our enemy knows of us, the better."

I've spent less than thirty minutes with this creature, and I can already tell half the things they say about them aren't true. They are still frightening, and I don't trust them. However, they are not the dumb and mindless beasts the soldiers call them.

"How long have I been out?"

It takes him a minute to reply. I don't think it's because he doesn't know the answer; it's more like he doesn't want to answer.

"Three days," he finally grumbles.

Three days? They must know I'm missing at this point. Surely, they have been looking for me.

"What happened to your eye?" he asks catching me off guard.

"Mishap with a dinner fork."

His face scrunches up at my reply.

"Wait, how did you know something's wrong with my eye?" For all he knows I could have been born like this.

"I sensed the injury when I checked you over the night I found you. It is old and cannot be repaired now."

Tell me something I don't know.

"Why did you help me?" The question pops out without much thought.

If my prognosis about these creatures is true, and usually when it comes to men I'm always right, this beast should have left me for dead. Hell, if it were the other one from the mating room, he probably would have finished the job if he'd found me.

Once again, Sigma doesn't respond right away, nor does he open his eyes. It takes him so long to reply; for a moment I think he won't.

"Did you want me to let you die?" He finally asks.

My brow dips. "Well, no. I guess."

Did I want to die? I mean life isn't really great right now, but was I ready to give up? The answer that comes to my head immediately is no. No, I'm not ready.

"I thought about it," he says still not opening his eyes or lifting his head from the wall.

"About letting me die?"

"Yes."

Well, at least he's honest.

"But you changed your mind?"

This time he cracks an eye open and raises his brow. Okay, yeah, I get it. Obviously, that was a stupid question.

He shuts his eye and goes still again. "Go to sleep. You need your rest."

I don't argue or call him bossy like I want to. Instead, I close my eyes and allow sleep to take me.

***

I don't know how much time has passed. When I wake this time, my body feels even more achy than the first time.

I try to turn over but groan instead. A low growl comes from somewhere in the room, and I lift my head to see where it came from.

I now have two of the creatures in here. The one I know as Sigma, and now another one. This one is only an inch or two shorter than Sigma, with a deep olive skin tone. His dark hair and dark eyes make me believe he's Latino. He's handsome but not nearly as attractive as Sigma.

He's watching me closely. I'm frozen in fear. The last time one of them watched me like that, he tried to rape me.

The shorter one looks over to Sigma, and although no words are said, it's obvious a conversation is being had. Sigma shakes his head slightly and the other one backs as far away from me as he can get.

"Are you in pain?" Sigma asks in his deep voice, causing me to turn to look at him

"Yes," I say breathlessly. My ribs are definitely injured because it's hard to breathe.

"Zee would like to help you with your pain. Is that alright?"

The moment he says Zee's name, I look over to the other creature in the room. He's still watching me intently, but I can also tell he's trying to be less threatening. It's in the way his shoulders slouch and how he presses his back against the wall as if he's trying to put as much space as he can between us.

"Okay," I say barely over a whisper.

Sigma turns to Zee, and another one of those silent conversations go on. Zee nods before slowly approaching me. He kneels at my bedside, and my heart starts to beat a little faster. I shut my eyes and try to take steadying breaths. So far, the one called Sigma has not done anything to hurt me, but I still can't separate my fear when dealing with them.

"He wants to know your name?" Sigma asks.

I open my eyes and stare at him. His brow is pinched, and he looks mad or disappointed.

"Shiloh," I reply, keeping my eyes on Sigma. Out of the two, I trust him a little more.

Zee gets my attention when he lifts his hands over my chest. I flinch, and Sigma growls. Zee looks over his shoulder at Sigma. Sigma narrows his eyes and march out of the room. My breath hitches. The desire to have him back in this room hits me hard. It's like I'm having separation anxiety. It's on the tip of my tongue to call him back in here.

Instead, I keep my eyes on the door; before long, a warmth fills my chest, and the pain from earlier slowly ebbs away.

Zee stands and backs away from me, his back once again up against the wall. Sigma strolls back in, and he looks to me immediately.

His gaze rakes over my body with precision. He then looks over to Zee where they have one of those conversations. It hits me then what the looks remind me of. It's the same way Dr. Hammond looks at Rowan as if they are communicating silently.

Sigma turns back to me. "He cannot heal your bruised ribs the way he did your broken fingers; he can only ease your pain." He doesn't sound too happy about that.

From what I've gathered, this Zee guy is the only reason I'm still alive. That knife wound should have taken me out; I can deal with a few bruised ribs.

"It's alright. Thanks anyway, Zee."

The one name Zee gives me a smile and dips his head. Admittedly, I didn't think these creatures could smile. They always look so serious and deadly. Zee's smile makes him look kind of normal. Still not human though. I return his smile with one of my own. He's actually much more handsome when he grins.

The low grumble draws both of our attention to Sigma, who does not look friendly at the moment.

Sigma tosses his head toward the door, and Zee quickly leaves. What's that about?

"Are you hungry?" he asks.

The question must have triggered my stomach because it immediately growls.

"I will bring you nourishment when I return." He turns away and take's a few steps to leave.

"Wait," I call out. He stops in his tracks but does not face me. "Where are you going?"

I'm not a clingy person. I think I've established how much I enjoy my solitude. However, it's something about this creature that makes me want him around. I can't explain it. Maybe it's because he saved my life.

"They expect me in the mating room. I must go."

Are you shitting me? Is this jealousy I'm feeling? What the hell, Shiloh? Why in the world does the thought of this beast with another woman make me want to claw the chick's eyes out?

"Okay," my voice breaks on the simple word.

He storms out of the room and shuts the door behind him.

I lie in my bed, alone, feeling completely torn and confused. What is going on with me?

CHAPTER SIXTEEN

My Uvonu

Sigma

Standing outside the hidden room, I fight my anger and desire to go back inside to her.

My fist clench and unclench at my side. I do not like this feeling. I nearly ripped Zee's head off when he tried to touch her. I know that his instinct to help her was driving him, but I do not want any male around her.

I force myself to walk away from her door. Not liking this lack of control bothers me. I head back up to my cell, making sure to clear my path with the cameras.

It's still early in the day, so the guards that usually roam the halls are still sparse. I get to my cell without any interference. Slipping inside, I sit on the floor facing the door. My mind fills with my Uvonu. Shiloh.

Her name repeats in my head over and over. I purposely did not ask her what she wants to be called, not desiring the familiarity of knowing her name. However, thanks to Zee, it will not stop circling my thoughts.

I have spent most of my time around her, trying not to focus on the clawing need for her. She fears me still, and though part of me wishes she didn't, the other part needs her fear. If she continues to fear me, then it will be easier to leave her behind.

A growl rumbles in my chest in distaste of my thinking. Not even my thoughts are mine anymore.

"Sigma, are you there?" Alpha breaks into my concentration. The desperation in his tone has me focusing on him.

"Yes," I reply. *"What's wrong?"*

"I need you to locate my Uvonu? Where is she?"

This has become a constant thing with him. Dr. Strong is refusing to let him see the female, and Alpha is not taking it well.

Standing, I walk over to the wall near the door, placing my hand up against it. I first check all camera systems to see if I can spot her on either of those. When that mission fails, I go to the camera outside of the room they've been holding her in. Donovan, Strong's personal guard, stands outside her bedroom holding a tray. There isn't much food on the tray, only an apple and a slice of bread.

Once the door opens, Donovan slips in briefly and comes out without the food.

"Nothing has changed. They are keeping her locked away." I allow Alpha to access my thoughts so that he may see what I see.

Alpha hums in my head. *"That is best for now. No attention is good. I need everyone to continue to act as normal as possible. Your job is to keep an eye on the cameras. I want to know every time they move her. Also, keep an eye on everyone that goes in and out of that room."*

Any other time I would comment on how much of a waste of time and how unnecessary this is. I would've even told him that I should use my abilities for more useful things. However, unfortunately, I understand his concern. In fact, it makes me want to place a camera in my Uvonu's room so that I may keep an eye on her when we are away.

The thought of some male stumbling into the room while she lies weak in the bed sends a flash of rage through me that I can't contain.

"Does my request anger you so much?" Alpha asks picking up on my rage.

I exhale and run a hand over the low-cut hair on my head. The lack of control is becoming a problem *"No. I will keep an eye on your Uvonu. My thoughts were elsewhere?"*

"Are you ready to tell me?"

"No."

My reply is quick and final. Alpha remains quiet.

"Alright. I'll be here when you're ready." He breaks the connection, and my head is silent again.

My guards come to retrieve me for the mating room. They take me to the showers first. I need to find a way for Shiloh to bathe.

I've searched the human's world wide web for everything I can find about making my Uvonu comfortable. One of the things mentioned multiple times was cleanliness. Females like to take showers. I will supply this for her when she is healthier.

Just because I do not tend to keep her doesn't mean I can't provide for her while she's under my care. It is built into me to protect my Uvonu; there is no way around it.

The moment the guards and I step foot on the mating unit, we hear the loud commotion of a rogue in a rage fit.

I recognize him from the other day. He is the rogue that was placed in the room with Shiloh. He must be out of lock down after his tantrum with her.

"Where the hell is his breeder?" Dr. Long shouts over the noise.

"I can't find her anywhere. It doesn't even show she was ever here," His assistance replies.

I smile inwardly. I erased her from their files the night I found her.

"Fuck," Dr. Long runs his hands through his hair. "Get me another breeder in here ASAP. And get his handler ready."

The guards yank another breeder out of one of the rooms and tries to place her with the rogue. His tantrum increases as soon as he sees her.

"Come on, Sigma. You don't want to watch this," Reynolds says, escorting me down the hall pass the rogue.

The rogue turns to me as I draw near, his head lifts, and he sniffs the air. His angry growl fills the space. The breeder covers her ears and sobs. I cannot help but think of Shiloh. This would have frightened her even more. She is slowly starting to relax around me.

The guards aim their weapons at the rogue. I stop and watch him. His anger seems to be directed toward me.

"Where is she?" his voice is gruffly shouted in my head.

I tilt my chin to the left and narrow my eyes.

"Who?" I suspect who he is asking about. However, I want to be sure. If his inquiry is indeed of Shiloh, then my fist will help ease his concerns.

He bares his teeth to me.

"What's going on?" Dr. Long asks as he looks between the two of us.

"I think they're talking," Reynolds replies. His gaze swings back and forth between me and the rogue.

"Nonsense," one of the other doctors says. "They are not capable of that. Are they?" he asks the last question as if he's unsure. It amazes me that these men are supposed to be the smartest amongst the human species, yet they can't decipher that we've been communicating with each other.

"You will give her back to me," The rogue once again draws my attention. *"She is mine."*

For the first time, my facelifts into a half-smile. I only wish my Uvonu could see it. It will make her smile the way she did at Zee.

"Come and take her from me," I challenge.

The rogue turns his face toward the ceiling and lets out a loud roar. Everyone around us shuffles nervously. The rogue charges toward me, and the guns fire off, shooting darts at him. Yet, he is undeterred. His anger is fueling him; the tranquilizers will have no effect on him. But I will be his tranquilizer.

He rushes to me, and I meet him halfway. Grabbing him around the neck, I toss him against the wall behind me. Rubble falls from the crater we make in the concrete. He snarls at me as he tries to break free of my hold. Tightening my grip on his neck, his face starts to turn purple.

"0140, let him go," Dr. Long shouts.

I ignore his plea. This rogue thought to claim my Uvonu. She is not mine to keep, but she will not be his. He will learn today to never ask of her again. The rogue begins to move less and less.

"Hey, Sigma, I think you proved your point," Reynolds says beside me. "You can let him go now."

Although I like Reynolds, not even he will deter me. The rogue begins to go limp, his life leaving him slowly.

"That's enough, Sigma. Let him go."

I roar in my head at Alpha's demand.

"No." he will not make me let him go.

"You plan to defy my order," I don't miss the challenge in his tone.

"If the order is to let this rogue live, then yes."

He's silent for a moment. If Alpha truly wants me to let the rogue go, he has the power to force his command. In the life before and in this one, he has never had to use his ability on me. He knows that it will change the dynamics of our relationship. It is a betrayal that I will not easily forgive.

"Either tell me why you want his death or let him go," Alpha calmly says.

My low hiss causes Alpha to chuckle. He knows which I will choose. I release the rogue and he slumps to the ground at my feet. My desire to kill him does not overshadow my need to keep Shiloh to myself for a little while longer.

"Your tricks will not always work," I grumble.

Alpha laughs. *"If you say so."* The connection between us cuts off.

The guns are now aimed at me. The guards shout for me to step away from the rogue. I comply, keeping my eyes on him as they come in to move his limp body.

"What the hell was that?" Dr. Long shouts at me.

Although my gaze is on him, I don't answer.

"Get him back to his room," Dr. Long says to my guards. "You will not be allowed in the breeding room today."

Even better. I'd much rather be somewhere else.

My team of guards leads me back to my cell. Reynolds stands in front of my door as I enter.

"I don't know what that other guy said to you, but I bet he regrets it now," he says with a wink.

I dip my chin to acknowledge his comment. After walking into the room, he shuts the door sealing me inside.

I have to wait a while before I can go back to her. Taking a seat on the ground, I watch the door.

With my hands on the floor, I search the building until I find a cellphone connected to the world wide web. I use it to browse more information about human females. I want to know everything about them.

I've learned in this new life as well as in my old life that to defeat your opponent, you must first study them.

With my eyes closed, I skim through many different articles and scientific studies about women.

I learned that my Uvonu would be considered African American, and though the anatomy is the same to all women, there seem to be some significant differences in preferences and behavior. For instance, lotion seems to be a requirement for my Uvonu.

I spent so much time scouring the internet for information that I don't realize how much time has passed.

Slipping out of my room, I make my way first to the kitchen. My research suggest that I ask her about allergies before bringing her food. It also tells me that she prefers food with lots of seasoning. However, time will not permit that.

Finding a large paper bag tucked under a shelf, I take it out and fill it with food that she might like. Once I have the bag filled, I make my way out of the kitchen. Avoiding all the heavy traffic areas.

After turning a corner, I bump into Beta. I'm not shocked to find him; I sensed him on the hall before I ran into him.

"Sig, what are you doing out of your cell?" His brows reach for his hairline.

"I can ask you the same thing?"

The commander connection flares to life in my head. I roll my eyes as I open the link.

"Where are you headed?" Gamma asks.

"Probably to recount the bodies we have stored. We know how many there are, Sigma." Laughter follows Omega's remarks.

"I bet he's headed to the control room to relearn the layout one more time," Beta chuckles through the link.

"Or maybe he is off to meet a female." The link goes silent after Alpha's comment.

Their curiosity sends vibrations through the link. Beta's dark eyes squint as he stares at me. I do not focus on their suspicion—my mind races to think if I may have given something away to Alpha. I have kept the news of my Uvonu quiet. The only person who knows about her is Zee, and he has kept his mouth shut as well. Did my blocks not hold? Does Alpha know?

Our leader's deep laughter fills my head.

"I'm kidding. We all know Sigma has no use for females."

The others laughter joins his, even I let out a brief chuckle.

"Don't stay out too late," Beta says patting me on my shoulder as he continues in the direction I came from.

Heaving a deep breath of relief, I quickly make my way to my next destination.

It takes me a while to finally get back to my hidden room. I open the door silently, not wanting to disturb her if she's sleeping. Shiloh is still lying in the bed. She's facing the door, but her eyes are close.

"You came back?" Her question catches me off guard. I expected her to be sleep.

I do not like the lull her voice seems to bring me.

"I did."

Her mismatched eyes pop open, and she slowly attempts to sit up.

"Don't," I bark causing her to flinch.

Frowning, I remind myself that she still believes I am the enemy. My anger has me rushing to the side of the bed. I drop her bag of food in her lap and then take my seat at my spot, back against the wall, eyes on her and still in view of the door.

Despite my warning, she continues to sit up. Her shallow breath and increase heart rate tells me she's in pain. I won't remind her again to lay down.

"Thank you," she says after looking into the bag.

She takes out a pack of Oreo cookies and opens them up. I make a mental note to get her more of those. She browses through the bag a little more.

"You are clearly not concerned with my weight gain," she says with a laugh.

I process her words and her tone of voice, along with the chuckle at the end. Sarcasm, Gamma is good at this type of language.

"You are a very slight human. Weight gain should not be of concern to you."

She looks up from the bag and narrows her eyes at me. "I'm not sure if that was a compliment or an insult."

"It is a fact. The way you perceive it is up to you."

She shakes her head and goes back to her bag.

I have upset her. She doesn't say it, but I can feel it.

"Would you like me to bring you fruits next time?"

"I don't want to be a bother. This is fine," Although she says this, I can still feel her sadness.

"Uvonu," I call out to her gaining her attention. I do not like the downturn of her lips.

"If my words have upset you, it was not my intentions." I remember one of the articles I read on human females. They do not like to be considered out of shape. "Your body is perfect the way it is. If you would like to eat only food that makes you gain weight, it is fine, but if you want fruits, I will bring that to you as well."

Earlier, I would have told you that her smile did not matter to me. However, watching her lips lift and her eyes light up has become something I will look forward to often.

"I don't mind the junk food, but a salad or some meat would be nice."

"I will bring these things to you tomorrow."

She nods and goes back to the bag. She busies herself by pulling out foods and placing them in groups. The way her nose scrunches at certain things, I can determine what she likes and don't like. The Oreos are a favorite, and so are the Doritos chips. However, she is not a fan of the Cheetos or the chocolate donuts. She pauses, and her brows dip. She pulls out the bottle of lotion and stares at it for a moment.

When she turns to me, I can read the confusion on her features.

"My research shows that your skin gets ashy, and your kind do not prefer that."

"My kind?"

"Yes, the African American female."

Her face changes, and I cannot determine if she is angry or smiling. "And what else does your research tell you about 'my kind'?" her tone is not helpful in determining her mood either.

"There were many confusing articles on hair. However, you do not have any, so I did not focus on those."

Her full lips lift again in a smile.

"Well, thank you for the lotion," she puts the bottle down on the floor near her bed.

When she tries to sit back up, she becomes winded. Her shallow breaths come faster, and her brow pinches.

This time, I do not worry about her fear. I stand and head to her bed. Taking the bag from her and placing it on the ground, I help her lie back down.

"You must try to take deeper breaths."

Her eyes close as she lies back, but her smile remains.

"Deep breaths hurt like hell right now."

I wish that I can take the pain away from you. I think the words but do not say them out loud. Thoughts such as those do not benefit us.

She cracks her eyes open for only a moment and then shuts them back.

"Standing over me like that isn't really helping."

"My apologies. I will give you your space." I turn to walk away but stop when her hands shoot out and wraps around my wrist.

The useless appendage between my legs jerks. I frown down at it.

"Do not make an appearance right now," I scold inside my thoughts.

"You don't have to leave. You can have a seat." She does not sound sure of her offer.

Yet, my body immediately follows her orders. I take a seat right beside her bed. My back to the side of the thin frame while my eyes stay glued to the door.

We are silent for a moment. Her breathing shallowly, and me, listening to her. I do not like the complacency I feel in this moment. I tell myself to move away, to put distance between me and her. However, my body refuses to listen.

"I feel like I'm at a disadvantage," she finally says, breaking the silence.

I am stronger, faster, taller, and nearly indestructible. She is human, small, breakable, and injured. She is definitely at a disadvantage. However, I believe it is unwise to point this out at the moment. It may remind her of the fear she has for me, and she will likely ask me to move. I find I do not desire that.

Instead of telling her the truth, I pretend that I do not know. "How so?" I ask without turning to look at her.

"Well, you researched all about my kind," she says the last two words with a laugh. I do not see the hilarity in the two words, but I do not tell her this. "Yet, I know nothing about you."

"I can see how that may put us on unequal ground." I did not think this was where she saw the disadvantage. Not with so many other reasons that place her below me.

"Can you tell me about yourself?"

There is a reason the scientist at this compound knows so little about us. We deliberately keep our secrets from them. If they knew about our connection or our gifts, even the way we communicate with each other, it would cause them to try to use it against us. They want to control us. So, we keep our secrets. Telling this human anything could cause her to share it with the humans here and could eventually ruin our plans of escape.

However, no is not what comes out when I open my mouth.

"What would you like to know?"

She sighs behind me. The bed moves and dips before she speaks again.

"Were you really made in a lab?"

"Technically, yes."

She seems to sit with this answer for a minute before asking her next question.

"Are you guys aliens?"

I think through all my knowledge of the human words I've memorized.

"Yes, I guess I am an alien."

She yawns behind me. Even without the gesture of her exhaustion, I can already tell she is sleepy. Her words are lazier than her average speech, and her heart rate is steady.

"Do you like this place?"

"No," I reply curtly.

She yawns again, and her breathing is finally evening out. She still isn't taking deep breaths, but they aren't as shallow as before.

"Me either," She admits in the throes of sleep. "I'm going to get out of here."

"Me too," I admit, but I'm not worried about her hearing it. Her soft snores alert me to her slumber.

For the remainder of the night, I stay in my spot. Listening to her snores while feeling her heartbeat in my chest. I'm at peace.

CHAPTER SEVENTEEN

Comfort

Shiloh

"Uno out," I shout happily.

Sigma's eyes narrow across the table at me as he studies my hands in disbelief.

It's been a little over a month since I woke up from the beating. Since then, Sigma has this little one room place looking like a studio apartment.

We have a nicer bed, although I am the only one that sleeps on it. There's two chairs and a small folding table. We have our meals together here twice a day. A small radio sits on the side table and a steamer trunk in the corner that holds my change of clothes, and all the other things Sigma has stolen for me. Every day he comes into the room, he has something new for me. It's never anything expensive. Yesterday I got a half-done word search puzzle book. The day before, I got a small bottle of nail polish.

"You are cheating again," he says glaring at me.

I don't blame him for his suspicion, I've cheated so many times in this game. I can't help it. Sigma is very competitive, but he's always so focused on his hand that it's easy to slip a card or two under my butt.

"Nope, I won this one fair and square, Siggy."

He squints when I use my nickname for him. It's obvious we've come a long way since that first night he came back to my room.

I've learned that he is always serious and does not have the ability to relax. Sarcasm drives him crazy, even though he understands it.

I also found out you do not ask him a question you don't want an answer to. I made the mistake when I asked him how my tight afro looked, and he replied dry and spongy. That prompted me to put in starter micro locs.

He's brutally honest and very protective. He hates disorder; in fact, he has arranged my lotion collection about fifty times, even if only one bottle is out of line.

He also relies heavily on research and does not stray from the facts. He's stubborn, bossy, and does not do well with jokes.

However, he is very observant. After the first time he brought me food, he knew right away that I hated chocolate donuts and Cheetos. He even discovered that I have a weak spot for cookies in any form.

Not once has he done anything or shown any sign of hurting me. I won't pretend like he doesn't still frighten me. I know that if he wanted to, he could kill me with his bare hands. I respect him the way you would a trained lion. Yes, he seems tamed, but I also know that he is still a wild animal at the core.

"I do not trust you. You are dishonorable in this game."

My mouth flies open. "Sigma, you hurt my feelings." I pretend to pout, poking out my bottom lip. He hates to upset me.

His gaze narrow as his head tilts to the side. I fight to keep from laughing.

"I will not fall for it again," he stands up and comes around the table. He lifts me easily out of my seat and toss me over his shoulder as he looks all around my chair for hidden cards.

Meanwhile, I'm laughing my ass off. I laugh so hard that I end up coughing.

Sigma quickly lowers me to my feet, holding on to my arms; he looks me over. He doesn't let me go as he stares me straight in the eyes. I know where his concern stems from.

Two weeks after the attack, I ended up with Pneumonia. Apparently, I wasn't breathing deeply enough. Sigma had to call Zee in to cure me. Turns out, Zee is young and too inexperienced as a healer. It drains him when he heals, so Sigma only calls him in for emergencies.

"I'm fine, Siggy. It's just a cough."

He frowns. "You need to lie down."

I roll my eyes. That is his answer for everything.

Suddenly, a song comes on the little FM radio he stole for me. It only gets country, but after a month of listening to the station, I've started to like some of the songs.

"Oh, I love this song," I say. "Dance with me." I don't give him time to say no, not that he will. Another thing I've learned about Sigma over these four weeks is that he can never tell me no.

I grab his hands, placing one on my lower back. I hold the other out to our side. I start to sway to the slow beat.

"I do not understand the importance of this activity," he grumbles.

I roll my eyes up at him. "The importance is to live in the moment. Everything doesn't have to have a purpose."

His brow dips. I know he's battling with that answer.

It takes him a minute, but eventually he starts to get into the music.

"See," I smile up at him. "This isn't so bad is it?"

"No. It is pointless and serves no other purpose than to keep you entertained, but it isn't horrible."

I laugh out loud, and he does that weird thing where he just stares at my mouth.

"This does serve a purpose," I say, allowing him to move us in a circle. "One day, you're going to get out of here and meet you a nice alien girlfriend. You're going to want to dance with her. Consider this your first lesson."

He scoffs. "There are no alien women here. And if it were, they would not care to dance."

I tilt my head up to look at his stern face. "What do alien women like then?"

He thinks this over for a moment, his eyes narrow. "The woman on Albatraum preferred battle. We fought for their attention. Especially if she were our Uv...." He starts but stops, clearing his throat. "If she were our mate."

"If she's your mate, doesn't that automatically mean you get the girl?"

He shakes his head. "The male of our species is mate tied. We feel the connection. The females are not aware. It requires the male to persuade her to form a mate bond with him."

That seems unfair and pretty shitty. "What happens if you can't?"

His eyes narrow again; it's the sign that he's pulling information from that large well of a brain of his.

"My memory does not show this ever happening. I imagine that it could. I would assume the male would suffer greatly. He would be unable to be with another and would constantly feel his mates' emotions. He will forever be tied to her."

That sounds depressing. I've never been in love. Even though I once thought I was in love with Miguel, I've come to learn that doesn't count. However, I can imagine loving someone as deeply as feeling their emotions, and not being with them would suck major balls.

"What will you do if you meet your mate?"

The thought brings mixed emotions. That twinge of jealousy sprinkled with a little sadness and then the confusion on why I should feel either of those emotions.

Sigma stops dancing abruptly. "I do not know," He admits sadly.

I think this is the first time Sigma has ever not had a plan for something. However, I understand his worry. What's the use of finding your true mate when you're locked away here like a prisoner?

The song changes, and even though the rhythm is more upbeat, we continue to sway slowly. I press my head to his chest, and he wraps both arms around me, pulling me close.

"You have two hearts?" I ask without lifting my head.

"I have only one, the other is an echo."

Okay, I don't think I'll ever understand alien anatomy.

When I look up at him again, his brows are pinched, and he's concentrating hard. Eventually, he blinks and focuses back on me.

"What were you thinking about?" I ask.

"I was not thinking. I was speaking with Zee. He wants to know how you are feeling today?"

I stop swaying, looking up at him with my mouth open. "I knew it. I knew you guys were communicating telepathically." I do a little shimmy at my brilliance.

"Congratulations, you have figured out what the scientist here has yet to understand."

Not just the scientist, but the soldiers as well. They accused Sigma and his crew of being dumb too, and I can definitely say that's wrong.

"So, how does it work?" I ask as I go back to swaying to the music.

He tilts his chin and stares over my head at the wall. "My research shows that the only thing in the human world that resembles how it works is like a cell phone. I can call a direct line, or I can talk to multiple people at once.

"Whenever someone wants to communicate with me, they open the link, and it rings or vibrates, alerting me that I have a caller on the line."

In some ways, that seems like a really cool trick to have, but then again, I think of constantly having someone in my head, and it doesn't feel that appealing.

"What if you don't want to talk, do you just not answer the phone even though they know you hear it ringing?"

With the most serious face, he looks at me and replies. "Yes."

I burst out laughing but stop immediately when I get a splitting headache. I step away from Sigma and clutch my head in my hands.

"Uvonu, what is it? What's wrong?"

I take a few deep breaths before I reply to him. "It's from my eye. I get these migraines often."

"Come, lay down," he directs placing an arm against my lower back.

I could tell him that I'm not tired and that the headache will eventually pass, but I don't. There's no need to argue with him, he's only going to stress himself out if I say no. He worries worse than a parent.

Sigma guides me to the bed. I lie down and pull the cover up to my chin. He then takes his usual spot. His back is to the side of my bed as he faces the door.

Although it's a little earlier than our usual routine, this is how our day ends. He will stay with me all through the night, sitting beside my bed as I sleep. At some point before dawn, he sneaks off to grab me breakfast. We share our first meal in the morning, and then he leaves to do whatever he has to do.

I don't like to think about how I'm sure some of what he's doing is sleeping with breeders.

"What are we talking about tonight?" I ask. Last night was all about TV shows and movies. He got a real kick out of the sci-fi movies.

"Tell me about you before you were brought here."

I freeze. We have never got this personal. We've discussed our likes and dislikes. He's told me about his other friends here, including the big scary one I met my first day.

However, this is the first time he's asked about my past. Part of me is a bit embarrassed to tell him about my time at Miguel's.

"It's not a nice story." I admit.

"I assure you it is nicer than mine. What could be worse than the complete obliteration of your planet and a loss of your memory?"

When he puts it like that, my small issues seem so minor.

I huff out a breath. "You have a point there." Turning on my back, I look up at the white lay-in industrial ceiling. "Before I came here, I was in another prison. Kind of like this, but different."

He's silent for a moment. "Did you have a male in that prison?"

I snort in laughter. "That wasn't a very subtle way to ask am I seeing someone, but yes. He wasn't very nice though."

He's quiet for a moment, and I wonder, not for the first time, what he's thinking.

"Did he hurt you?" he finally asks.

Turning my head to see him, I don't miss the tension in his shoulders. I roll over to my side to face his back, then twirl my fingers aimlessly in the sleeve of his shirt. The tension quickly fades from his shoulders.

"No, he never hit me. But you don't have to strike a person for them to fear you. Miguel was always really good at making sure I understood that he held my life in his hands. He owned me."

Admitting that out loud hits me hard, but it's true.

"He told me what to wear, what to do, and who I could and couldn't speak to. He treated me like property. Something he could take off the shelf when he wanted to and place back up when he was done. He tried to tell me it was love, but it wasn't."

"So, you escaped your prison?"

"Yep."

"But why come here?"

Sigma already knows that I'm a volunteer. I told him the first week after he found me; I guess to him it does sound crazy to leave one prison just to go to another.

"I've escaped before, and Miguel always found me. This was the only place I could come where he couldn't track me down."

"I am sorry that your experience with him was unpleasant."

I grin, continuing to tug on the sleeve of his shirt. "It's okay. It's my own fault, I should have known better."

"Why do you say this?"

I sigh. "I don't have good luck when it comes to men. Everyone I've ever loved let me down."

For the first time ever, Sigma turns his back to the door. He's looking directly at me now. From where he's sitting and how I'm lying, his face is so close to me I can feel his breath on my lips.

"Explain," He demands with a pinched brow.

I roll onto my back again, not able to deal with the intensity of his gaze.

"Do you remember your parents?" I ask.

He's explained to me once that his memory of his past life was splotchy. However, sometimes if he focused long enough, he could recall things.

When he doesn't answer right away, I glance over to him. His nose is crinkled, and his expression is even more pinched. He blinks and then looks back at me.

"My father's skill was a craftsmen, like Beta, able to build anything. My mother was a healer, which is why I have extensive knowledge of them. They both died when I was still a boy." He looks shocked that he remembered all that information.

I turn back to face the ceiling.

"I was a daddy's girl. He was a musician. Did you have those on your planet?"

"Yes," he answers after a brief pause.

I continue. "My daddy played the keyboard, and he had a band. I used to watch him and the guys practice. I thought he was the coolest man I knew. He called me his shadow because I followed him everywhere. He was my first true love." I take a moment to fight down the burn in my throat.

"I knew things had gotten rough. Even at eight years old, I could feel the tension between him and my mother. They were fighting a lot over bills and my father's dream of being a successful musician. Mom wanted him to give up on it and get a job, but daddy couldn't give it up."

Now, I can see how selfish that was of him. When I was younger, I blamed my mother for the fights. But we were struggling to make ends meet, she was working like a dog, and he didn't want to let go of a dream that wasn't supporting his family.

I let out a staggering breath. "The morning my life changed, he dropped me off at school, and he was quiet. I remember, before I got out of the car, he told me he loved me and that he would pick me up after school like he always did." I pause, once again fighting emotions.

"I waited in the rain for two hours for him. The principal kept trying to tell me he wasn't coming, but I didn't believe her. My trust in men was forever shattered."

"Did he ever apologize for leaving you stranded?" Sigma asks.

"No. Daddy never came back that day. He's remained vacant from my life ever since."

"I am so sorry, Uvonu."

I laugh, but it isn't cheerful. "I wish my disappointment in men stopped there but no. After daddy left, my mom took it hard. She blamed herself for him leaving and ended up on drugs. They became her everything. She was in and out of the house on binges so much we hardly saw her.

"My brother Jonesy stepped up to the plate to raise me. He was five years older than me. He taught me how to survive and how to read people. He showed me how to determine who I could trust and who I couldn't."

It's his life lessons that got me through my few years in foster care. Without Jonesy, I'd probably be worse off than I am now. I can only imagine what that would look like.

I continue, "He was all I had for so long that I forgot about the lesson I learned from my father. I started to trust that Jonesy would always be there for me. Then one day he too didn't come home. I had no idea where he was. For three days, I stayed in a cold apartment with no food waiting for him to come back. I was thirteen at the time. Eventually, a neighbor found me and reported me to the authorities. I learned that he had been arrested for robbery. He died after only serving two years of his fifteen-year prison sentence."

"What happened then?"

I shake my head because the story doesn't get better.

"I was put in foster care where I met even more untrustworthy men. At sixteen, I was done with it all, and I ran away. I took care of myself until I eventually met Miguel, and well, you know where that lead me."

"Here with me," he says. I turn this time to look at him and smile.

"Yes, here with you."

"Good," he says before turning his back to me to face the door again. "Sleep now, Uvonu. You are safe from the untrustworthy men."

I don't argue with Sigma. I don't tell him that I will never be safe. Not as long as Miguel is out there. Instead, I roll over to my side and twirl my finger in the short sleeve of his shirt. I allow his presence and the sound of my breathing to ease me to sleep.

CHAPTER EIGHTEEN

Test

Sigma

Reynolds leads me to the cafeteria; behind us are two more guards with their guns aimed at me.

The compound is in an uproar. A few of the rogues tried to impregnate some of the breeders. Their lack of knowledge has led to the death of those breeders.

I take my seat beside Alpha. Gamma is across from me, and Beta is beside him. Omega is on the other side of me.

"Where's your best friend?" Beta taunts with a smile.

The others chuckle beside me. Zee is with Shiloh.

After her confession last night, I have not wanted her to be alone. I do not like the story of heartache and disappointment my Uvonu told me. I especially did not like when her eyes filled with tears. My need to protect her has grown exponentially.

So even though her ribs are fully healed, I cannot allow her to go back to the breeders' quarters.

"He is not my best friend," I grumble, cutting into my meat. It is some type of animal, fried and covered in a thick gravy.

"Leave him alone," Alpha says with a laugh. *"Give me an update on the Rogue's breeders?"*

Leaning back on the bench seat, I place my hands to the ground and quickly find the hospital records.

"The final breeder has just died," I say sitting up straight.

Alpha hums in my head.

"What do you think caused the Rogues to defy your orders?" Omega asks through the link.

"They are testing my control. The longer we stay here, the more they will try to push back. I do not blame them. The substance in their blood is slowly driving them mad."

"How much closer are we to putting our plan in action?" Gamma asks the question that is normally reserved for me.

"Statistically speaking, the odds are not in our favor at this time. With Alpha's Uvonu still unaware of their connection, it would be unwise of him to leave without sealing their bond first. Not to mention there are records of her coming here. If he takes her, they will suspect the bodies we have placed are not all ours. Also, I still have not figured out what is going on with Strong. I believe he has another weapon he thinks will kill us. I have not found the design or any other mention of the weapon to dispel or prove his theory. Plus, we do not have the sufficient number of bodies that will cover our tracks."

When I look back up from my plate, the others are staring at me.

"Okay what is going on with you?" Beta asks.

"I know this is not my common stance on the situation. However, it is the right decision to wait a little longer." I go on to explain.

"He's right," Alpha adds. *"I have no right to ask you to wait, but I need to establish my bond with my Uvonu first. I cannot leave here without her."*

"We will stay," Gamma says, and we follow with the same declaration.

We go back to eating, until I notice Strong enter the cafeteria. Every time he comes into a room with me, my hackles go up. I cannot pinpoint why I have such an adverse reaction to the man. I dislike him; that is obvious; however, this is something else.

"Heads up," I say to Alpha. *"Strong is up to something."*

"I feel it," he says without turning to acknowledge the man.

We all freeze when a soldier walks in. He's young, but not one I've seen often. We all register the scent on him the same time Alpha does.

My leader vibrates beside me with rage.

"Why is her scent on him?" he questions in the link.

Before I can respond, the young guard hurries to Asim and pulls out a piece of fabric from his pocket. Immediately we know what the white cloth is.

"This is not going to end well," Gamma mutters.

Alpha roars loudly and leaps to his feet.

"Calm yourself," I say in our private link. *"This is a trap."* Even if I didn't just see Stronghold up his hand to stop the guards from tranquilizing him, I would have known this was a trap. No one has been allowed in his Uvonu's room except Donovan and Strong. Donovan only drops off food, and he immediately leaves.

My words are ignored as Alpha charges for the soldier and kill him easily. We all stand in unison, awaiting his next orders.

He bends down, picks up the underwear, and brings them to his nose to sniff.

"Prepare yourself," Alpha says in the main link. *"Today we will add more bodies to the count."*

The soldiers attempt to subdue Alpha, but he takes them down one by one.

"Zee," I call out to him through a private link. *"Is my Uvonu safe?"*

"She is well, Mr. Sigma, but have you heard of this Superman character she speaks of?"

I see Shiloh is introducing Zee to all of her human depictions of aliens. *"Yes,"* I grumble as I remember how the red undertones in her skin became more pronounced when she spoke of that particular alien. *"We need bodies. Alpha is causing a distraction, time to collect. Anyone that dies or go missing now will get lumped in with the ones he will kill."*

"I'm on it."

I break off the connection to Zee knowing he will do what I ask of him. Meanwhile, we use one of our ancient war tactics from the old world. The grunting confuses and disturbs our enemies in battle.

The main link opens, and the body counts start to roll in. As of now, we can add four to our secret stash.

The door to the cafeteria opens, and more guards pour in. We aren't worried about them overpowering our leader in any way. A few of the rogues become antsy to join in with Alpha. Omega and I both snap at them to get them under control.

Then finally, the game Strong is playing comes to an end. Donovan rushes into the room carrying Alpha's Uvonu. Strong hurries over to her and pulls her from Donavan. She whispers. Alpha's name, and we all stop.

I study the human, comparing her to mine. Her skin is slightly lighter than my Uvonu's. Her eyes softer and down turned. They look sad and scared, but they lack the same fire like Shiloh had. Her lips are just as full as my human's, but her face is more rounded. She wears a scarf over her hair, whereas my human has twisted hers into a small individual twist. I wonder would Shiloh prefer a wrap like Alpha's Uvonu?

"Hey," The human whispers through chattering teeth.

Alpha rushes to her side. Watching him with her, has me longing for the human I have stored away.

I open the connection to Zee.

"Where are you?" I demand of him.

"Back with Shiloh. She heard the commotion. She is asking for you."

I do not have words to explain the feeling that now warms my limbs. Her concern for me is humbling.

"Tell her I am alright."

Silence follows my command. *"You're allowing me to speak to her?"*

I understand his caution. I first forbade him from talking to her and even threatened to kill him if he did. However, I do not want her to worry over me, and I will not be able to get back to her until it is time for our dinner.

"Yes. Do not make me regret this decision."

His excitement causes the connection to crackle.

Alpha gets our attention as he lifts his human in his arms. The main link opens.

"Do not disturb me for the rest of the day," he growls and then cuts the link off completely.

More than half of the guards leave, following Alpha out. The other small handful starts to grow nervous when they notice they are outnumbered.

"What do we do?" one of the soldiers asks.

"Take them back to their cells," Another answer. "They have training in two hours."

Beta opens the main link. *"I need all those bodies brought to the lower level. Sigma will meet you there to help dispose of them. Everyone else head back to your cells. We need to keep a low profile for the rest of the day. Alpha is busy, and we will not be the reason he is disturbed."*

Most of us agree easily, but anger vibrates the link from a few rogues. Beta cuts away from the main link to connect to the commander link.

"Keep an eye on those that aren't pleased," He warns. *"I know Alpha is not worried, but I don't like how they are challenging him."*

"I agree, and I'm on it," Gamma replies eagerly.

The guards that are left begin to separate us; their guns aim shakily as they escort us out of the cafeteria.

As soon as we are sealed in our cells, and the floor is clear, I make my escape. I met Zee and a few others in the area we are storing the bodies. With each body that is tossed in the pit, I work my gift to remove their names from the system.

"Is that all of them?" I ask Zee.

"Yes."

We ended up with a total of five bodies. Once the others have all went back to their cells to await training, I head to see her.

I dislike the edgy feeling when I am away from her. She is a hindrance to me. It is time I let her go. Today, I'm going to send her back to the unit with the other breeders.

Pushing open the door, I stop in my tracks when my eyes fall upon her. She's lying across the small bed, wearing only one of my t-shirts. The hem of the shirt stops right where her thighs turn into the curve of her buttocks.

Her body glistens, and I can smell the powdery soap that I found for her. She must have recently showered. She's on her stomach, her feet up in the air swaying back and forth.

She looks over her shoulder at me and smiles so big, my breathing becomes labored.

"Hey, Siggy. What's a six-letter word that means strips in Geography class?"

I run through my knowledge of the English language. "Isthmi."

She laughs. "I knew you would know the answer."

She then turns back to her crossword puzzle. I remember once again what I had planned to tell her when I came in here. I move further into the room and then take a seat on the side of the bed.

Shiloh rolls to her side and peers up at me. Her brow creases, and her puzzle forgotten.

"Everything alright?"

Her concern quickens my heart. I am thankful she cannot feel mine the way I feel hers.

"Is it about the noise from earlier? Zee said nothing was wrong, but he then ran out of here like he was late for work."

"Everything is as it should be. What would you like for dinner tonight?" I berate myself in my head for not being strong enough to tell her what needed to be said. When I send her back to the breeder's unit, I will no longer be able to visit her as I wish. Their floor is much more patrolled than ours.

"Ooh, what are my options?" She rolls over and sits up in the bed, folding her knees under her.

I reach around her, bringing my face so close to her that I not only hear but feel her breath hitch. Placing my hand on the wall behind her, I find the cafeteria computer and pull the menu off.

"Lasagna and cobb salad, or baked chicken, mixed vegetables, and baked potato."

Her eyes are close, and her breath comes out in little pants. She swallows before she replies.

"Lasagna sounds good."

I've studied my human reactions very closely. This one is new; it also comes with a scent that has my meaty appendage leaking. Peculiar.

I lean away from her, giving her space again. Her eyes open, and she lets out a breath followed by a chuckle. Yet, neither of us has said anything that would warrant a laugh.

"I will bring your meal tonight." I stand, needing to put distance between us. I'm not sure why I desire suddenly to taste that unfamiliar scent on my tongue. Where is it coming from?

I go to leave, but she quickly climbs off the bed.

"Wait." Her fingers twirl in the fabric of my shirt she's wearing, causing it to ride up and give me a glimpse of her legs. I tilt my chin to the right; the scent seems to be radiating from between her legs.

"Do you have to leave right now?"

It takes me a moment to register her question. That scent is maddening and distracting. My tongue slips out and runs along my bottom lip. I must distance myself from her and this new magnificent, yet unfamiliar scent.

"I must return to my cell, Uvonu. It is imperative that I do not risk getting put in lockdown." The thought alone makes my hands tighten in fist. If I'm in lockdown, I cannot be with her nor protect her.

Her head drops, and she takes a step back. "I understand."

This is when I should leave. Yet, instead, I step closer to her and place my hand on her shoulder. Her sad eyes look up at me.

"I can stay for only a little longer."

The smile on her face is worth the pain of resisting the scent.

"How about a round of Uno?"

I roll my eyes. "If you wish."

**

I give my human two hours of my time before I leave. Though the sweet scent subsided, it still lingered in the room. Thankfully, I was able to maintain control.

I slip back into my room as quietly as I slipped out. I have a few hours before I take Shiloh dinner. I find my favorite position against the wall. My member has been hard and painful since I stepped into her room. It isn't unusual, it is always painfully stiff when she is near. However, today feels different.

I tug at the heavy girth and blissful pleasure has my toes curling and a hiss coming from my mouth. What was that? I repeat the action and get the same outcome as before.

Loosening my belt and unzipping my pants, I pull myself out to examine it. It stands stiffly in the air. It has never been this hard; it feels like steel in my hands. The veins on the side seem to throb, the head looks purple, and continues to leak the useless substance.

I tighten my grasp on it, my large hand wrapping around it, allowing my thumb and forefinger to touch. I move up and then down. My eyes close, and my head falls back against the wall as pleasure fills my limbs.

A vision of my Uvonu pops in my head. Her bright smile and mismatched eyes causing my length to jerk in my grasp. My grip moves faster, causing my stomach muscles to tighten.

The memory of her lying across the bed, her thighs shimmering with the substance called lotion. Just like today, the vision in my head looks over her shoulder at me. However, instead of her asking about a crossword puzzle, my mind conjures up the image of her asking me to taste the scent from between her legs.

I groan in ecstasy as my legs begin to tingle. The image in my head then turns into Shiloh standing before me smiling. Her shirt riding up showing me that glimpse of her legs. My fist tightens onto my steel, and I work hard, even pumping my hips into my grip.

Then it happens, a feeling I have never experienced erupts through my body. I roar up into the ceiling as ropes upon ropes of pearly white substance shoots from me. It continues to spew as my body shakes from aftershocks. When it finally subsides, I fall to my side feeling completely spent.

The pounding of footsteps coming near my cell gets my attention. I have just enough time to tuck myself away before the viewing window on my door slides open. Reynolds peers through the opening; he scans the room until he finds me.

"Hey, Sigma, you alright?"

No, I am not. I've never felt this weak, not even when Alpha first woke me for my rebirth.

I push myself off the ground and ever so slightly give Reynolds a nod. He seems unsure, but he shuts the viewing window.

"False alarm," he tells the others, and soon after their footsteps recede.

I take a seat on the bed I never use. Dropping my head into my hands, I ponder on the turn of events. Not even when I am in the breeding room has my release felt this good. My muscles are still tense from it.

I try to search my memories of the old world for any guidance of what just happened. When I come up unsuccessful, I begrudgingly stand and walk over to the door. Placing my hand against the wall,

I find access to the world wide web and search everything I can about human intercourse. It looks like I will be here for a while.

CHAPTER NINETEEN

Mating Room

Sigma

I land a punch on Gamma's jaw. Knocking him into the dirt. He quickly gets to his feet, swiping a hand under his lip to wipe away the blood.

Despite what Strong and the scientist here think, we can be harmed, just not by them.

"Someone has been training," Gamma mocks in my head.

"Or someone has just grown lazy."

The others laugh at my taunt.

We've been on strict training orders since the incident in the cafeteria a week ago. There is a mission he wants us to go on. Apparently, Dr. Strong has one last chance to prove his findings to his superior, Stewart Scott.

We aren't worried about the job. We are more than capable of handling whatever it is.

Gamma charges at me, and I barely avoid his blow to the side of my face. I counter with a swing to his, but he leans away from it and comes back with a kick to my stomach, sending me flying back into a jeep denting the side.

"Enough," The guard in charge of training says.

I stand, chuckling through the link. *You must be soft on me, Castian. That was nearly a love tap.*

"He must think you are his Uvonu," Omega teases his brother.

We all laugh through the link. Gamma takes the joking in stride. I move to the end of the line, allowing the next two fighters to take my spot.

"Why isn't Alpha here leading this training?" Gamma asks. He's standing on the opposite end of the line. They always line us up side by side when we are together.

I watch as the two new reincarnates battle in front of us.

Alpha has been on his best behavior after Strong pulled that stunt with his Uvonu. I knew they placed devices inside the breeders to track their ovulation and to determine if they are pregnant. However, we had no idea it could be used as a weapon. It took me a while to figure out how to disarm the device that was set off in Alpha's mate. I took care of Shiloh's while she slept that night.

"He's being detained today," Beta supplies. *"He has a meeting with Strong."*

"Let me guess, they have him in the interrogation room?"

"Yes," Beta replies to Gamma.

Gamma chuckles through the link. *"When will they learn."*

The two reincarnates in front of us finish with the rogue being thrown to the ground. The soldier in charge calls for the next two. Beta steps forward with Iota. Iota is a great fighter but is no way a match for Beta.

"Hey, Sigma. What's with the rogue?" Omega's question has me lifting my head from the battle in front of me. I glance across the field we are

on to the other set of reincarnates. They are doing a different drill lead by another soldier.

It takes no time to spot who Omega is referring to. It is the rogue from the mating floor, the one that was in the room with Shiloh. His gaze is on me.

I open a private link to him. *"Were my last two lessons not efficient enough for you?"*

He bares his teeth at me from across the field. *"Give her back to me?"*

"You are wasting your time, rogue. Find something else to fixate on. This will be my last warning to you." I cut off the connection between us.

I do not understand his fascination with my Uvonu. The next time he crosses me for her, not even Alpha will keep me from killing him.

The commander link sparks to life in my head.

"Sigma, where are you?"

Alpha's voice sounds desperate and urgent.

"Outside in the training yard. What's wrong?"

"I need you to pull records of my mate. They are held in a place called Vita labs. Strong has suggested that she was abused. I want to know if he speaks truth. There is also video of her on his tablet. I want his cameras disabled and all videos erased." The last sentence is growled causing all of us to shuffle restlessly.

"Yes, as soon as I am inside, I will handle this for you."

The link goes silent, and immediately after, soldiers run onto the training field.

"We need Gamma, Beta, Sigma, and Omega," The short soldier says out of breath.

Although we do not turn to look at each other, I can feel our unease through the link.

The four of us, guided by our personal guards, walk back into the building. We bypass the floor with our cells and head down to the mating unit.

"Why are they cutting training for mating?" Beta asks through our link.

"I don't know, but something seems off," I reply.

Silently we allow them to lead us to a door on the mating hall.

"They want you all to go in and disrobe," Reynolds says. Even his brow is pinched in confusion.

Never have we all been in the same mating room. Although we are not fans of the intercourse, we are still territorial males who do not like to share.

"Hey, get moving," One of Beta's guard's shout.

Beta is the first to enter the room. We follow him, one of each of our guards' trails in behind us. We disrobe and hand our clothing off. The guards back out of the room and close the door. Immediately the artificial pheromones start to pump into the room.

While here, I decide to do what Alpha asks. I place my hand against the back wall and find the connection I need.

"I think I know what this is about?" Gamma says through the link.

We give him our attention.

"They want me to show you all the proper skills for intercourse," his joke is followed by his laughter.

Omega scoffs, *"You wish, little brother."*

"My research shows that heterosexual women are the most likely to be unsatisfied in the act of sexual intercourse," I say still focused on getting Alpha the information he requested. I've already looped the cameras in Strong's office and deleted the many videos he has of Alpha's mate.

"What does that mean?" Gamma asks getting my attention back.

"It means there is a high probability you are not as good as you think."

They all laugh as if I was telling a joke. I do not inform them that I wasn't.

Suddenly, the pheromones in the room increase. My heavy appendage grows solid. My first instinct is to tug it like I've learned to do every time I leave my Uvonu's room. How I only wish that I could be placed in a mating room with her.

I shake my head at the thought. That would not be wise.

Looking around the room, we have all grown more tense. I still do not know what their plan for us will be, but it needs to happen soon. I want to get out of this room.

Gamma grows impatient and steps toward the door.

"No," Beta barks through the link. It comes out as a growl. *"Stay calm something is wrong."* He says the same thing we are all thinking.

Gamma grunts his annoyance, but steps back.

The door flies open, and Alpha's Uvonu is shoved into the room. She turns and beats at the door crying and pleading for someone to let her out.

"What is the meaning of this?" Omega growls. His anger is felt throughout all of us.

Beta opens the commander's link to Alpha and shows him what is going on. Our leaders anger burns through us like molting lava.

"Touch her and die," He warns unnecessarily.

"Relax, those are not our intentions," Beta says remaining the calm headed second he's trained to be. *"How do you want us to handle this?"*

The female's body sags against the metal; she then turns around and slides down the door. She looks helpless sitting here among us. My anger builds as I think of what would happen if it had been my human thrust into this room. I would destroy this place without a second thought.

Beta takes a step toward her. She trembles as she calls out for our leader. Complete sadness and worthlessness fill me. I know it is not my feelings but Alpha's.

Beta kneels in front of her, and very lowly tells her, *"I am a friend of Alpha's. Do not worry."*

The human seems to relax a little; she nods. Beta helps her stand and then lifts her up in his arms. On the other side of the wall, Strong is throwing a tantrum that rivals a rogues.

Dr. Strong shouts for them to send in more of us. I convey the information to Alpha.

"His obsession of me has grown dangerous," Alpha has calmed a little knowing that we would not hurt his mate. *"It's starting to place my mate in serious danger."*

"We are not prepared to leave yet. Beta's secret project is not complete. I have not secured all the things we will need once we are free, nor have we found a location that will keep us hidden." I point out very important facts.

Maybe I am being selfish for not wanting to leave right now.

"We will figure it out," he says.

I turn my attention back to the metal door. It swings open, and five other reincarnates walk in. One of them is an unnamed rogue. The other four read the room clearly. Beta quickly explains that the female is to go untouched. The four back away. However, the rogue takes a step forward, intending to defy Beta.

"If you want to live longer than this moment, you will sit down," Alpha's command comes so strong through our link that it almost causes me to sit.

The rogue quickly scurries away and takes a seat.

"Beta, I need your eyes. Show me Strong," Alpha says.

Beta turns to the wall using his exceptional vision; he peers through the mirrored glass.

I keep my eyes on the human writhing in pain on the bed. If pheromones are strong enough to affect us, I can only imagine what it is doing to her. Her scent fills the air, and though it is sweet, it is nowhere as fragrant as my Uvonu's.

"She's going to be in pain," I tell Alpha.

"Can you do anything," He pleads.

Before I can respond or research, Beta cuts in.

"They are about to pull us out of the room."

The doors open, and one of the handlers is ushered in carrying a useless object. I want to roll my eyes at the control they think they have over us. It is a brilliant plan Omega came up with. He advised us to give our enemies a false sense of control. We made them believe simple objects or obsession as they call it, had power over us. It keeps them compliant and allows us to have more freedom.

The handler attempts to calm one of the reincarnates that came in last. Meanwhile, Donovan lifts the human out of the room and rushes her away.

"I need eyes on her," Alpha growls.

The first handler escorts his guy calmly out of the room. Another one enters with a similar box. Thankful for the distraction, I place my hand on the wall and follow the cameras as they carry the human to Strong's personal room.

I allow Alpha access to my thoughts so that he can see what I'm seeing.

Strong enters his private quarters, and Asim hands him a syringe. Quickly, Strong dismisses Asim. For some reason, Asim hesitates, which angers the doctor

"I said, that will be all, Asim," Strong shouts at his assistant, but his eyes are glued to the bedroom where Morgan lies.

Asim leaves and Strong enters the room where the human is tossing and turning on the bed. I move our view to the camera inside the bedroom.

"Mmmmmmmake it sssssssstop," the human cries as she rubs her thighs together.

Strong holds up the needle, he takes off the top and some of the liquid squirts out.

"Inside this needle is the cure you crave. Right now, your body is pumping a very strong substance through your system. Without the proper cure..." Dr. strong says waving the needle back and forth.

"I want that medicine," Alpha's voice is a low hiss in my head. *"Find it for me."*

I too wanted that medicine. I don't like the idea of them using the pheromones to harm my mate.

"I'll have it for you soon," I tell Alpha.

We focus back on the cameras in Strong's room.

"However, there is another way to cure you of your ache, Morgan. Sex." Dr. Strong says to the human. His voice is low and husky.

Alpha growls in my head at the same time I do. I do not like where this is going.

"*Prepare the others, if he tries to touch my mate, I will kill the Doctor today.*"

On screen, Dr. Strong continues to speak. "If you would like, I can help you. I can help you take the pain away without the medicine."

The human grimaces before replying, "I'd rather have the needle."

Alpha laughs, and I join him when I see the disappointment in Strong's face.

I stay connected to the camera system long enough to see Strong put away the needle and storm out of the room.

"*Even if I get the medicine, there will be no way I can get in Strong's office. With your mate in there he will keep it guarded.*"

Alpha grows silent, seeming to think this over. "*Just get the medicine. It will be good to have if we need it again.*"

I disconnect the connection as my handler comes in carrying a computer mouse. I allow her to escort me out of the room. From there, my guards lead me back to my cell. As soon as they close me off, I dress quickly and escape.

I will have to wait until nighttime before I can sneak away and get the medicine, but right now, the pheromone in my system has me wanting to see one person only.

Shiloh is sitting up in the bed reading a book when I enter the room. It's nearly dinner time for her. She drops the book on the bed and jumps to her feet when she sees me.

"You're early," she smiles. Her excitement has my hands trembling. I want to touch her so badly, but I worry it will reverse all the effort I have made in calming her fear of me.

"Are you alright?"

"Yeah, is everything okay?" she looks over me, her mismatched eyes going from my head to toe.

All I can picture is my Uvonu locked in that room with nine rogues, me unable to get to her. A growl slips from my lips and her eyes widen.

"Siggy, you're scaring me. What's wrong?"

"I need to touch you," my words are spoken through clenched teeth. "Please, Uvonu. May I hold you?" I have never pleaded for anything, not in this life or the old. But some part of me needs to have her in my grasp to know that she is safe with me and not in that room.

She takes a tentative step back. For a moment, I am afraid I have scared her away, but then, she sits on the bed and lies down, scooting her back against the wall; she then holds her hands out for me. I do not stop to think. Even though I can feel her heart pounding in my chest, I will not refuse this opportunity.

Climbing on the bed, I lie on my side facing her. I make no sudden moves. She grabs my arm and places it around her waist. I pull her into my chest, and she comes easily. Burying my face in the top of her head, I take a deep breath. Peace comes over me. She is safe in my arms.

"Are you going to tell me what happened."

"No, Uvonu. I would rather just hold you."

CHAPTER TWENTY

The Mission

Sigma

The anxious energy in the aircraft is stifling. Alpha was allowed to choose who he wanted to bring on this mission with him. We were unsure what to expect when we got here, but we weren't concerned.

Our anxious energy came from being away from the compound. This is the first time we've been allowed to step foot outside of the barbed fence.

Much of the knowledge I have of this human world is from my research on the world wide web. In some ways, we are sheltered. We understand the way this human world works. We understand that currency is required to sustain us. We also understand the inner turmoil and wars amongst the human population. We are not unprepared to join the outside world.

However, even I know that researching something isn't the same as having firsthand experience.

Looking around the aircraft, I take in the others. Beta is busy studying the plane. When we first saw the aircraft, he asked me immediately to get him everything I could on the model and build. I know his mind is working overdrive on how to recreate a CH-47.

Omega and Gamma are having a heated conversation on how many kills they will get and who is the better fighter. A few of the other reincarnates with us are studying the guards and the scientist.

A tickle in the back of my mind has my gaze shifting to Alpha. There is only one person that has the ability to sift through my knowledge.

"You could have asked," I say to Alpha.

He grunts. *"Don't worry, I am not searching for your secret."*

I already knew that. I have my Shiloh buried so deep in my mind that it wouldn't feel like a tickle if he was searching for her.

"Then what do you want?"

He sighs. *"I need all the information you have on human intercourse."*

Although my face does not change on the outside, on the inside, I'm laughing. *"Why do you assume I have that knowledge stored in my memory?"*

"Because I know you. Even if you didn't enjoy the act, you still researched it. Now show me what I'm searching for."

I chuckle once more before I bring up all the knowledge I have of intercourse. I show him the articles along with the videos most of the soldiers enjoy.

"And the human women enjoy this?" he queries.

I show him the video of cunnilingus that I've discovered is very well received by human females.

"Particularly this." I tell him.

He goes silent as he continues to study my thoughts. After going over everything, he pulls back. I know that Alpha plans to use this new knowledge on his Uvonu.

My attention immediately turns to mine. The desire to have intercourse with Shiloh has been strong lately, especially since every time I enter her room, that scent between her legs seem to grow stronger. I wonder will she enjoy the cunnilingus like the women from the videos.

"Heads up, King. Your boyfriend's watching you." Omega says in the commander link breaking into my thoughts.

We all turn to look at Dr. Strong.

"I know," Alpha replies. *"He's nervous. He's starting to understand that he's not as in control as he thinks he is."*

"Should we be worried?" Gamma asks.

Most of our plans revolve around the scientist and soldiers at the compound, believing that we lack knowledge and are no real threat to them.

"No," I reply, easing their fears. *"My research and evaluation of the doctor shows that though he may realize he is not in control, he will never accept it. He believes in all things; he is still the superior."*

Just as I tell the others my thoughts, Asim's question fills the space of the aircraft.

"What do you think he's thinking?" Although he spoke quietly, we all heard him.

Strong turns to Asim briefly before turning back to Alpha. He watches our leader with a challenging gaze in his dark eyes.

"Nothing. They don't think, Asim."

At this we all laugh through the link.

"Told you," I say.

"Let him think what he will. It will be more enjoyable when I kill him." Alpha adds.

The plane begins to descend.

"Alright, listen up," Alpha's voice no longer has the humor from earlier. *"We run this smoothly. The quicker we get this done the faster I get back to my mate. I don't want anything to deter that."*

"We got you," Beta says, and we all agree.

They load us off the plane in a single file line. We stand motionless as we take in our surroundings.

The area we are in looks similar to our compound. The air is a lot dryer and the temperature is hotter. Although the landscapes look similar, the ground here is a type of red sand rather than the packed earth we're used to. I search my intensive knowledge of this planet's landscape to figure out where we are.

"We are somewhere in the middle east," I tell the others.

Before anyone can reply, the man we know as Steward Scott approaches Strong.

"I hope you are ready to prove your worth."

Strong frowns at the statement, but Scott doesn't see it. He's already turned back to the other men with him. Judging by their uniforms, they are high ranking in the US military. I explain this to the Alpha.

"Gentlemen," Scott goes on to say to the men. "Are they not all that I told you they would be?"

"Yes," a general says. "It is one thing to look like a soldier, but another to perform like one, and I am a true believer real soldiers are not made in a lab, but on a field."

"They doubt us," Omega growls through the link. *"On Albatraum, I would have cut his head off for his comment."*

"Relax, Gakos. Let them have their doubts," Alpha says in a placating tone. We all know how volatile Omega can be when he believes someone doubts his skills. Even in the old world, he did not take kindly to others challenging him.

"Then allow me to prove you wrong," Strong says stepping forward as if he is the reason for our strengths. "Gentlemen, I know you are skeptics. I would be too if I weren't the one who created these magnificent soldiers."

"Ugh, can we please kill him now," Gamma grumbles. We all feel his sentiment.

Strong continues to boast over his perceived accomplishments. "But I assure you, they are faster, stronger, and better equipped than any born and bred soldier on your battlefields."

One of the soldiers standing with the men laughs. The link sizzles with tension—neither of us finding humor in what was said.

"Do I have a doubter?" Strong asks.

The soldier that laughed looks to a commander. "Permission to speak, sir?" he asks.

"How can someone that cannot even speak without permission find humor in us?" Beta queries. We all laugh.

"Of course, Lieutenant," The commander replies with a grin.

The Lieutenant looks back to Strong. "With all due respect, sir, these… things have never been on a live battlefield. Everyone is fast and tough when in the safety of a practice facility." His reply garners a few more laughs.

Omega moves sightly toward the soldier. *"I will show him how much experience I have when I rip his tongue out of his mouth."*

Alpha stops him by shifting in front of him. The movements were so quick that none of the humans noticed it.

"I see," Strong says. "Might I see your firearm for a moment?"

Once again, the man looks to his superior. The officer nods at him. The lieutenant takes his firearm from its holster and hands it to Strong.

"Be careful with that. Those are real bullets," the soldier says, and laughter rumbles through the crowd again.

Strong's shoulders tense. I can tell he is not a fan of the laughter and taunting either.

"Heads up, men. Strong is going to shoot one of us. Prepare yourself," Alpha warns as Strong checks the magazine of the weapon. I do not understand the humans' love of their guns.

It has proven to not be successful in harming us. Our bodies will just heal the damage.

Strong aims the gun at Gamma's head and pulls the trigger. The blow hits him in the center of his forehead. Gamma leans his head back, not allowing the men or Strong to see the hole. They believe we are indestructible. We will keep it that way.

"What the hell is this, Scott?" one of the men shouts.

"Wait for it," Scott tells him with a smirk on his face. His eyes still glued to Gamma.

Gamma lifts his head back up, and his skin has already mended. The bullet falls to the ground showing no sign of injury.

"Unbelievable," one of the men says.

Strong turns to face the laughing soldier that gave him the gun. He aims the weapon at his forehead. "Now, your turn."

"For once, I think I'm on Strong's side." Omega says through the link.

The soldier holds up his hands, begging Strong not to shoot. I think we all know Strong is unstable enough to pull the trigger. However, he drops the weapon back down to his side and laughs.

"Gentlemen, shall we get this show on the road?" Scott announces causing the other men to turn and leave.

"Alright," Alpha says gathering our attention. *"We know what we are up against. Sigma, see what you can find about this mission."*

I crouch down and place my hand to the ground. It's much easier to search for the information if I'm inside the building, but this works too. Strong and Scott are in a heated conversation, so they aren't paying attention to me.

"Hey, get up," One of the guards Strong brought with him says. He didn't bring any of our personal guards.

I ignore the soldier until I find what I'm looking for. Standing back up, I bare my teeth to the guard. His eyes widen as he steps away from me.

"It's a rescue mission. Two weeks ago, five American employees for the embassy were kidnapped by a terrorist group. The hostages are being kept in an underground

tunnel. They need these people back because they all hold important jobs. The government is afraid the hostages will be forced to give up valuable information."

"*We know the mission. Can we get a layout of the tunnel?*" Omega asks.

"*No. They cannot get footage of the inside of the hidden tunnel. They fear going in blind and they want all hostages back alive.*"

"*We're going to be smart about this,*" Alpha says, but gets interrupted when Strong walks over with Donavan and another man.

"Ok, men," Strong says facing us. "This is what you were created for. We need to make sure this mission goes well in order to continue with our program. If they shut us down, they will take everything, including the girls."

Fear like I've never experienced before hits me. The thought of not being able to see my Uvonu has me grinding my teeth.

Strong goes on to speak. "They will probably terminate you all or lock you up forever, so I need your best work out there. If it goes well, you will receive your obsessions as soon as we are back at headquarters. Now, with this being said, this is your leader, Captain Willard. You will follow his instruction."

"*What did he just say?*" Gamma asks.

"*Sounds like he said we were going to let this measly human tell us what to do.*" Beta says.

Omega starts to grunt, and we join in. We have no intentions of attacking. The sound is only to irritate Strong and show our dissatisfaction.

Every soldier around us points their guns at us. I laugh to myself. Did they not see what Gamma did with their useless bullets?

"Strong, what the hell is going on?" Scott shouts over the noise.

Strong doesn't reply; he continues to have a staring match with Alpha. My leader keeps his calm even though I can feel his anger through our link like flames lapping at my mind.

Strong turns to Asim, who hands him a tablet. After pressing a few buttons, Strong flips the tablet around, and the screen comes to life with Alpha's mate. We all immediately feel his rage subside.

"Alpha," She hums his name. Her face lights up with happiness. It is how Shiloh smiles at me whenever I walk into the room. Her excitement always wakes the sleeping appendage between my legs.

Morgan continues to speak to Alpha. I take this time to check on my own Uvonu. I left Zee in charge of watching her. He should be with her by now.

"How is she?" I ask as soon as Zee opens his link.

For the first time, I am envious of Alpha. I wish that I could see Shiloh instead of hearing of her from Zee.

"Sleeping," he answers, and I realize it's still early there. *"She was restless for a while."*

She sleeps better when I'm near her. She twirls her fingers in my shirt sleeve as she talks. It brings me comfort to know that I am the only one she does this with.

"She will want to shower when she wakes. Make sure that she does," I tell him before closing the link.

I tune back into my surroundings when the sound of Alpha growling catches my attention. Strong ended the video chat with Morgan. The human male Strong introduced as Willard pulls his handgun.

"That's your reward, Alpha. Is she worth it?" Strong grumbles.

For a moment, Alpha doesn't reply, but then he holds up his hand, and we stop grunting. It was all for show. Our leader needed the men here to see who is really in charge. Although they believe we will follow their orders, we will not.

"Listen for my command. I want this over as soon as possible. My mate needs me, and I will not keep her waiting."

Strong and the others walk away, and the one named Willard is left behind.

"Let's start getting these creatures loaded up." Willard says.

The soldiers begin to circle us as if we were livestock. With their guns aimed at our heads, they guide us to large vehicles. Alpha, Omega, Beta, Gamma, and I are all in the first truck with Willard.

All the soldiers in the truck keep their eyes on us.

"Freaky, isn't it?" One of the soldiers asks Willard. "They almost look human."

"They aren't," Willard replies, eyeing Alpha. "No matter what that psycho Strong says. These things will never replace us."

At this we all smile, causing the men to pull up their weapons again.

It doesn't take us long to get to our location. We climb out of the truck only to meet more soldiers. Willard immediately starts barking out orders to the others.

"Is everything set up?" he asks as he walks into a tent.

We follow behind him. I take in my surroundings. Large computer screens with surveillance of the tunnel the hostages are being held. There is a camera in the corner, and behind it is another screen that shows the room Dr. Strong and the other men are in. On the far left of the entrance is a map showing the direction of the tunnel.

"Sir, we're ready and awaiting your command," Willard says to the camera.

One of the men on the screen nods his head at Willard. "Good, we will wait until nightfall to strike. I want to make sure you have enough reconnaissance. Once we get inside those tunnels, we will be going blind. We don't have a sure layout of the tunnels."

"Night fall?" Gamma asks. *"They plan on keeping us here that long?"*

Alpha growls through the link. *"Omega, have you memorized the map?"*

"Yes, we're only three miles away."

"Sigma, can you get me visual of the hostages."

I wrap my hand around one of the exposed wires that connect to the computers and quickly find the images of the hostages. I share the info with the others.

"They want a survivor," I explain to Alpha. Then I show him the image of the leader of the terrorist group.

"That's all we need. I'll go in first; you four will follow me. I'll get them their survivor, and you will get the hostages. Everyone else, make sure these idiots don't get hurt in the process. Let's go."

We storm out of the tent. Willard and his men shout after us, but we don't stop. Omega leads us directly to the tunnel, the men guarding the entrance fire their guns as soon as they see us.

Before the human soldiers can catch up with us, we take down the terrorist outside the tunnel. Once inside, it breaks off into two hallways. Omega lifts his nose into the air and sniffs.

He points to the left side of the tunnel. *"Survivors are there."*

We all go left while Alpha goes right. We come up against many of the terrorist party, but without breaking a sweat, we kill them all.

The hostages are in a cell all the way to the back of the tunnel. Beta rips the metal door off, and we enter the room. The people look tired and malnourished, but they are alive.

"You are free. Go," Gamma tells them.

They rush out of the cell. Beta leads the way back out to the front entrance.

The survivors step out first, and then we follow. The soldiers we left behind are here with their guns trained on us.

Finally, Alpha steps out of the tunnel. It looks like he came into contact with a lot more enemy fire.

"Looks like you had more fun than we did," Gamma says teasingly through the link.

"We are done here," Alpha announces before charging toward Willard. He snatches the camera out of his hand and stares into it before smashing it onto the ground.

"We're leaving," he demands storming away.

I too, shared his sentiment. I am ready to go back to the compound. I need to see my Uvonu.

CHAPTER TWENTY-ONE

Shiloh

Sigma has been gone all day on some kind of mission, and I'm not okay. Ever since a week ago, when he came to the room asking to hold me, things have changed.

I never thought I'd crave something so bad yet fear it at the same time. My desire to be in his presence alarms me. At first, I chalked it up to the hormones they have pumping through my system. I've never been so horny in all my life.

When Siggy asked to hold me, my body trembled with want and terror. I didn't know how much I wanted him to touch me until the moment came. My body went from slightly warm to burning hot within seconds; I won't even talk about how I got so wet that my thighs felt sticky.

It's probably a good thing he only held me and didn't ask for more. It would have made things even more awkward.

Lately, he seems uncomfortable in the room with me. There has been no repeat of his need to touch me; in fact, he almost looks pained when he's around me now. He started something that night a week ago that my body is in desperate need to finish, but my brain is screaming no.

Not paying attention, I run into the back of Zee. He's on babysitting duty, and I'm heading to my daily shower.

"You are distracted," Zee says, turning around to frown at me.

I'm happy Zee is allowed to talk to me now. Having one-sided conversation with my scary babysitter wasn't fun.

I clutch my toiletries and towel to my chest as my gaze runs away from Zee's.

"Can I ask you something personal?"

I look back at him when he doesn't reply. He's doing the staring thing. Sigma does it often. I know it's when he's on the group chat with one of his friends.

"Mr. Sigma says it is alright for me to answer personal questions."

I shake my head. Zee does nothing with me without Sig's permission.

"Do you guys enjoy the breeding room?"

His face turns a shade of red and he cuts his eyes to the left. "Sometimes," He admits.

"But do you find pleasure in it?"

He looks back at me and narrows his eyes.

"I suppose it was pleasurable."

My head jerks back. "What do you mean was?"

He runs his fingers over his shaved head. "We are no longer permitted to have intercourse with the breeders."

My head draws back quickly. "Why?"

"Our leader has forbidden it. They are keeping his mate from him, so he will stop their research."

Okay that's messed up. "So, because he can't get any, he's keeping everyone else from it? That doesn't sound like a very good leader."

Zee shakes his head. "Alpha is a great leader. They are torturing his Uvonu, and he will not stand for it."

"Wait," I say holding up my hand. "What did you call her?"

Zee frowns. "Uvonu."

"What does Uvonu mean?" I've asked Sigma this many times whenever he calls me the name. He says it has no real significance and is used as a term of endearment. However, why would Zee use it for Alpha's mate.

"It is the name we call our soul mates. The person that is created just for us." His face softens, and his voice takes on a wistful tone. "I hope to one day find my Uvonu."

This doesn't make sense, why does Sigma call me Uvonu? He told me that he hadn't met his soul mate.

The noise behind us causes Zee and my head to swing in the direction. I've been living down here for a month and a half, and other than Zee and Sigma, there is never anyone down on this level. However, today there are footsteps approaching from the hallway we left.

Zee walks around me, stepping in front of me.

"Stay here," he demands before heading back the way we just came.

Too nosy to stay put, I follow him as soon as he bends the corner. I'm smart enough to stay out of sight though. I peek my head around the wall.

Two of the creatures are standing in the hallway. It looks like they have something between them. I can't quite make out what it is, but I can tell by the way they are angled something is there.

Zee seems tensed as he stares at them with his back to me. It's obvious they're having one of those silent conversations. Although, Sigma and Zee have kind of grown on me, the rest of the super soldiers still terrify me.

Apparently, Zee has said something that angers the other two. The dark skinned one bares his teeth.

Zee shifts and I spot the unconscious woman lying on the floor between the creatures. I gasp, and the two creatures look up directly at me.

One of them growls and charges toward me. Zee steps in his way and throws a punch, knocking the creature to the floor.

"Run, Shiloh," Zee shouts. However, I'm too terrified to move.

The other creature swings at Zee, smashing him into the wall. He bounces off and falls to the ground. The creature that hit him turns his attention to me and starts my way. Zee grabs the creature's pants leg. The beast kicks Zee in the head, but Zee does not let go.

The Dark-skinned one gets back up. He shakes his head before stomping toward me. Finally, realizing I'm in danger, my fight or flight reflexes kick in. Choosing flight, I drop my stuff and run, heading for the shower room

The shower room isn't anything fancy. The white tiled room has a single shower hose sprouting from the ceiling. The floor dips in the middle with a drain, a half wall blocks the view from the one single toilet and industrial sink with rust stains.

I was so happy when Sigma found it and brought me to it the first time, I overlooked the bare minimum of it. Now as I run for my life to the safety of the nearly empty room, I realize just how little it offers by way of protection.

Rushing inside, I attempt to hold the swinging door closed. The creature shoves it open causing me to crash onto the floor. He grins down at me, which is probably meant to be charming. He's gorgeous— I don't think I've met one of these things that wasn't—however, he is terrifying.

He takes a step forward and I scurry back from him like a crab. My heartbeat is thrashing in my ears. He grabs my leg and yanks me forward; I cry out at the sharp pain. What the hell is with these things and my ankle.

Zee runs through the door and tackles the creature. I have only a second to roll to the side before they come crashing down on where I was lying. Stumbling to my feet, I run out of the shower room only to slam into the chest of the other creature. Damn it, I forgot about him.

Once again, I'm knocked on my ass, this time hitting the ground so hard the breath whooshes out of me. Pain shoots through my side and I'm pretty sure my ribs are going to be messed up again.

The creature stands over me with a frown. My body shakes in fear. I let my guard down, being around Sigma and Zee. I started to believe that these things weren't bad. However, I can see the fury in his unnatural gaze.

He reaches for me, and I cover my head, tucking my body into the fetal position. I don't want to die here.

A growl pierces the air, and then something wet rains down on me.

I peek up through my arms to find the creature with a pained look on his face. His mouth is open, and his eyes are wide. I trail my gaze down and nearly pass out when I see a fist shooting out through his chest. The hand is yanked back, and the creature falls to the ground right beside me. I look from his frozen face of pain to the man standing over me now. Sigma is here. His chest rises and falls rapidly.

Zee runs out of the shower room and comes up short when he sees Sigma. They have a silent conversation. I only know this because Zee replies out loud.

"Yes, he's out cold," He answers, but his eyes are on the body lying on the floor at my feet. The way Zee is looking at the creature, I don't think he was expecting this outcome.

"Take your guy back upstairs; he will come too soon."

"And the female?" Zee asks Sigma, but his gaze hasn't left the one beside me.

"Take her with you," While Zee is focused on the fallen super soldier, Sigma's eyes are still locked on me. I wonder if he is watching me because my body is still shaking from fear.

"What about that one?" Zee asks.

For the first time, Sigma looks away from me and turns to the fallen one. "He will heal soon. After you deal with the other one, come back for him."

Wait, he's not dead? He has a hole in the center of his chest, and you mean to tell me he's not dead. Every day I'm around these super soldiers, I learn more and more that if we ever have an alien attack, we're doomed.

"What are you going to do? Alpha knows," Zee says somberly.

Sigma's head turns to Zee quickly. "I will deal with him."

Zee nods and goes back into the shower room. When he comes out, he has the dark-skinned creature thrown over his shoulder. He looks to the fallen one again and then rushes off.

"Are you alright?" Sigma asks, drawing my attention to him.

No. No I'm not. I want to scream those words at him, but nothing comes out when I open my mouth.

Sigma's brows dip. He reaches his bloody hand out for me, and I flinch away from him.

Part of me is yelling at how stupid I'm being. I should know that Sigma would never hurt me. He's had plenty of chances but never has. Not to mention, I'm supposedly his soulmate.

However, that other part of me, the one that was locked away in Miguel's home for six years, understands that people change. At the core of his being, Sigma is one of these creatures. Can I trust that he would never snap?

"You fear me again," his voice is low as if he were talking to himself and not me—the pained expression on his face tugs at my dead heart.

I go to stand, but hiss when my ribs scream in pain.

Sigma reaches down and lifts me off the ground. He holds me as if I'm fragile, yet so close to his double beating heart that I can feel them pounding against my chest.

He walks into the shower room and gently place me on my feet.

"I do not wish to cause you fear. I will take you back to the breeders' unit and leave you alone." His shoulders sag, and he looks everywhere but at me. "But I plead with you, Uvonu, wash the rogue's scent off first. You do not understand how maddening it is to smell him on you." His eyes close, and his head dips. I've never seen him look so distraught.

It brings me back to a memory. Miguel said something similar to me after he blinded the drunk man at sample night. He said he didn't want anything of another man to touch me, not even his blood.

That night those words sent a cold chill down my spine. They did not warm my soul the way it does now when I see the pained expression on Sigma's face. I truly believe he may go mad if I don't wash.

"Okay," I reply, my voice sounding hoarse.

He lifts his head and looks at me. For a moment, I don't see a creature or something unnatural. Looking back at me is a man who has done nothing for the last month and half but try to take care of me. One who spent time with me so I wouldn't be bored despite having many things to do. One who made sure I was safe and protected. I can't speak for the other creatures at this compound, but I can vouch for this one.

Sigma turns to leave.

"Wait," I call out to him. He stops and turns back to face me. "Don't go."

He seems to think this over for a moment. Or maybe he is waiting for me to give him further directions. I have no idea what I want. I only know that the thought of him leaving me here or taking me back with the breeders where I may never see him again has a tingling in my chest that isn't caused by fear.

He walks over to the wall and turns the water on. The shower spurts to life, already making the room muggy. Sigma walks back over and stands in front of me. His dark brown eyes peering down at me. He tugs at the hem of his black shirt I'm wearing. I lift my arms, and he pulls the fabric up over my head.

Tossing the shirt to the floor, his gaze is fixed on my eyes, but I want him to look at me. I want him to see my body. Maybe it will make the ache in my lower belly stop.

With only two pair of panties, I often go without any until my others are cleaned and washed. Today is one of the days I'm bare underneath. He takes a step back, but I don't want him to put distance between us.

I move forward, taking back the space he placed between us. Grabbing the bottom of his shirt, I lift it up. He lowers himself, allowing me to pull the fabric over his head. I discard it on the floor.

Squatting down, I start to unlace the combat boots on his feet. He kicks out of each of them. I then remove his socks. Before I can take off his pants, he lifts me under the arms and carries me to the water.

After setting me back on my feet, I lean my head back allowing the hot water to rinse the blood off me. Sigma places his hands on my shoulders and slowly eases them down my body, helping to wash away the other creature's scent.

His palms are rough and add wonderful friction to his sensual touch. He stops and cups my small breasts, rolling his finger around the chocolate nipple. My breath hitches, and a moan slip out. His eyes narrow at the action.

He takes his time cleaning my body, using his hand to gently bathe me. There is no soap, but he does a good job cleaning me.

When he gets to the apex of my thighs, my breathing is so ragged I feel as if I may pass out. He cups my pussy and growls. I wonder is it because he can feel how hot and wet I am.

When the heel of his palm presses against my clit, I whimper his name. My head drops forward landing against his stomach as he continues to grind against me.

Sigma uses his free hand to lift my chin so he can look into my eyes. He moves the other one faster, slipping a finger inside me. I grab a hold of his biceps to keep myself upright.

"Sigma, oh god," my mouth falls open, and my eyes drift close.

"Open, Uvonu. I need to see your eyes."

I obey his command. Locking my gaze with his. The intensity in his stare is just as much of a turn-on as what he's doing to me.

I ride his hand, feeling the euphoria build up inside me. It rises and crashes over me like a wave causing me to cry out. My nails dig into his skin as pure bliss has me jerking against him. My eyes blur, and the sound of my heartbeat rings in my ears.

Once my orgasm subsides, I start to get lightheaded. My head drops to his stomach; the echo of his double heart beats out of sync. One is beating erratically like mine, and the other is strong and steady.

He lifts my face and gazes down at me. Lifting on my tiptoes, I wrap my hands around his neck, bringing our lips together. He seems stiff at first. I don't know if it's from shock or maybe he's never kissed before. However, it only lasts for a moment before his tongue dives into my mouth, swallowing my whimper.

He cups my face in his large hands, completely taking over. He kisses me as if he's a man starving, and his next meal is in my mouth.

I move my hands to his waist, fighting to get his bottoms off. I've never been this desperate to feel someone inside me before. His boxers along with his pants fall; wrapping my hand around his length, I gasp at the size.

I'll admit, some of my eagerness drains when I feel the size of him. Everything about these super soldiers is big. I thought maybe the guy in the mating room was an anomaly. Apparently, he is not. In fact, he is smaller than Siggy.

Sigma brushes my hand away from his length as he wraps one arm around my middle and lifts me off my feet. I lock my hands at the back of his neck and my legs around his waist all without breaking our kiss.

He carries me over to the wall and presses my back against it. Pulling back only slightly, he lifts me higher, placing my thighs over his arms. He spreads me wide and lines the head of his cock to my opening.

With his eyes on mine, he waits. It takes my sex-hazed brain a few minutes to realize what he's waiting for. He wants my consent.

"I need you, please," I can hardly recognize my voice; it's so husky and needy.

My words seem to appease him. He lowers me onto his length, and I cry out at the deep intrusion. It's a tight fit, but glory to the heavens it feels divine. His hips roll back and then forward, and I squeal at how deep he goes. My toes curl as he continues to pull out and drive into me deeply. My nails dig in his back.

"Oh shit. Oh Fuck. Sigma, yes."

My words spur him on, and he starts to move faster. His balls smack against my ass, sounding as if they are applauding us.

My cries of pleasure can surely be heard throughout the compound, but I don't care. His fist smacks against the tile on the wall above my head. Pieces fall to the shower floor. The veins in his neck and head protrude and throb. He's holding back.

It's then I realize that everything he does is to take care of me. It goes without saying that he could easily hurt me if he wanted to, but even now he's thinking of me first. He's always thinking of me, from bringing me food to making sure I'm looked after when he's gone to supplying me with enough lotion to last a lifetime. Despite what he is, he is unlike any man I've ever known.

I take his lips again, needing the connection to him.

In no time, I roll into my second orgasm. I lean my head against the wall behind me and cry out his name. He fucks straight through my release, burying his head into my shoulder.

I notice that he's speaking in a foreign language. I have never heard anything like it before. It has a lot of sharp words and guttural sounds. Eventually, it turns into a chant that goes from foreign to English. He's repeating the word Mine.

"All yours," I whisper back to him.

He lifts his head and stares at me, and his eyes are glowing. This should freak me out. It is a reminder that the man that is fucking me so good isn't entirely human. However, I am not frightened. I lean forward and place a chaste kiss on his lips.

"I'm all yours, Sigma. I'm your Uvonu."

He pistons into me so fast and deep I have to hold on for dear life. He then tosses his head back and roars as hot jets of his cum bathe my walls. Shockingly, his jizz goes from hot to cold leaving me shivering.

Sigma lifts me away from the wall, falling out of me. He walks us back under the water. Instantly, I'm so tired all I can do is close my eyes and lay my head on his shoulder.

"Rest now, Shiloh. Rest," his deep voice rumbles.

Over exertion, the hot water, and his warmth sends me straight to sleep.

CHAPTER TWENTY-TWO

Repercussions

Sigma

Watching my Uvonu as she sleeps brings me peace. I thought I would feel remorse after taking her body today. I do not.

However, I do feel a mixture of sadness and concern. Sadness that my brothers are forced to do the intercourse that is meaningless, and they may never know what it feels like to make love to their soulmate. There is no comparison.

Being inside Shiloh, feeling the connection between her soul and the wet grip of her heat, is the greatest feeling in the world.

My concern stems from wondering how I will keep her with me. There is no question of me letting her go. Even when we leave this awful place, I will bring her with me.

I do not know much about the outside world on this human planet. However, I will supply her and my offspring with the best life that I can. No matter what it cost.

The pounding in my head grows even more intense. Since I attacked the rogue, I've been blocking everyone out. The moment I injured him; I could feel the others anger.

I am not allowed to kill or severely harm the rogues. Not without good reason or Alpha's permission. Though the rogue will recover from my beating, I know I crossed the line.

My head explodes in pain, and a roar pierces my thoughts. Alpha has grown tired of me blocking him.

"Explain yourself?" his voice is like thunder in my head.

"I am not ready," I reply.

"That answer no longer suffices. You will tell me why his blood was shed."

"I do not owe you an explanation for everything, Tovian. This is not Albatraum." I will not back down in this.

Alpha is silent, yet I know he has not disconnected—his rage sends tremors through our connection.

"If you will not give me the answer I seek willingly, I will take them by force." My head explodes with pain. I groan and clutch it in my hands.

He's trying to pluck the answers out of my thoughts. I use every technique that I know to fight off his attempt. It feels as if hot pokers are stabbing at my brain. I crumble to the floor, groaning as I fight my leader in my head.

"Siggy? What's going on? Oh God. Please talk to me," Shiloh is at my side. Her soft touch soothes my soul but does nothing for my head.

My body convulses as Alpha continues to attempt to rip my secrets from me.

"Sigma," she cries for me. As much as I want to assure her that all is okay, I cannot.

The only way to fight him is to focus on something else. Something that will take all of my attention. The war. My thoughts immediately go to the great war. I fight to pull up a single memory of the event.

A blurry memory starts to take form. A room with a throne. Alpha in his true form. His dominant arms are crossed over his chest, but his secondary arms are down at his side and clenched in tight fists. Large black horns jut out from the side of his head curving upward. The white lines that signify his status as king curve around his mouth and down to his chin.

We're having an argument, which isn't new for us, but something tells me this one is different. As soon as I try to focus on the words that are being said, Alpha shoves against the small glimpse. The memory immediately fades leaving not even a trace of what I saw.

The pain stops, and I'm left on the ground panting for breath.

Shiloh wraps her arms around me, and places her head on my chest. She's crying.

"You left me no choice, Vulto," Alpha says in defense.

"You've crossed the line, Tovian." The betrayal I feel shakes the link. In the many years I've served him, he has never violated me in such a way.

"You went against my command and shed the blood of one of us."

"He was a rogue, not one of us. And he had intentions of harming a human," I growl feeling much better that Alpha was unable to find out about Shiloh. *"I was protecting the female he and his partner kidnapped."*

"You do not get to make that call," He shouts in my head. *"You and your secrets—"*

"Do not speak to me of secrets." I cut him off matching his tone. *"Why can I not see the war? I have seen every memory of the past that I search for. Yet, that one still eludes me. Even now, you cut off the memory."*

"Some memories are best left in the past. Consider it a gift."

"I do not need your gift. I want the truth."

Our line goes silent once again, I know he is not gone.

"My first seed has planted. My Uvonu is now with child. I choose to live in the present and not the past. Your actions today will require repercussions. You will be on your own with that. I will not help." The disconnect is immediate, leaving me feeling cold.

Placing my hand on Shiloh's back, she lifts her head and looks up at me. Tears track down her face.

"I'm okay," I say. Sitting up against the wall, I lean my head back.

"I don't think I've ever seen you in pain or sweating." She sits beside me tucking herself into my side. She swipes the tears from her face. I wrap my arms around her back drawing her closer. "I didn't think you guys could feel pain."

"I feel it. I don't always react to it."

She hums. "You want to tell me what just happened there?"

Sighing, I turn to look at her. "My leader is not very pleased with me for hurting the rogue."

"But he was going to kill me. Did you tell him that?"

Shaking my head, I answer. "No. He does not know about you."

"Wait. Why?" I do not like the dip in her voice or the way her brow pinches.

"You are my weakness, Shiloh. You are also my one source of happiness in this prison. I'm not ready to share you with anyone else. You are mine, and I owe no one your existence. Not even Alpha."

She lifts up to kiss me, and I find that I enjoy this human sexual activity. My research says that women enjoy this as well. I gently bite into her bottom lip and then suck the plumpness into my mouth. My Uvonu has full lips. Much plumper than my own.

I grip the side of her head slanting my face so that I may take this kissing thing further. She groans, causing my need for her to grow.

My penis extends and hardens. I tug her into my lap, and she straddles me. Gripping her hips, I lift mine so that she can feel my desire for her. She hisses and pulls back with a smile.

"Whoa, lover boy. As much as I would love to ride your dick right now, I'm a bit too sore. You're really big, Sigma."

I frown. "My apologies for my size."

She chuckles, and I've grown to cherish the sound of her laughter.

"Hey, I have no complaints. You just have to give me more time to recuperate."

I nod, willing to give her anything she needs as long as we don't have to stop the intercourse.

"Come on," she stands, then reaches down and grabs my arm.

"Where are we going?" I ask allowing her to believe that she's pulling me up.

"To bed."

"Uvonu, I do not sleep," I explain following her over to the bed.

She climbs in and scoots back toward the wall. "You don't have to sleep, but I want you to hold me."

I have no intentions of denying her this request. I climb in the bed and pull her to my chest. I rest my chin on the top of her head.

"Siggy," her breath fans across my skin as she calls my name.

"Yes?"

"What are we going to do if they take me away from you?"

My arms tighten around her. "That will not happen. I'll never let them take you. Now sleep."

She snuggles closer to me and eventually slips off to sleep. However, her question stays with me. Not even Alpha will be able to restrain me if they take her away.

CHAPTER TWENTY-THREE

Sigma

"Oh shit, Sig. Don't stop, baby."

Three days has passed since I first had my Uvonu in the shower. I had no idea that I would begin to crave her so much.

Pushing her legs up into her chest, my tongue dips inside her wet heat. She squeals as I drink from her well. Slipping my tongue out of her, I focus on her clit, sucking the hardened nub.

She comes hard, soaking my face with her essence. I don't stop tasting her; I do not think I will ever tire of her flavor.

"Too sensitive," She cries scooting her bottom away from me.

Coming up for air, I wipe a hand down my face cleaning up the residue of her. I climb up her body, lying between her legs. Her fingers interlock behind my head as she lifts up to kiss me. She moans as she sucks on my tongue.

I line my cock to her entrance and slowly push inside. She whimpers as I make room. I call it cock or dick now because Shiloh says that penis sounds too clinical.

"My god, you feel so good," Her head falls back on the pillow as I roll my hips and pull out of her, only to shove back in.

"I promise, it is not as good as you feel," I grit out between clenched teeth.

I must remain in control when I am with her. I'm much stronger than her and do not wish to cause her pain. Burying my face in her pillow, I brace my hand against the wall over our heads. With each thrust into her depths, my hand tightens until my fingers dig craters into the wall—concrete rains down over us.

"Sigma, look at me," She demands.

I look down at her and her brow creases.

"Make love to me, stop fighting it."

"I can't, Uvonu. I will hurt you."

She shoves at my chest, pushing me off her. I move, even though my heart is beating fast from the disconnection. The bed is pushed up against the wall, and I sit with my back leaning on the flat surface.

"What is wrong?" I ask not liking the distance between us.

She doesn't answer my question; instead, she climbs into my lap straddling my legs. Hovering her mound over my erection, she grabs my length with one hand. She stares into my eyes as she slowly lowers herself down onto me.

I grip her hips tight as her walls squeeze me like a vice.

"Shiloh," I hiss as she fully seats herself.

She cups my face and places a gentle kiss on my lips. "If you will not make love to me the way I want, I'm just going to have to do it myself." She places her hands on my shoulders and rolls her hips as she lifts herself off me and then drops back down.

I groan as her wet slit swallows my length. She bounces up and down on me giving me pleasure beyond anything I have ever experienced in this life and the one before.

Her head is tossed back, as she screams. "Shit, Sigma. It's good."

She is beautiful as she rides my cock. Her dark brown skin glistens with perspiration. Her chocolate-tipped breast bounce in my face. I lean forward and suck one of the puckered nipples in my mouth.

"Fuck, yes," She hisses. "Don't hold back, Siggy please. I want all of you." She pleads.

I release her breast and stare into her eyes. I want to be sure she knows what she is asking.

"Do you mean it? Do you want all of me?"

Shiloh stills, cupping my face between her hands. Her eyes shift back and forth between mine. "Yes," she whispers.

"Then all of me you shall have," I growl. I can never deny my heart what she desires. I wrap my hand around her back, pulling her pert nipple into my mouth.

When she drops down on me, I lift my hips slamming up to meet her.

"Fuuucccckk," she screams.

I use my tongue to lick her sweat from her chest to her neck as I continue to lift my hips to meet her center. Her body jerks as she convulses over me. Hot cream squirts into my lap, and I become starved.

I flip her off me, placing her face down on the mattress with her bottom in the air. I bury my face in her wetness and lap up her essence. She grinds herself on me and claws at the bed as I clean her mess.

Once I'm done, I lean up on my knees and wrap my hand around my wet dick. I tap it on her butt, watching as it causes the flesh to jiggle. I then line myself up with her entrance and shove in. I will give her what she wants to the best of my ability.

I drive my hips forward rapidly, feeling the aftershocks of her orgasm rippling around me.

"You ask for this, Uvonu. I will give you what you want."

"Yes, baby. Yes." She cries as she takes my powerful thrust.

I desire her kiss as I take her this way. I grab her neck and lift her from the bed. Her back remains arched, but her head rests on my shoulder as I take her lips. She grinds against me, and the beginning of my end starts to tingle my balls.

My woman has asked for all of me, and I shall give her my all. I cup her center in my hand and massage her clit, encouraging her to meet my climax with me.

"Will you accept all of me, Shiloh?" I need her approval again. I want to hear her grant me the permission to plant my seed.

"Yes, Sigma. Yes," she screams as her walls clench down, ripping my release from me.

We both shatter together. My body becomes too weak to stay upright. I fall to the bed, pulling her down beside me.

Her breaths come out in quick pants, and her heart beats rapidly inside my chest.

"That was incredible," she says, trying to catch her breath.

Pride swells my chest.

She rolls over and faces me. I wrap my arm around her and tug her body flush to mine. For a moment, we are suspended in time. Her hand cups my jaw as she strokes my scruff of beard. I stare into her eyes, taking in the color changes in each iris.

When I first researched human relationships and what it required to make my mate happy, I did not like what I saw. The thought of spending most of my time with her and preferring her company over being alone sounded like torture. However, now it is all I want. I would much rather spend my day lying between my mate's legs, bringing her to the climax.

"It feels unfair to be this happy," she says, a crease forming between her brows.

I've learned the crease means she's thinking hard about something.

"Why is it unfair?"

"Back home, I know people are dying, and here I am, happier than I've ever been. I know eventually reality will set in, and my run of bad karma will come and snatch this away from me."

I frown at her words. "Nothing will take you away from me."

She smiles, but it doesn't reach her eyes. "Not even my big strong monster can promise me that. If my life isn't anything, it's consistent. Whenever I feel the happiest or safest, the rug is always pulled from under me. I'm sorry your Uvonu comes with such bad luck."

"My Uvonu is perfect," I say. I will not dispute with her on this. No matter what happens, she will always be mine, and she will always be safe.

The clock I brought her last week goes off. I hate the way her face falls at the reminder it's time for me to go. She rolls over and hops out of the bed to stop the alarm.

I climb off as well and start dressing.

"I never thought I'd be one of those girlfriends that doesn't like to be away from her boyfriend." She laughs, but it lacks true humor.

After pulling my pants up, I go over to her and wrap her in my arms. She hugs me tight, burying her face in my stomach. I lift her head to look in her eyes.

"You are not my girlfriend, you are my soul mate," I clarify. "And I feel the same as you."

I get a real smile this time. She lifts on her toes, bringing her lips toward mine. I bend to meet her halfway.

She breaks the kiss off too soon and pulls away.

"What's on the schedule for today?" She picks up my shirt off the back of the chair and hands it to me.

"Mating first."

She laughs. "The guys still on strike with that?"

"No. They have resumed."

She bobs her head as she pulls one of my shirts on. She doesn't have to ask if I'm participating in mating. She knows that I will not touch another female other than her.

"What happens after mating?"

"Training," I sit down on the bed to put my combat boots on.

"How much training do you guys need? I mean you're super soldiers for goodness sakes."

She plops down beside me, one-foot tucked underneath her. She opens a bag of fish-shaped crackers and starts to eat.

"We do not attend training to learn, we do it to study?"

Her head tilts to the side. "Study what?"

"Our enemies. Every time they train us, they are teaching us their war strategies. Which in turns, teaches us how to defeat them."

She stares back at me with her mouth open. Using my finger under her chin, I close it for her.

"The human race would be destroyed in an alien attack," she says shaking her head.

I kiss her forehead before standing. "We do not wish to destroy your planet. We only want our freedom."

She hums and continues to eat her crackers.

"What about you," I ask. "What will you do until I return?" I did not expect to be this interested in her plans until I asked the question.

"Well, I need to retwist my hair. It's growing way too fast. Then I'm going to rearrange my lotion collection."

I look to the steamer trunk at the foot of the bed; it is covered in half empty bottles of lotion. Her favorite one is the body butter I took off one of the female scientists. It is from someplace named Sugah Bae, and it is called Star Crossed. When I get out of here, I will buy every bottle they make for her.

"And then," she goes on to say. "I'm going to finish up that weird alien book you got me. Hey, can you check and see if they have the second one."

I nod. "Yes, I will check this for you."

She walks over to me and wraps her arms around my neck. "I'll see you for dinner tonight. Don't get in any trouble before then,"

Placing my hands on her hips, I lift her off her feet. She wraps her legs around my waist.

"I can make no promises."

She laughs and then kisses me. I regret when she pulls away. I place her down and walk out of the room. I cannot risk staying in her presence a moment longer. If I do, I will cast my duties aside and never leave her.

**

I make it back to my cell upstairs before morning call. Heavy footsteps alert me to my guard's approach.

"Give me a second guys," Reynolds says moments before he opens my door. He seems shocked to find me in my room.

He then does something he has never done before. He shuts the door behind him as he enters.

"I know you left your room last night," he holds his hands out in front of him. "Look, I'm not going to rat you out. You just have to be careful about that. They're starting to patrol the halls at night. A breeder said she was kidnapped, and she's pointing fingers at one of you guys."

I knew there were going to be consequences for what the rogues attempted to do. If the guards are making rounds at night, it will be unsafe for me to leave my room. My thoughts go immediately to Shiloh. She is expecting me to return to her tonight.

I don't say any of this to Reynolds; instead, I nod my head.

Reynolds turns back to the door and opens it. The guards rush in with their guns aimed at my head. I walk out, ready to get this day over with so that I can figure out how to get back to my human.

We bypass mating and head straight to the cafeteria. After getting my tray, I find an empty table. Everyone's gazes land on me causing my skin to prickle. There has never been a time that I have not joined Alpha and the others at the head table until today.

Taking my seat, I ignore the vibrations in the link from the others trying to communicate with me.

Today for lunch we are having spaghetti; I think of my Uvonu and how much she loves it.

I huff out a breath when Zee sits in the seat across from me.

"If it was not made clear by my absence at the main table, I wish to be alone."

"Yeah, I figured," Zee says as he takes a bite out of his garlic bread. He does not show signs of leaving. I roll my eyes and dig into my food.

"I found a puzzle in one of the guard's rooms. I'm thinking about taking it to Shiloh. Do you think she will enjoy it?"

Though by nature, I am very possessive of my mate, I do not have issue with Zee around her. Something deep down in me trusts the young man.

It also helps that she has mentioned he reminds her of a little brother. My research has proven that human females do not desire close family members sexually. In the rare cases that they do, it is frowned upon by society.

"She would like that," I say to him.

The moment I look up from the table, I lock gazes with Beta and the others. They are all frowning at me. Their ire has the commanders link buzzing.

"Did Alpha tell you he has seeded his Uvonu?" Zee asks, unaware of the tension between me and the others.

"Yes."

"Do you think he will give you permission to seed yours?" he queries.

"I have no intentions to ask his permission." Considering I have already planted my seed in Shiloh. The thought of my offspring growing in her uterus has my dick hardening again.

After that first night in the shower, I researched everything about human female anatomy and how their reproductive system works. Turns out, they do not hold babies inside their wet slits.

Zee finally gives me the peace I crave as he quietly eats.

After Lunch, they haul us out to the training field. We run through a few everyday courses and then we are paired to fight. I enjoy this time the most. It allows me to express my pent-up anger and frustration.

"Alright, we're going to have soldiers 0140 and 2106," The soldier in charge of training says.

I step out of line and to the open spot where we fight. Tau, or 2106, steps forward but then immediately steps back in line. The group starts grunting around me, and I know this sound.

I turn to glare at Alpha as he steps forward

"Wait," the soldier in charge of training calls out. "I said 2106. Get back in line 0041."

As usual, we ignore him.

The link between Alpha and I flare to life. *"I told you, you would have to deal with the repercussions. Your slight this morning will also not go unpunished."*

Alpha and I pace around each other.

"We're going to need back up," the head trainer calls out. "Get those guns ready."

I turn to Reynolds without speaking. I shake my head subtly.

"Wait," Reynolds holds up his hands in front of the soldiers with their guns up. "I think they're hashing something out."

"Shut the fuck up, Reynolds. When did you become an alien whisperer?" Another guard calls out.

"Just wait and watch them," Reynolds argue.

I turn my attention back to my leader. *"Now you are worried about what others think of you?"*

"I have to show them what happens when I am disobeyed, you know this, Vulto. Being my oldest friend does not exclude you from punishment."

"Friend," I snarl as we circle each other. *"I ask you for understanding and you invade my mind. Have I not served you loyally for many years?"*

"Yes, but your complacency has made you bold."

As angry as I am about this, I also knew this is his only option. The rogues have been challenging him more and more, and the only way to keep control of them is to show his power. It doesn't mean I have to comply easily.

"So be it," I snarl.

We charge each other. I throw the first punch, but Alpha counters with a brutal blow to my face. The hit sounds like thunder cracking across the sky. I fly backwards and land on my back. My face splits open, but quickly reseals. I push off the ground and face him again.

This time I charge first. Once I'm close enough, he grabs for me, but I quickly duck out of his reach. Grabbing him around the neck, I spin around, bringing his back to mine. Bending forward, I lift him over my head and slam him into the dirt. The ground shakes, and a crater form around us blowing debris up.

Alpha is back on his feet fast. I knew that move would not keep him down long. He kicks me in the chest, sending me hurling into a jeep. I rip through the vehicle, cutting it in half and coming out on the other side.

This time, he doesn't give me a chance to get back on my feet. He leaps through the air and lands over me. Kneeling, he grips my shirt and repeatedly pounds his fist into my face. My exhaustion is slowing my healing capabilities—blood rains in my eyes.

The grunting around us grows louder as the others call for my submission. I refuse. I will not make it that easy.

With as much energy as I can muster, I twist my legs around Alpha's waist and roll him underneath me. Gripping his arm in an arm bar, I shove against it, dislocating it from the shoulder.

Alpha growls before pushing off the ground. I roll off him and quickly get to my feet. He stands and easily pops his shoulder back into place.

We charge at each other again; this time our movements are so fast; I know the soldiers around us can't make anything out. One powerful blow breaks my jaw, but I counter with a kick to his chest that caves in his sternum.

The pain in my jaw causes me to slow down, and Alpha takes advantage of this. He grabs me by the neck, picking me up off my feet he slams me hard into the earth.

Pain is immediate, and I know wherever the ache is coming from, I will not recover from it quickly.

"Do you submit?" Alpha roars through the main link.

Though his words are said for the group, his eyes implore me to give in.

Our private link opens up. *"Do not make me extend this punishment, Vulto. This is not what I wish for you."*

"You know I will not submit. It is not my nature, old friend."

Alpha huffs in my head. He stands up straight, then brings his foot down on my face.

I go into oblivion with the thought of my Uvonu on my mind, and her steady heartbeat in my chest.

CHAPTER TWENTY-FOUR

Baby Maker

Shiloh

My nerves have my leg shaking. I've bit my nails down to the skin. It's way after midnight and Sigma has not come. He is never this late.

Climbing to my feet, I rub my hands together as I begin to pace. This has been my routine since around nine o'clock. I'm either sitting and nervously shaking my leg or I'm pacing.

I don't know what brings me more fear, thinking of Sigma hurt and unable to get to me or thinking he's abandoned me. I know I'm supposed to be his soulmate, but I don't know exactly how it works. Maybe he has more than one, or maybe his need for me wore off.

Let's face it, it's not like this should be new for me. Miguel never left me, but his love for me wore off if you can even call it love. He had always been intense, but in the beginning, he was kinder and gave me a lot more freedom. His obsessiveness didn't come until later. Maybe, my time with Siggy has run its course.

As soon as the thought briefly skitters across my mind, the squeaking of the metal doors alerts me that I have company.

I race across the room, my heart knocking so hard it feels as if it will leap out of my chest and land on the ground at my feet.

Zee walks in with Sigma over his shoulder.

I gasp and hurry to him. "What happened?"

Scanning over what I can see of his body, he seems to be covered in blood and bruises.

"Our leader made him pay for his insubordination," Zee says, walking over to our bed. He places Sigma down like a sack of potatoes. I rush to his side. His face looks like he's been used for a punching bag.

Tears leak from my eyes. How could their leader do this to him?

"Can you heal him?" I ask Zee.

"I have been forbidden to aid in his healing."

My head swings in his direction and I glare. "By who?"

"Alpha," Zee says staring down at a beaten Sigma. From the frown on his face, I can tell he isn't happy about this rule either.

I don't blame him. The more I hear about this Alpha, the more I dislike him.

"What kind of leader would do something like this to his own people?" I kneel at the side of the bed and stroke Sigma's bruised face. He's black and blue at the moment. His eyes are swollen, and the blood coming from his nose tells me it may be broken. The beautiful lips that I love to kiss have been split open. Alpha really put work in on him.

"Do not hold it against him. The rogues called for Sigma's death. This was Alpha's compromise. Sigma disobeyed orders and Alpha has to keep control over the others, or everyone will start to test his boundaries."

I guess that made sense but fuck him I don't care about logic right now.

Leaping up, I grab one of my clean face cloths off the trunk at the foot of my bed. I then wet it with water from a water bottle. Taking my position back by his head, I gently wipe the blood from his face.

Sigma's eyes pop open and stare right at me.

"Uvonu," he whispers.

Placing my finger to his lips I shush him. "Don't talk. Let me take care of you." I continue wiping the blood from his face, rewetting the rag each time it dries out.

"He can stay here tonight," Zee says behind me. "He's supposed to be in a holding cell for a few days. They will come to check on him first thing tomorrow morning."

"Are you sure they won't look for him?" I ask glancing over my shoulder.

"No. It is part of the punishment in holding cells. They leave us for days to suffer in the darkness alone."

Zee slips out of the room, leaving me alone with Sigma. I spent the remainder of that night wiping blood off Sigma and forcing him to drink water. I really had no idea what to do to help him. After the water ran out and his face was clean, I climbed into the bed on the other side of him and held him until I finally dozed off myself.

***

Soft kisses on my stomach wakes me from a restless sleep.

"You will be protected. I swear this to you both."

I yawn, covering my mouth. "Baby, who are you talking to?"

Sigma lifts his head and smiles at me. It is the most beautiful thing I've ever seen. Thank goodness his face has completely healed. I look over at the digital clock and see that it's nearly five in the morning. It only took him four hours to look normal again.

"I am speaking to our children."

I laugh and then slowly stop when I realize he isn't joining in on the joke. Pushing up on my elbows, I look down my body at him.

"What are you talking about?"

"You are with child, Shiloh. Well, two. It is rare in our kind for more than one seedling to plant at once, but the boys were eager."

Wait, hold up. Look, I'm not stupid. I know that Sigma and I have been fucking, and not once did we use condoms, but I assumed after no other pregnancies have been viable that they were shooting blanks. My breathing becomes labored, and I feel hot all of a sudden. I push away from him and jump out of the bed.

"What's wrong?" Sigma stands up and takes a step in my direction.

I hold up a hand to stop him.

"What the hell did you do?" my anger is misplaced. I know that, but fear has me unreasonable.

"You asked for all of me; I gave you my all."

I stare at him with my eyes wide. "Don't play that shit with me, Sigma. I was asking you for more dick, not your fucking offspring."

His face pinches as if my words are confusing him.

"I do not understand your ire."

I scoff. "You don't understand? Look around you, where the hell do you think we are?" I shake my head in frustration when he actually looks around the room.

"Why does our location matter?"

I cup my hands in front of my face to gather my thoughts. "We are prisoners, Sigma. I know that being locked down here like this makes it seem like we're living in a small protective bubble, but we're not. Outside the walls of this room, they're ready to snatch these babies away from me. And what do you think they're going to do with them?"

My pulse races, and the sound of my heartbeat thrashes in my ears. When I sat in that research lab, and they told me about the plan to take my child, it didn't bother me. Hell, I didn't even want kids. Why should I care about some nameless and faceless baby that I didn't even have yet? The only concern I had was getting away from Miguel. However, the idea of these babies being taken by the government now does not seem so simple.

I look down and notice that my hand is involuntarily clutching my flat belly.

"You need to trust me…"

I cut off the rest of his sentence. "Trust?" I repeat. "Are you kidding me? You think I'm supposed to trust you?"

"Yes. You gave me your body. My research says that it proves you trust and love me."

My mouth falls open. For the first time since we started having sex, I am reminded again how little Sigma knows of humans.

"Sex and trust are two different things. Hell, love and trust don't always go hand and hand." I let out a breath and take a minute to compose myself.

The time he and I have spent alone has been the greatest time I've ever shared with a man. Sigma has made me feel respected, protected, and yes loved. But I don't know if I can ever trust him or any other man again.

"I love you," I admit to him, and the reality of those words smack me in the face. This isn't like with Miguel, where I say what I have to in order to survive. I am completely and stupidly in love with this creature. Yet even knowing this, it changes nothing. "You're asking something really big from me, and I don't know if I'm capable of doing that."

"Do you still think of me as a monster? Is that why you do not want my offspring because you fear me?"

Looking up into his brown eyes, his hurt and pain stare back at me.

"No. You are not the monster I fear. Have you forgotten why I'm here? Even if by some miracle I find a way to get out of here and keep them from finding out about these babies," I point to the door to indicate the government. "I'm still on the run from a man that has no qualms about killing innocent children. Miguel will never allow me to keep these babies. He will kill me first."

Flopping down on the bed, I bury my face in my hands. I don't know what to do. This made everything much more complicated. I never thought I would form a tie to children I never wanted, but I'm not leaving here without these babies.

"This was so stupid of me. I've put myself in a lot of really fucked up situations, but it has always just been me I had to worry about it. I don't know what I'm going to do?"

"You will do nothing," He moves my hands from my face as he kneels down in front of me.

"I am not asking you to keep them safe from the scientist or your ex. All that I ask of you in this moment is to trust me."

I shake my head. "You don't understand."

"Have I ever let you down?" he asks, cutting me off.

"What?" his question catches me off guard.

"Have I ever let you down?" he repeats his question as patiently as he said it the first time.

From the moment I first met him in that hallway, he has protected me. He has provided for me when I couldn't even stand up and take care of myself. And every time that I've needed him, he has been there.

"No," I admit. "But that doesn't..."

He silences me with a finger to my lips. "Then trust me when I say I will handle this."

I open my mouth to argue once again, but he shakes his head.

"Just trust me, Uvonu."

Trusting has not been easy for me in many years, not since that rainy day in third grade. Every ounce of me, every single cell in my body is telling me that in the end, Sigma will be no different from all the other men.

All the years that I spent coming to terms with the fact that hope, dreams, and love were figments of people's imagination. They were just pretty words to make those that believe in them sound credible. Yet, here I am, pulling those words out again as I stare in the face of the man that makes me hope for a happy ending.

He makes me dream of a place somewhere no one can find me, and we can raise our family. And he makes me believe that in three months, I have fallen head over heels in love with someone that isn't even human.

Glancing away from him, I blow out a slow breath.

"Okay," I whisper

Sigma wraps me in his arms and kisses me so deeply that I forget my worries. In this moment, we're not prisoners, I don't have a crazy ex, and we aren't confined by these four walls.

When his lips are on mine and his tongue claims my mouth, we are two people in love celebrating exciting news. However, too soon, we are forced apart when my stomach grumbles loudly.

Sigma laughs, and it is the first time I've ever heard the sound from him.

"What's so funny?" I ask.

"They are communicating with me. They're demanding to be fed and do not like the way I'm making your body feel right now."

"Wait, they can talk?" Having alien babies is going to take some getting used to.

"They do not communicate the way we do. They can only share their feelings or relay a message."

"How do they relay messages?"

"Like this." It takes a few seconds, but his voice appears in my head.

"Oh my gosh," I cup my hands over my mouth. "That's so cool."

"You will find our sons have many tricks." He wraps his arms around me and pulls me close. I reach up on my tiptoes and wrap my arms around his neck, placing a quick kiss on his lips. Slowly the thought of these babies are starting to settle on me.

"Why do you believe they're boys. I could be having girls."

He shakes his head. "We always produce male heirs first. It is part of who we are. And even if that wasn't a fact, they have both let me know they are males."

I cannot believe I'm talking about being a mother. Before this experience, I wouldn't even discuss kids. I still don't know if I will be a good mother. After daddy left, mama was present in body only. I guess if I'm being optimistic, at least she taught me what not to do.

The alarm goes off. Sigma and I both look over at the clock.

"Zee, said you needed to be back by the start of first shift."

Sigma sighs and turns back to me. "I will send you breakfast. You must eat. The babies will require a lot of nutrients."

"Okay daddy." I laugh, but Sigma does not join in.

"Tonight, I will take you from behind and you will call me daddy."

The laughter dies on my tongue. My body goes from warm and fuzzy to hot and wet. I can only nod my head in response.

Sigma kisses me one last time before turning and heading out of the door.

**

After cleaning my room and reading for a while, a noise at the door has me hoping up off the bed.

I pat my belly. "Looks like food is here, boys." Ugh, already I'm turning into that person.

Before I could make it to the door, it swings open. However, it isn't Zee or Sigma standing on the other side of the door; it's the super soldier from the mating room.

The sneer on his lips and the way he shuts the door behind him, let me know he isn't here to bring me breakfast.

I was waiting for the shoe to drop, looks like that bitch just landed.

CHAPTER TWENTY-FIVE

Truths

Sigma

After closing my holding cell door, I take a seat on the ground, shut my eyes and lean my head against the wall.

Pride fills my chest as I think of my boys. My lungs expand as I take in deep breaths, feeling unstoppable. This is all the common behavior for my kind after planting our seeds. However, something inside of me tells me this isn't new to me. I have a vague memory of experiencing this before.

I try to latch on to the memory, but like the ones dealing with the great war, I cannot pull it up. For the first time since my rebirth, I take Alpha's advice, and I do not focus on the past. This moment is more important; I have a mate and sons.

The pressure of getting out of here and keeping Shiloh safe falls heavy upon my shoulders. I now know that I can no longer wait for

Alpha to make the decision to leave. When the time is right, I will have to take my family and go no matter if he is ready or not.

I am finally ready to tell Alpha about my mate. I open the link only to immediately shut it back when I realize he is involved in the intercourse with Morgan. I'll save the news for later. I hate when they interrupt during my intercourse time with Shiloh.

"You look really pleased for someone who got their ass handed to them yesterday."

The metal grate on the door is open, and Reynolds is peeking inside.

I stand, eager to get back to my old room. It's easier to make it to the kitchen from there and I need to feed my young.

Reynolds opens the door, and ten guards shuffle in, their guns aimed at me. The extra guards have me on high alert. There are usually only three or four, and Reynolds is always in the lead.

As soon as I step out of the room, one of the guards approaches me with heavy chained cuffs. I cut my gaze over to Reynolds for answers. Surely, they are not still paranoid about my fight with Alpha yesterday.

He tugs at his collar. "Sorry about this, Sig. With you and Alpha fighting and now another of you guys gone missing this morning, the compound is pretty much on high alert. It's just a safety precaution."

I lose focus on most of his words when a rush of fear hits me so hard, I nearly buckle. The emotion isn't coming from me, I know by the way her heart beats rapidly in my chest where it stems from.

A roaring growl slips from my lips as I take off down the hallways. Reynolds and the rest of the guards are shouting behind me. Someone is calling for back up while the others chase me.

I don't stop running. I leave the guards in my sprint to get to Shiloh. Her exhaustion and fear is pushing me to run faster. Shoving the door to the stairwell open, I rush halfway down the steps. I stop when the door opens again, and my guards burst through.

"Sigma, stop," Reynolds pleads.

But I don't stop. Placing one hand over the banister, I use it to spring up and jump over the side. I fall from the second story all the way down to the bottom fifth floor, landing on the balls of my feet. Not stopping even for a second, I run into the hallway on the basement level. From here, I can hear her cries. My anger propels me to move faster.

The door to our bedroom is closed, but that does not deter me. Rushing inside, I stop in my tracks when I find the rogue with his hands around my mate's neck, and the front of her shirt ripped from her. Shiloh's eyes turn to me, and tears spill down her cheeks over a split lip.

Since the day of my reawakening into this new form, I have never allowed the rage to take hold of me. I have always been able to feel the substance Strong created moving inside of me. We all can feel it. It's almost as if it's a foreign body inside me, not a part of me but still there. Well today, I allow it to take over.

I charge the rogue knocking him into the wall on the other side of the room. He tries to shove me off him, but he is no match for my strength. My fist pounds into his flesh repeatedly. Blood flies everywhere. Even when his body goes limp and slumps down to the ground, I continue to beat on his face until it is unrecognizable.

"Sigma, that's enough," Reynolds shouts from behind me. "If you don't stop, they will shoot."

It's not enough. This rogue has touched my mate for the last time. He cannot live in the same space that she does. My job is to protect my family; this is what I must do.

When I do not stop, the darts hit my back, plunging into my flesh pumping me with the medicine that puts me to sleep. It is not enough to stop me. I continue to pound the rogue's face, the bones breaking with each punch.

The links inside my head are rattling with everyone trying to break through, but there is no hope. No one will stop this outcome.

I grab the rogue's head in my hands, placing one foot on his chest, I rip him apart. We can recover from many things, but not a beheading. Dropping both body parts to the ground, I turn around. The room is filled with guards; all their guns are aimed at me. Even Strong's assistant is here. He watches me warily. I scan through the faces for the one person I care about.

Reynolds has his arms wrapped around Shiloh as if he is holding her back. He isn't looking at me or her; his eyes are busy scanning the room around us. I guess that's why she easily breaks free and runs toward me. A few of the other guards try to catch her, but my growl has them pulling back. Shiloh wraps her arms around me as her body shakes with sobs.

"You came. You came," she repeats over and over with her face pressed into my stomach.

Although the anger has receded and I'm back to my normal self, I do not let my guard down. There are too many unknown variables in the room around my family.

Alpha's link roars to life in my head causing me to flinch.

"Explain," he demands so forcefully that even if I wasn't ready, I might have been forced to tell him.

I open myself up allowing him to feel my connection to my Uvonu. He skims my thoughts going back to the first time I met her. I allow him access to her, but I keep the boys to myself. I'm still not ready to share them yet.

"You were protecting her all this time." It isn't a question, but I answer it as if it was.

"Yes."

There is a pause in the link. *"Why didn't you tell me?"* the accusation and pain in his voice makes me feel guilty.

Initially when I found out about my Uvonu, I didn't tell anyone because I didn't want to keep her, but that wasn't the only reason I kept her to myself. I've shared many things with Alpha in our lifetime, in this life and the old. Yet, something deep inside me kept me from telling him about Shiloh.

Even now, I keep the information about my young to myself instead of sharing it with my oldest friend. I cannot explain the uneasiness, but it is there.

"I was not sure I'd keep her until now," the untruth comes naturally. *"She is my Uvonu, I claim her as mine."*

"Then your actions were justified, my friend." The link ends as abruptly as it started.

I push my thoughts to my boys, allowing them to pass it on to their mother.

"Are you okay?"

Her gentle nod against my stomach lets me know she heard my question.

"They're going to take me away now." Her thoughts are passed to me.

Pride fills my chest at the sound of her voice in my head. *"I will always protect you, Shiloh. No matter where you are."*

Those are the last words I say to her before the tranquilizers finally do their job. The sound of her screaming lulls me to a black sleep.

CHAPTER TWENTY-SIX

Dream Over

Shiloh

I'm sitting in a room that looks like the set of a cop sitcom. A metal table with cold metal chairs are the only furniture in the room. There are no windows, only a double-sided plexiglass mirror on the wall.

The soldier that held me back when I tried to go to Sigma during the fight stands silently in the corner, watching me with a hawk like expression.

"Did you hear what I said?" The man that introduced himself as Asim asks.

I turn my gaze away from the soldier and back to him. He's a clean-cut man, very well put together with no facial hair and an angular jaw. His nails are clean and manicured; his cologne has a slight musk and floral scent.

None of those things aid in me realizing he's gay. My radar for these things is exceptional. It's why I was so good at making money at the strip club. I can pick out a high roller and a gay man with absolute ease. It's the bad boys I clearly have trouble with.

"No, I don't know how dangerous my actions were. Maybe you should tell me?"

The soldier standing in the corner snorts, I guess he picks up on my sarcasm.

Asim frowns before leaning back in his chair. "You're not the first female to try this, you know. They all try to saddle up to one of the super soldiers hoping to make them fall in love with them and save them," He rolls his eyes. "It never works out. These creatures don't know anything about love or commitment. At any given moment, he could have snapped your neck and killed you."

I keep my face blank, not giving anything away. He clearly doesn't know anything about Sigma. I can't vouch for the other super soldiers, but I know mine would never hurt me. Is he capable of it, obviously by the way he pulled that other super soldiers head off his neck like he was a Barbie. However, I know he would not hurt me.

"I don't know what you think was going on, but I got lost and I found that space. I was taking a nap when the other one found me." That's my story and I'm sticking to it.

I have a feeling if they knew how Siggy and I were living like a couple down there, they will start to dig too far.

My only concern right now is to keep my babies safe. If these people find out that I'm pregnant, they will never let me see Sigma again, and I can only imagine what they have planned for the boys.

No, I will not put these babies at risk. I only need to be strong until Sigma comes and gets me. He told me to trust him and that's what I'm going to do.

"All the records of you coming to this compound was somehow wiped clean. Can you explain that?" Asim asks.

No, I cannot. In fact, I had no idea Sigma cleared my records.

"Let me see if I have this right, one of your guys messed up, but you want me to explain how it happened."

Asim's eyes narrow at me. He really doesn't like my attitude. Noise at the door has everyone in the room turning to look. The scientist from my first day on the tarmac is here.

He doesn't look as put together as the first time I saw him. His lab coat is wrinkled, and his hair looks tousled as if he's been pulling at it.

"What the hell do you want, Asim? Alpha is in the mating room with Morgan. I have to be there."

Asim jumps up from his seat and scurries over to the man. Clearly, this is the guy in charge. Even the soldier in the corner seems to stand up straighter now that he's in the room.

"Dr. Strong, we have a situation." Asim quickly explains to Dr. Strong what happened.

Strong's shrewd eyes lock on to me. Something is seriously off with this man. I've been around dangerous men for most of my adult life. Not only Miguel, but he often kept me with him when he met his work associates. Dr Hammond being one of them

I've grown to be able to read danger in men a mile away. This Dr. Strong is dangerous, and the frazzled look and dilated pupils tells me he's also on something.

Strong walks further into the room; he never takes his eyes off me. He scans over my head scarf, something Sigma picked up for me one day. My locs peak out the front and hang over my forehead like long bangs. His gaze stops at my face, I imagine he's taking in my mix match eyes by the way his brows scrunch.

He takes a seat in the chair Asim recently vacated, placing his hands together on the table out in front of him.

"What is your name?" His direct attention is unnerving.

"Shiloh," I say.

"Did you sleep with him, Shiloh?" he's definitely blunt.

I have a feeling my usual snarky and sarcastic attitude will not go over well with him. This Dr. Strong guy gives me bad vibes.

I sit up straight. "No," I reply quickly.

He doesn't say anything for a long moment, only continues to eye me up and down.

"Give her a pregnancy test and keep her in isolation until the results come back. If I find out you're lying, you won't like what happens next."

Fear washes over me like ice-cold water. I don't like this man and everything in me is telling me to trust my instincts. I clutch a hand to my stomach under the table grasping for strength I don't think I have.

"I really need you right now, Sigma." I plead in my head and hope my babies pass my message to their daddy.

"If I may, Sir," The soldier asks. I have to turn to look at him because he's on my blind side.

"Yes, Reynolds?" Dr. Strong says.

Reynolds takes a step forward. "As Sigma's head guard, I can vouch that we have kept eyes on him. There is no way he has had any involvement with this woman outside of today."

The Soldier is clearly lying through his perfectly white teeth. My question is why? I didn't trust any of these people in this place. It's hard for me to believe he lied out of the goodness of his heart. I don't have time to think on it too long.

"Then explain that room. Someone was living down there," Asim argues a good point.

"It was the other Super soldier." I blurt out without thinking.

All eyes turn to me.

"How do you know this?" Strong asks.

Another good point that I didn't consider before I spoke up.

I clear my throat before I speak. "He told me. When he woke me up, he said I was in his room."

Strong's eyes narrow. "He spoke to you?"

Licking my lips, I reply. "Yes."

Strong and Asim look at each other. I have a feeling I've said something wrong. Sigma and Zee spoke to me so often; I forgot that when I first got here, everyone said the creatures didn't talk.

Strong turns back to me. "What else did he say to you?"

"Nothing else. He grabbed me and started to yank my clothes off."

Which is kind of what happened. The super soldier never spoke a word to me, but he did go straight for my clothes.

He seemed to get angrier when he buried his face in my neck and took a deep breath. I'm assuming he didn't like how I smelled. However, I don't tell them any of this.

"Peculiar," Strong says with a smirk. "You are nowhere as beautiful as she is. Yet, you seemed to have caught the attention of one of our soldiers. I wonder why that is?"

Okay, fuck this doctor and his opinion. Who is this female he is talking about and why is he comparing us?

"Asim, when does Morgan's two weeks with Alpha run out?"

"She still has twelve days left," Asim says without even thinking about it.

"Hmmm, put this woman back in rotation. I want her in a room with Alpha as soon as his rotation with Morgan is over."

Vomit nearly rips up my throat and out of my mouth. The idea of being in a room with the big scary leader has me nearly passing out.

Dr. Strong stands. "Let's see if you have any real value around here." He turns and walks out.

Immediately once he leaves, the air in the room seems to grow lighter and less stagnant. Asim follows him out, leaving me and the soldier alone.

"Did he hurt you?" His voice is so low, for a moment, I think I might have imagined his question.

I turn to look at him, his eyes are narrowed, but oddly, I don't see anything that causes alarm. I still don't trust any of them, but something tells me this one isn't all bad.

"Who?" I ask.

"Sigma, did he ever hurt you."

I make sure to keep my gaze directly on his as I answer his question. "Never." This seems to placate the guard. He nods his head and leans back against the wall.

I turn back to the door as Asim walks in.

"Time to go," he says.

I stand and Reynolds comes up beside me as if he's ready to offer a hand.

"That will be all from you Reynolds. We will have a guard from the breeding unit to come and escort her back to her room. You should go back to your post."

My gaze connects with Reynolds, and I wonder if he can see the fear in them. He nods to me and steps out of the room. A new guard walks in and ushers me out into the hallway.

Asim steps in front of me; he looks me over warily. "Are you sure there is nothing else you need to tell me?"

Hell no, I think. Yet I simply reply. "No. I've told you everything."

Asim steps back and the guard grips my arm painfully, dragging me away.

The walk to the breeding unit is too short for comfort. When the double doors open, I get that sinking feeling in my stomach. I do not want to be back here, but I don't have a choice. The hallway is still as boisterous as it was when I first arrived at this compound. I guess three months isn't enough time to change anything.

Everyone turns to glare at me. I'm not sure how much they all know, but judging by the frowns and the angry looks, I'm guessing enough.

Standing in front of one of the doors is Carter. He's the one that helped Frankie kidnap me that night. His eyes nearly bug out of his head when he sees me. He turns to the girl standing beside him, and I recognize her from that night as well—the urge to kick her ass battles for dominance inside me. I compose myself, not wanting to get in any more trouble. I have to think about the babies.

From the way they are both eyeing me, they are most definitely not happy to see me.

We quickly walk past them. The soldier gripping my arm stops me in front of my old room. He shoves me inside so hard I crash to the floor catching myself with my outstretched hands.

"Asshole," I mumble under my breath as I stand.

"Oh, my goodness."

I turn to face Fatima. She hops off the bed and rushes over to wrap her arms around me in a tight hug.

"I thought you were dead. I asked Frankie what happened to you, and he told me to mind my business. I told everyone I could that you were missing, but they said they had no record of you." She says all this with me still buried face first into her shoulder.

I smile against her. It feels weird to know that someone actually cared that much about me. I haven't had a female consider me a friend in so long I didn't think it was possible.

I pull back so that I can get a good look at her. She still has that flawless dark brown skin and those upturned cat-like eyes. She is still as stunning as the first time I saw her, but I couldn't help but tell she seemed unusually tired.

"Are you okay?" I ask her.

She steps back releasing me. "I haven't slept a full night since you left. It's starting to get dangerous around here." She pulls me over to the bottom bunk and we both take a seat. She leans in making sure to keep her voice down before continuing.

"Some of the girls have gotten ruthless. Word is, Alpha now has a favorite, and she's getting all kinds of special treatment. The women here are dying to become a favorite of one of the super soldiers. So much so, they are basically attacking any female they think is competition."

Not the best news for me, considering I'm pregnant by one of the super soldiers. As if I needed any more reason not to tell anyone about this.

"That's insane. What are they trying to accomplish?"

Fatima shrugs. "I used to think it was all about the money, but now I don't know. It's like some kind of weird power trip."

I guess I'm the last one to judge these women for falling for a super soldier. Hell, I'm in love with one myself. However, I don't think they understand what they're asking for. Plus, Alpha doesn't have a favorite, the girl is his mate. It isn't something that can be won, it's fate.

"Don't worry about any of that. I need you to stay out of their way," As a victim of what these women are capable of, I don't want Fatima to fall into any danger. I can't promise she will have the same fortunate outcome as me.

"Well, well, well," Fatima and I both leap to our feet and turn to face the door. Frankie is here with Carter.

"The dead has risen," Frankie jokes. "Carter, what's that show you like so much?"

Carter laughs. "The Walking Dead?"

"Yeah, seems like we have a real-life Zombie on our hands. I guess this time, we need to stick around and make sure the job is done."

These assholes lured me to what they assumed would be my death. The more they talk, the angrier I get. Thank goodness for Sigma because I have no doubt I would have died in that room.

"Is that really how you want to play this?" I challenge.

Frankie's gaze narrows, but he doesn't speak.

"Come on now, Frankie. Think about it. How do you think I survived that attack?" I wasn't going to give anything away. I wanted him to come to his own conclusion; most likely it will be more exaggerated than anything I could tell him.

"She didn't go deep enough," he says, and it doesn't sound as if he believes that at all.

I laugh. "You and I both know that's not true. No, I was saved because I made friends in high places. Friends that would take it very personal if something else happened to me."

"You're lying," he snarls.

Lifting my chin, I stare him right in the eyes. "Are you willing to take that chance?"

I'm pretty sure he knows how I was found, and even if he doesn't, he can always ask. I didn't admit to anything, but one can deduce that something suspicious happened. Especially since he knows I was left in that room for dead three months ago. I have no problem throwing my man's name around for protection if I needed to.

Frankie's face changes from doubt to terror in seconds. "Just stay out of our way," he snaps, turning around and storming out of the room. Carter follows silently behind him.

"What was all that about?" Fatima asks.

"Frankie was just coming to terms with me being off limits," I say turning to face her.

She smiles and goes back to her bed. Although I had solved my Frankie problem, I still had a few more issues that needed to be dealt with. I have no idea where Sigma is. I'm still very pregnant, and no telling how long I'll be able to hide it, and I know I'll have to face Candace again soon. The honeymoon phase is definitely over.

CHAPTER TWENTY-SEVEN

Going Crazy

Shiloh

I pace the mating room they have me in again. My hands wring in front of my belly. Nearly a month has passed, and I'm starting to notice a bit of a pudge to my lower belly. Nothing that stands out to others, but I definitely see it.

I have yet to hear from Sigma, and I'm starting to get worried. I refuse to believe that he has forgotten about me. My soul knows that isn't true. Something is wrong.

When the door to the mating room opens again, I expect more of the same thing. They put me back on mating rotation the very next day after they found me. Every single time that door opens, and a super soldier walk in, he looks at me and then takes a seat. Not one of them have touched me. It's driving the scientist crazy, trying to figure out the reason.

I know why. Sigma must have finally claimed me. The first day it happened, I realized what he'd done, and I cried my eyes out at how much I missed him. Even in his absence, he's still protecting me.

This time when the door opens, however, it's Zee that walks in. I squeal before sprinting into his arms. He wraps me up in a tight hug and lifts me up. I wrap my arms and legs around him.

Yes, we are both naked, and people are watching us on the other side of that window. I don't care, I'm just happy to see my friend. Burying my face in his shoulder I cry.

"Where have you been?" I whimper out.

"I cannot get free. Mr. Sigma is not here to control the cameras or the locks." He whispers against my neck so low I'm sure no one can pick up the sound.

I lean back to look at him. Before I could speak again, he shakes his head subtly before burying it back in my neck. He places me up against the wall. His back is to the double-sided window in the room.

"Where is Sigma?" I ask him as I pretend to place kisses on his neck.

"I do not know. We cannot reach him or Alpha. Something is wrong."

He confirms my fears, plummeting my heart into my feet.

This time, I don't pretend to make out with him. I lift my head from his shoulder and stare down at him.

"How do I find him?" I keep my voice low.

Before he can respond, a loud roar has us both turning toward the door. Is it odd that I know it isn't from Sigma? I've heard him roar in anger before; that isn't him.

Zee turns back to me and shakes his head. "Too dangerous," he mouths.

I don't care how dangerous it is. Every time I have needed him, Sigma has come for me, it's my turn to come to his rescue.

"Please," I plead.

Zee's gaze shifts away from my face for a moment usually whenever he does that, it means he's talking to Sigma, but I know this time he isn't. When he looks back at me, his eyes are a little surer.

He leans in and drops a gentle kiss on my forehead, and whispers, "Reynolds."

He steps back, and I drop my legs to the ground. He releases me and walks over to the mirror before tapping it twice. Within seconds, a man comes in with a small box that contains a green gemstone. They usher Zee out of the room before ordering me to get dressed.

I slip the red robe on quickly, anxiously ready to get back to the breeding unit. They escort me out of the room and across from me is Morgan. It's the first time I've seen her since the day we arrived, and they whisked her away. I know why Alpha reacted the way he did on that tarmac, she's his mate.

She looks nothing like she did the first time I saw her. She still has those sad eyes, but she has lost so much weight it looks jarring on her.

When her gaze turns to me, I see in her eyes the same drive in mine. We are both doing whatever we can to survive in this hell hole.

They escort her away; her head is down until she walks past a brown skinned super soldier with golden eyes. As soon as she's close enough to him, she lifts her head, and they make eye contact briefly. I don't know what's going on between the two, but a lot was said in that one gaze.

The guard drops me off in my room, and I quickly redress in my jumpsuit and head back out into the hallway. I'm on a mission, one that demands I stop hiding in the safety of my room.

I search the hallway of unit A until I find who I'm looking for. Frankie is hanging out with some of the other volunteer girls. They flock to him as if he's a local celebrity.

I march right up to him. "I need to speak to you."

He turns to me for only a second, barely giving me his attention. Ever since that last conversation, he has avoided me at all costs. I'm pretty sure it's him that's keeping Candace out of my face as well.

"I got nothing to say to you," he sneers before turning back to the girl he was talking to.

Not in the mood to be dismissed, I scoff before squeezing my way in between the female and him.

"They asked me how I got down to that room, but I told them I couldn't remember. It would be really awful if I suddenly got my memory back, don't you think?"

I'm pushing my luck with Frankie. He could honestly snap my neck and get away with it. Do I think Sigma would brutally murder him, yes, but I'd be dead by then.

Frankie scowls at me before grabbing my arm and dragging me away from the girl. He rounds a corner and peeks inside a room before shoving me in and slamming the door.

The room is empty, and for a split second, I don't feel as brave as I did before. However, I take a deep breath and pull my shoulders back.

"I need to see a soldier named Reynolds."

Frankie's brow wrinkles. "Why the fuck do you need to see that ass licker?"

"The reason is none of your concern," I say putting my hand on my hips.

Frankie takes a step toward me. My arms drop to my side as I take one back keeping distance between us.

"You're talking a lot of shit for someone who's all alone here."

"And you're being quite annoying for someone that can so easily be killed with just a whistle from me. Would you like to see how fast the super soldiers really are?"

I'm bullshitting like a pro right now, but I've survived most of my life from mastering the gift. How else do you think I lived in the house with Miguel.

It takes a moment for Frankie to give. I keep my face neutral the entire time, giving nothing away.

"Fuck," he finally swears. "Fine, I'll get you Reynolds." He turns around and storms out of the room, and I let out a deep breath. That was close.

An hour later, Reynolds steps inside my room. He looks around the space, spotting Fatima on the bed.

"I'll give you guys some privacy," she says getting up. She gives me a thumbs up behind Reynolds back before walking out of the room.

"What was that about?" he asks, pointing his thumb behind him.

"She thinks we're going to have sex." I shrug.

His eyes widen. "That's not what's about to happen right?" He looks disgusted at the thought.

"Relax, Reynolds. No."

He lets out a long breath. "Well, what do you want?"

"Sigma."

He's shaking his head before I finish my sentence. "No way. That's too risky, if they find us there, they'll kill us both."

"Please," I plead stepping toward him. This is my only shot at finding Sigma. Wherever he is, I know he needs me. It may seem strange, but I can feel it. Something is terribly wrong. "He said that you're his friend. Told me you were one of the only decent guards here."

"He really said that?" One of his brows quirk up.

No. "Yes, he even told me that if I needed anything to look for you. Why do you think I asked for you?"

I had time to think about that day in the interrogation room. Initially, I had no idea why he lied for Sigma, but when he asked about his treatment to me, it got me thinking. I think Reynolds actually respects Sigma. It's why he was quick to lie for him. And why he asked me if Sigma had hurt me. I think he knew he hadn't and was just verifying. I also believe Reynolds knows that I was living in that room.

He runs his hands through his short brown hair. "If you're doing this because you have some sick hope that he will get you out of here or if you're just looking for a payout, don't drag me into it."

His comment pisses me off. "I don't expect someone that can watch people be caged up and mistreated to understand what love is, but I love Sigma. I don't give a fuck if you don't understand it or if you don't believe me. This has shit to do with getting out of here or making money. And rather you help me or not; I will save him."

He stares at me, his eyes narrowing. Yet, I don't back down. I'm serious about what I told him; I'm going to save Sigma even if I had to do it myself.

His shoulders slump, finally relenting. "Alright. I'll be here around midnight. Be ready."

Although I was hoping this would turn out this way, it still takes me by surprise when he agrees to help.

"You're really going to help me?"

He looks away from me, folding his arms over his chest. "Despite what you think of me, I'm not a bad person. I have a wife and kids back home, and this is how I feed them. I don't like what goes on here anymore than you, but what else can I do?"

I guess it was pretty shitty of me to judge him. Especially since I volunteered for this bullshit, we were both trying to make do with the hands we were given.

"Sorry," I say meekly. "You're right. That wasn't fair."

He nods before turning away and heading toward the door. He stops with his hand on the knob. "This isn't going to be easy. That place is off limits for a reason. You're going to want to prepare yourself for what you see." With those final words he slips out of the room and leaves me. I spend the rest of the day stewing over those last words.

**

Reynolds walked through my door twenty minutes after twelve. I was still wide awake when he came in.

He tossed me a pair of fatigues the same as his.

"Put these on," He demands.

I waste no time slipping out of my jumpsuit and getting dressed.

"What do you need from me?" Fatima asks.

I told her my plans of saving Sigma and she was a little worried about my choice, but she's offered to help.

"If anyone comes asking, tell them I was here all-night sound asleep," I tell her as I tighten the laces on the black boots.

She tilts her chin down letting me know she understands the assignment.

"Let's go," Reynolds says heading toward the door.

I snatch my scarf off my head and toss it to the bed before following him out.

"Keep your head down as much as possible," He scolds as we walk by a few guards in the hallway. They barely spare us a glance as we hurry pass. Finally, we make it to the stairwell and quickly descend. We don't go as low down as the old room Sigma and I shared, but we go pretty deep into the compound.

We stop at a door with bold red letters saying restricted, special clearance needed.

"Wait," I say placing a hand on Reynolds' shoulder. "Do you have clearance?"

"No, but I know someone that owes me favors, and he does," he pulls out a badge and presses it to the small machine on the side of the door. The light turns green, and the door clicks.

The hairs on my arms stand up, and my skin feels clammy. Something about this place has me feeling terrified. Whatever is going on behind this door, I'm sure I don't want to know, but for the man I love, I will find out. Reynolds pushes the door open, and we enter the restricted level.

It doesn't look too different from any other floor I've been on. Doors line the hallways, and they all require a keycode in order to get in the room. Big, bold letters paint across each entryway to the rooms reminding you of the restrictions.

Reynolds and I hurry down the corridors; we take a left and then pull up short, ducking back behind the corner when we spot two men in lab coats outside one of the rooms.

"That's the room they're holding Sigma in," Reynolds whispers.

I peer around him to get a peek. The two scientists are in deep conversation. They both turn and head in the opposite direction before stopping at the elevator. They are so distracted by their conversation they never look back. When the doors open, they climb on and disappear out of view.

"They're gone," I say stepping around Reynolds.

"Slow down," he whisper-shouts as he catches up to me.

"I can't. He's here and he's in pain. I can feel it." I'm not exaggerating. My stomach is in knots right now. I think the babies are trying to tell me it's bad. We stop at the door marked Bay Eleven.

Reynolds pulls out the card he used to get into the hallway and place it to the door. The light flashes red.

"Shit," he curses under his breath. He tries it again, but it flashes red once more. "He must not have access to this room."

"No," I place my hand against the door. No way did I get this far to get turned back. I won't leave him here.

Tears spill down my cheeks. "Siggy, please. I don't know what to do." I say out loud.

An electric current shoot through my belly and out through my hands shocking me. Immediately afterward the light turns green, and the door clicks. I step back staring in disbelief.

"What the hell just happen?" Reynolds asks.

I don't answer because I don't care how the miracle worked as long as it did. I push the door open and rush into the room. My feet fail me when my eyes adjust to the dim light. I stop suddenly. My stomach flips upside down, and I have to rush to the large silver sink. Everything I ate today rushes up burning my throat as it splashes into the metal basin.

"What the fuck," Reynolds curses behind me.

I quickly rinse my mouth out and turn to face the horror. Pinned to a surgical table is the man I love. Someone has cut him open like they were dissecting a frog. His insides are on display like a sick museum exhibit.

My knees go weak, and I nearly collapse. Reynolds wraps his arms around me, keeping me up. Sobbing uncontrollably, I never take my eyes off Sigma.

My gentle giant, my monster is gone. The first time I truly experience love and have it given to me so purely, these people take it from me.

My heart feels like it's shattering against the ground. My boys will never know their father. They will never meet the man that cared so much for them, that protected us with his life. Sigma did not deserve this. He was the only good thing in this hellhole.

"I'll get you out of here," Reynolds says. "I won't let his death be for nothing." He continues to rub my back as I break down in his arms.

Groaning startles us, and we jump apart. Brown eyes pop open and peer at us. My jaw drops as I rush to Sigma's side.

"Baby, oh God. Sigma." My hands hover over his body. I don't know where to touch him. I settle on his face, cupping it between my hands I rain down kisses that mix with my salty tears.

"Uvonu," he whispers my name, and I've never been happier to hear someone's voice before.

"Help me," I shout to Reynolds.

I move to the metal clamps on Sigma's feet. We need a key to open them. Reynolds comes to my side with a set of keys he must've found somewhere. It takes a few tries, but he finds the right key.

We free one foot, and then Reynolds goes to the other side of the table to free the other foot. We move up toward Sigma's head.

Reynolds frees his hand then hands the keys to me so that I can free the other one. I'm shaking so hard I can barely get the lock open. The moment I do, I drop the keys and lift his wrist, placing kisses up his arm.

Sigma cups my face. His thumb rubs over my bottom lip before his hand falls weakly back to the table.

"I thought they didn't have any weaknesses," I say to Reynolds.

He shakes his head. "They don't naturally. But imagine being cut open and left like this for days. The fact that he is still alive is a testament to his strength. He needs time to heal."

"We don't have time," I say. I move to his torso. The skin is being held back by metal spikes hammered into the table beneath us. I pull at the spike, but it is not budging. The thing must've been driven in with Thor's hammer. Reynolds tries to pull out one of the spikes on his side but is unsuccessful.

"It's no luck. If Sigma couldn't pull these out, there is no way you and I can get it."

That's when I remember we have one ally that can help.

"We need Zee."

Reynolds' brows pinch together. "Who?"

"Zee, he's another super soldier. He can help us. He's Sigma's friend."

Reynolds shakes his head. "Only five of these guys have names. Everyone else is just a number; you would have to tell me his tracking number."

Ugh, I have no idea what his number is. Suddenly the numbers appear in my head out of the blue.

"4765," I repeat.

Reynolds nods his head and rushes for the door. He stops before exiting. "Do not leave. I'll return with 4765. If anybody other than me come to this door, you need to hide."

"Okay," I say.

Reynolds runs out leaving me alone. Turning back to Sigma, I grab his hand and clutch it to my chest.

"I'm sorry. I should've come sooner."

"No, it was too dangerous. Your job is to take care of our boys."

I place his hand on my slight swell. "They are safe, Siggy."

He smiles, placing his hand palm down against my stomach. "Their gifts have manifested." My eyes water at the proud look on his face. "One is a healer like Zee. The other is like me."

"What's your gift?"

He closes his eyes as if he's in pain. "I can manipulate anything electrical."

It explains how he deleted my records and how he was able to get around for months without ever being discovered. It also explains how we got into this room. I press my palm over his, sending a silent thank you to my baby.

"I want to get out of here, Sigma. I want us to run away somewhere no one will ever find us. I just want to be with you."

His eyes pop back open. "I will take you away from here. You are my Uvonu."

I smile and lend down placing a kiss on his lips. "And you are my monster."

I love when Sigma smiles. It's so rare to see that it feels like a gift whenever he does.

Tapping at the door has me spinning around.

"Shiloh, it's me." Reynolds says.

I quickly rush over, hitting the green button on the wall panel. It makes a loud clicking sound. Reynolds pushes the door open and steps in with Zee on his heels. I hug him briefly before letting him go.

When Zee approaches Sigma, he lets out a low growl.

"We can't get the spikes out," I say, pointing to the objects.

Zee grips the metal spikes and easily yank them out as if they were toothpicks stuck in little sausages. He goes around the table removing them all.

Once he's done, I fold the skin back over Sigma's torso. We watch in wonder as the skin mends and knits back together, leaving nothing but a red welt where the wound once was.

Even though the injury is healed, Sigma still doesn't look like himself. Zee grabs one of his arms and lifts him off the table. He places him over his shoulder in a fireman carry.

"Whoa. Whoa. We can't just take him out of here," Reynolds says, holding his hands up in front of him.

Zee snarls showing his teeth. Reynolds steps back.

"We're not leaving him here," I say. "I don't care where we take him, but he is not staying in this place another second."

Reynolds runs his hands through his hair. "Shit, alright. We will take him back to his cell. If they find him there, they may not get too pissed. It won't be the first time these guys have gotten around without us knowing. They will have questions about how he got out."

"Don't worry about it. We will take care of that." Hopefully, whatever gift my little one possesses, he can use it to fix the cameras like his dad does.

Reynolds leads the way, making sure the coast is clear. We make it back to Sigma's cell. Zee places him down on the floor. It's sad the way they're living.

The rooms are small and nearly vacant. Only a small bed that would barely be big enough for me, let alone Sigma's tall frame. The walls are bare and a dreary gray color. A single recess light in the ceiling gives the room minimal visibility.

I take a seat on the floor beside Sigma and place his head in my lap. I'm not leaving his side until I know for sure he is better.

"I'll come back to get you before we have to make our first rounds," Reynolds says looking down at Sigma lying so weakly in my lap.

"Okay," I mumble the single word. My attention is glued to the man in my lap.

I don't see Reynolds and Zee leave the room, but the door closing alerts me of their absence.

"I'm here, Siggy. I'm going to take care of you this time." Leaning my head back against the wall, I prepare for a long night. No matter how uncomfortable it's going to get, I'm not leaving his side.

CHAPTER TWENTY-EIGHT

Plans

Sigma

"Shiloh," her name comes from my mouth in a guttural growl.

I thought nothing could feel better than being inside of her tight wet walls, but having her hot mouth wrapped so snuggly around my cock is pure bliss.

It's been three days since she came to get me from the pain room. That is what we call the restricted area. It is where scientists experiment with our bodies. They aren't just using us to create weapons. They take our blood and organs trying to make everything from cures for their disease to creams that fight wrinkles. So far, they have been unsuccessful, but it does not stop them from trying.

I stagger back against the wall, my legs feeling unstable. As soon as Reynolds let Shiloh in the room, she immediately went to her knees and pulled me out of my pants. I had little time to step out of them before I was in her mouth. I close my eyes tightly as she swirls her tongue over the tip of my cock. What sorcery is this?

She hums around me as she continues to work her mouth up and down my length. Both her hands work the base of me, moving in motion with the rotation of her head. My toes curl as I feel my release rushing to erupt from me.

I open my mouth and begin to speak in my native tongue. I've only used the language once before since I've been reborn. It too was when I was with Shiloh. It comes naturally when I'm with her.

Shiloh continues her madness, taking my length to the back of her throat. She starts to gag, and it is my undoing. I roar as my orgasm erupts from me, spewing into her mouth. She drinks me down, not allowing any of it to spill.

When there is nothing else I can give her, she sits back on her knees. Running her tongue over her lip, she giggles.

"Why is your cum so sweet? It tastes like melons."

I do not answer her. Instead, I grab her around the waist, lifting her off the ground. I spin her around, placing her front against the wall. Grabbing the collar of her jumpsuit, I rip the heavy fabric down the middle exposing her skin.

She squeals and then laughs. "Whoa, slow down, baby."

I finish ripping the rest of the clothing off her. Using my foot, I kick her legs further apart. Wrapping an arm around her waist, I lift her off the ground. She places her hands against the wall as I line the head of my cock to her entrance. I run the tip of my erection between her slick pussy lips. The sloshing sound letting me know she's fully prepared. I push forward, and she sucks me in easily, accepting my girth. I sink into her all the way to the base. My pelvis bone is pressed to her round ass.

"Oh. oh. Sigma. You're so deep," she purrs.

Using my grip around her waist, I lift her up and then slam her back down on me. She screams and I bask in the sound.

I continue to work her up and down on me, using my hips to drive into her. Then, stepping away from the wall, I take her with me as she dangles in my arms. She wraps her legs around my thighs, the heel of her feet resting under my buttocks.

Her hands reach back and grip my wrist. Her back is arched, making her look like a figurehead on the front of an ancient ship. She bounces on my manhood as she sings my name like a chant.

Carrying her over to the bed, she lets go of my wrist placing her hands flat on the thin mattress. One of her feet drops to the ground while I keep one knee bent over my forearm. From this angle I can watch my large member as it glides into her pink center. Her creamy essence coat me as I drive in and out of her.

My orgasm builds, causing my legs to shake, but I do not stop. My hips power into her as she fists the blankets and call out for a man named God.

Her walls clench down on me as she leaks cum all down my balls. Her body jerks with her climax. The clenching of her tunnel sucks my release from me. I toss my head back and roar as my blank sperm fills her womb.

When we are both spent, I tuck her into my chest as I climb onto the bed without pulling out of her. I do not wish to break the connection yet.

Her heart pounds inside my chest. I pull her tighter pressing her back against my front.

"I missed you," she admits quietly.

Since I woke with my head in her lap three days ago fully recovered, Shiloh and I have spent time together each day. Not as much as we did when she was hidden away for three months.

"I know that sounds crazy," she says with a chuckle. "I never thought I'd miss someone that I see every day. Yet, the intensity of my need to be with you is crazy. Is this normal?"

Running my hand over her flat belly, I enjoy the feel of her soft skin. "Yes. I'm afraid it does not get any easier." My brow creases as I think over her words. On my planet, mates are a way of life. It is all we know. Did I rush Shiloh into this?

"Do you wish to not feel this way?"

She turns over to face me, my semi-hard cock slipping out of her wetness. She cups my face as she stares up at me with one amber eye and one gray eye.

"Don't you for one second ever doubt that this is where I want to be. I had to nearly die in order for you to find me. And I would do it all over again to be right here, right now, with you in the end."

Her words warm my heart and tighten the bond of our mate link. Suddenly, a memory flares to life in my head. I shut my eyes chasing the faded image before it disappears. It is of a female. One with pale white skin and glowing gray eyes. The large black horns growing out the side of her head points down like those of a ram. Long brown hair is braided in a ponytail that hangs down to her hips. She smiles up at me and whispers my name.

Suddenly the memory fades. Who was the woman, and why does my cock swell so suddenly for her?

"Babe, are you okay?"

My eyes shoot open, and I'm back in the small room with my Uvonu. Shiloh's brows are furrowed as she stares at me. Why do I have such a reaction to the female in that memory?

"Okay, maybe I came on too strong just now," Shiloh chuckles nervously.

I grab her face and kiss her, trying to erase the unease I'm feeling about the other woman. She moans in my mouth, and I roll her underneath me separating her legs with my body. I pull away from her lips and stare down into my eyes.

Her heart beats steadily in my chest.

"You are all I want," I say the words before forming my lip back to hers.

I am unsure if I am telling her the words for reassurance or am I saying them to remind myself. Lifting on one hand, I use my other to slide my length back into her. She whimpers upon my entrance. I spend the rest of our afternoon solidifying my bond with my Uvonu,

**

Rapping at the door has both of us looking up.

"Sigma, times up. I have to get her back now," Reynolds calls through the door.

After having the intercourse several times, Shiloh eventually passed out from exhaustion. Thankfully no other memories of the mystery woman appeared.

Reynolds knocking at the door rouses Shiloh from her slumber. I hate when her body slumps with disappointment when she realizes what time it is. I wish that I never had to send her back, but I can't keep her.

"Come, my love. You must get dressed."

She sighs before climbing out of the bed.

"I like it better down here. It's much quieter." She hums as she walks over to her ruined jumper and picks it up. She then turns to me and lifts a brow.

Yes, maybe I got a little carried away with her clothing.

"My apologies for your clothing and the noise."

Strong's attempt to drug Alpha and break the bond he has with Morgan has caused us to protest. All day long, we grunt in our ancient war tactic. It does not cause us any discomfort, and we do not get tired. However, our plan is to slowly drive everyone else crazy in order to get our way. We do not doubt our plan will work.

Pulling my shirt over my head, I hand it to her. She takes it and puts it on, the hem brush against her knees.

"It's okay. It doesn't bother me as much as it does the other women and the guards. It's kind of calming."

Once I'm fully dressed in my pants and boots, I wrap my arms around Shiloh and bring her into me. I kiss her in the human way that I like, where my tongue slips into her mouth. Her nails scrape the short hair at the back of my head, and I must fight myself to pull away from her.

"I'm glad that you are not affected by the sound." I don't explain that is because of her connection to me that the sound does not disturb her. Instead, my thoughts go to more pressing issues. "Do you have enough food?"

She laughs and shakes her head as she stares up at me. "Siggy, you gave me two trash bags full of junk food yesterday. I promise you I have enough food."

Dropping a kiss on her forehead, I let her go. I cross over to the door and open it. Reynolds stands outside, looking back over his shoulder. The guard has become somewhat of an ally since the day he helped rescue me.

He pulls the earplugs out of his ears. "I'll take her back to Unit A. Can you get back on your own?"

This is the routine every day for the last three days. After dinner, he goes to get Shiloh and brings her here to meet me. He allows us two hours of time before we have to part ways.

I nod my head. Shiloh walks past me to leave. I grab her arm and pull her back. With one hand cupping her face, I kiss her deeply. The memory of the mystery woman still haunts me.

Shiloh sighs and sinks into the kiss. Pulling away, I glance down at her face. Her eyes are close, and her lips are slightly open. Dropping my forehead to hers, I inhale her scent which is a mixture of mine, and the sweet, powdery smell of her favorite body butter.

"Rest well tonight," I send the message to the boys to deliver to their mother.

"I will. I love you." Her words come through the link.

I hate the simple words. There isn't a word for love in our native language. Because what we feel when we mate with our Uvonu's can't be summed up by such a simple term. My research says the word love means strong attraction or assurance of affection. I live and breathe Shiloh. She is part of my soul and my way of life. Her happiness and safety are my only concern. However, there is no English word that explains this. So, love has to suffice.

"I love you too."

I let her go, and she walks over to Reynolds. He slips the earplugs back in his ear and leads her away from me.

As soon as they are out of sight, I head toward the location we have the bodies stored. We still need a few more to cover our disappearance. I've already made sure that our Uvonu's have been erased from their files. Yet we have not established where we will find permanent residence once we're free.

With most of us now having Mates, we need a place that will assure they are safe as well. Though our plans have not changed, we are still faced with delays.

The commanders link opens up and Gamma speaks.

"Sig, I need you to clear the cameras tonight," he says gruffly. He's been on edge ever since he found out his mate was being assaulted by guards. It was Morgan that notified Beta of the attacks.

He's been bidding his time until he could get a hold of them.

"That will not be a problem." I reply.

"Keep the link open," Alpha says. *"I need to be in her presence, even if it's only through our link."* I feel sorry for my leader. He has gone too long without seeing his Uvonu. I can't imagine the pain he is feeling. Through our relationship has still not recouped after he tried to rip my secrets from me; I do not wish him this hurt.

"Someone needs to help him dispose of the bodies," Beta adds.

"I can do it," I volunteer.

"No," Gamma says quickly. *"We will leave the bodies. I want them to be found. It will be a warning to anyone else that tries to touch what does not belong to them."* No one misses the growl in his voice.

"In this I agree. Leave the bodies, but make sure you make a statement." Alpha says.

"Will do," Gamma says before leaving the link. One by one, the others disappear until it's only Alpha and I left.

"I miss this side of you, old friend."

"And what side is that?" I ask even though I already know what he speaks of. My skin tingles with it. It radiates off me and through my link like sparks from a powerline.

"Happiness," Alpha simply says.

Yes, for the first time in this life and the old, I am happy.

"It is well deserved, Vulto," He goes on to say, his voice hollower.

"Why does part of me still feel as if I am missing something? As happy as I am, something in the back of my head pleads with me to remember the war." To remember the woman in my memory.

Alpha is silent for a while, even though the link still vibrates from his presence.

Finally, he speaks. *"Sometimes, memories do more damage than good."* With those words, he breaks the connection, and I'm left alone.

CHAPTER TWENTY-NINE

It Ends

Shiloh

Standing under the hot shower water, I rub a hand over my small belly.

I'm only two months pregnant, but already, my stomach has a slight swell. Still nothing noticeable yet, but by next month, people will start to notice.

I'm going to be a mother. My fear of that word is slowly ebbing away. I don't know if it's because the thought of having Sigma's babies fills me with a warmth I can't explain, or maybe I'm just now accepting the fact that I'm not my parents. I don't have to hold onto their generational curses.

"You got five more minutes ladies," The guard yells from outside the shower room.

I smile at how much has changed in the last month. Since those guards were found outside of a breeder's room, not one guard has stepped out of line with us. They won't even come in the shower stalls anymore. They used to love to leer and watch us bathe.

This place is almost bearable now. However, I won't allow myself to get blinded. I am still in a government ran shithole. One that will undoubtedly take my babies from me the moment they realize they're here.

Turning off the shower, I wrap my big white towel around me. My locs have gotten so long they hang past my shoulders now. I can say one thing about the hormones they've pumped in us, they have my hair growing and my skin glowing.

I twist the water out of my locs running my hands through my fuzzy roots. It's time for a retwist.

I was so lost in the thought of my pregnancy that I didn't realize that the bathroom had cleared out and I'm the only one inside. Well, not the only one.

"I seem to keep making mistakes when it comes to you," Candace's voice has me spinning around to face her.

She's here with those same three friends. Her blue eyes glare at me with more hatred than usual. She has a gun in her hands pointed right at my head. The barrel nearly touching me.

Rocks knot my stomach. Candace has proven to be unstable enough to shoot me.

Taking a step back, I hold my hands out in front of me.

"Don't move another step," she warns."

I stop retreating. "Aren't you tired of this?" Because I know I fucking am. "I'm not your enemy, Candace."

She shakes her head. "He loved me. But you wouldn't let him go."

If I didn't think I was going to die soon, I would've laughed in her face. Did she truly believe I was the one keeping myself prisoner in that house?

"You can't truly believe that? I tried to leave. You were there to witness it."

She and the other girls laughed as Miguel drug me back into that house by my hair. They taunted me when he made me kneel in the blood and guts of the security guard he'd gutted. The guard's only crime was that he didn't know I could fit through the bathroom window at the boutique.

"Only because you wanted him to come find you," she screams. "You wanted him to abandon us to go look for you. You were so selfish"

"I didn't want to be there," I shout back before lowering my voice. Screaming at her is probably not the wisest thing to do right now. "I was a prisoner in that house. I was suffocating under him, and all I wanted was to be free."

This time, I can feel when my sons break through my thoughts. It feels like a tickle in the back of my head.

"Why is your heart rate elevated?" Sigma has the boys pass the message to me.

"She's going to kill me this time." I send back to him.

"What? Where are you, Shiloh?" The urgency in his tone is not missed.

However, I don't get to answer. I have to keep my attention on the crazy chick in front of me.

Candace shakes her head wildly as she grabs at her hair with her free hand. "You're lying. You were always a good manipulator. He told me the things you did to him."

What did I do to him? This is news to me, but I guess if I think about it, it shouldn't be. Thinking back on my time in his house, Miguel enjoyed the drama. He liked making the other girls jealous. It's why he constantly asked me if I was. He wasn't doing it because he wanted me to love him. No, I think he got off on the fact that we vied for his attention. The other girls' hatred toward me and each other fed the narcist inside him.

"I'm coming for you," Sigma says in my head.

I don't tell him that it may be too late by then. I continue to keep my focus on Candace and that gun.

"We're not even there anymore, Candace," I try to lower my voice and keep her calm. "We don't have to hate each other here."

I stare into her eyes, hoping realization and clarity will take over. However, it doesn't. It's in this moment that I realize she is damaged. I never put much thought into the emotional trauma living the way we did have on us. I was so much in survivor mode that I couldn't see how traumatic it was. We were locked away from the world, some of the women were kidnapped from their homes. We were then forced to sleep with a man that made us believe that having his favor on us was the reward. He made us question if we were truly victims when we were. Miguel destroyed her mind so much that she believes I am her offender and not him. My hatred for Candance evaporates. Instead, I feel sorry for her.

"He loved me," She shouts.

"He didn't love any of us. It was a game to him," I try to explain.

She shakes her head and holds her gun up toward me.

"You were the problem, just like you are now. You won't take another one of our men."

I'm not going out like this. I let her get away with a lot of things in the past. Rightfully, I should have dealt with her when she stabbed me in the eye. But I won't make that mistake again. This time, I have a lot more to fight for.

I react without thinking, shoving her arm up just as the gun goes off. Her weak grip on the weapon has it flying out of her hand when I shove her as hard as I can. We fall to the floor, me on top of her. She grabs at my hair, but my fist to her face loosens her grip. She screams as she tries to scratch my eyes out.

Wrapping my hand in her blonde hair, I hold her head still as I punch her repeatedly. I allow my anger and frustration to work its way out of me. This bitch has been a thorn in my side for years. Although I don't hate her, I'm going to beat her ass.

The other girls are trying to pull me off her, but I don't let go of my hold on Candace. Pounding footsteps run into the bathroom, and I'm finally lifted off of her. At the same time, Frankie picks Candace up off the ground, examining her face.

He looks over at me and snarls. "Lock that bitch up. She attacked first."

Funny, he says that when his ass wasn't even in here.

The arms around me tries to pull me away, but I fight against his grip.

"Let me go," I argue. "I'm going to finish this."

Candace yanks away from Frankie and takes a step toward me. "The only good thing that came out of this is that he finally got rid of you. I take comfort in knowing he sent you here to suffer," She mocks.

I laugh. "You dumb ass, thin-lipped, bitch. He didn't send me here. I ran from him."

Watching her face fall is the best feeling ever. She now realizes that he kicked her ass out with the intentions of keeping me.

"Get her out of here. Lock her down in the box," Frankie shouts to the soldier holding me.

I've heard of the box. It isn't a place the compound knows about. Apparently, the soldiers on this unit found a small closet-like room and have been using it to punish the breeders when they don't follow their orders.

I try to get away from the guard holding me, but his arms tighten around my chest.

A low growl at the door has everyone's head swinging in that direction. It is then that I realize during my scuffle with Candace, my towel fell off, and I'm now butt naked wrapped in another man's arms while my very possessive baby daddy stands at the door.

"What the hell is going on?" Reynolds ask walking further into the shower room. His eyes scan the area quickly.

"None of your business, Reynolds. This is our domain, and we are handling it." Frankie says. "What the hell is that thing doing here?" he points to Sigma.

Sigma let's out another growl. His eyes remain on me and the man still holding me.

"Carter, if you value your life, I strongly advise you to let that one go," Reynolds says.

Carter releases me so quickly I stumble forward. Sigma is there to catch me without delay.

He scans over me as if he's checking to see if I'm harmed. Other than a few stinging scratches on my face, I'm good. Once he's satisfied, he drops his head to mine.

"No more fighting, Uvonu," his words are chuckled in my head.

"She had it coming." I argue.

He smiles, and it immediately has my nipples hardening.

"All you ladies out," Reynolds says. The other females start to run out of the door.

"You don't make any demands here," Frankie argues. He's still trying to remain in control. Around the breeder's unit, Frankie is the man and apparently, he has let that little fame go to his head.

"Go back to your room. Get dressed," Sigma says letting me go.

Reynolds holds out a towel for me. I take it and wrap it around my body.

"What are you going to do with them?" I ask in regard to Frankie and Carter.

"They owe me a debt. I'm here to collect." I eventually told Sigma what happened to me the night he found me beaten and left for dead. I also ratted out who was involved. He would never hurt a female, so I guess he's here to deal with the men.

I don't argue with him. I scurry out of there putting space between us.

That night when Reynolds comes to get me, I don't mention the shower or the missing soldiers. We pretend that it never happened.

CHAPTER THIRTY

Madness

Miguel

"Please. Miguel, I swear I don't know where she is," The private investigator I hired pleads.

It's been over nine months since my Sweets has been missing. Not a day goes by that I don't still search for her. And each day that passes, I grow angrier and angrier with her. How could she leave me?

My Sweets was good for playing this game when she felt as if she wasn't getting enough attention. She would try to run in hopes that I'd find her. Every time I'd fall for her game. I won't lie; I enjoyed the chase, but not as much as the punishment afterward. However, this time she has gone too far.

"I gave you a job, and you failed me. You will pay the consequences." I swing the ax splitting the man's skull nearly in half. I don't stop there as I continue to swing; blood flies through the air

243

soaking me. Yet, I don't stop hacking until an unrecognizable mass is hunched over the chair where a man was once tied to.

I step away from the investigator and drop the ax down on the ground.

"Find me another investigator. This time make sure it's one that's actually fucking good at his job," I say to my baby brother.

Carlito looks everywhere but at me. He doesn't approve of my actions. However, my little brother didn't lose the love of his life, so I couldn't care fucking less about his distaste.

"Bring me one of my bitches," I shout to a security guard standing nearby. My blood lust isn't quenched; the only other thing to take the edge off is pussy.

The guard looks nervously to Carlito.

"There aren't anymore," Carlito says speaking for the first time since we came down to the basement.

"What?" I ask as I pick up the towel off the table where all my torture instruments are kept.

"I said, there aren't any more girls. You killed them all."

Damn, I forgot. "It's an easy fix. We can ride over to the warehouse, and I can get a few more."

That is the bonus of running a sex ring. I had girls coming out of my ears. I could always get more.

Carlito sighs. "Why, so you can do them the same way you did the last set of girls you got. This is your third time going to the warehouse and getting girls."

"I collect and sell pussy, Carlito. It's not like I have a short supply. I can spare a few bitches until I get Sweets back."

"That's the problem, Miguel. What if you never get her back? I think it's time you let Shiloh go."

For a moment, I do not move as I keep my gaze on my little brother. He shuffles his feet uncomfortably as I continue to watch him.

I wipe the blood off my face using the towel in my hands before placing it back down on the table. Slowly, I stroll over to Carlito.

"The day we moved those girls for your CEO," I say watching him closely. "You and I checked every single one of those buses before they rolled out of here, right?"

His gaze darts away before coming back to me. "Yes, I told you. I made sure that every girl on the buses I checked were supposed to be there. She wasn't on any of the buses, Miguel."

I nod, trusting that my little brother is telling the truth. He is the only man in the world I trust. Even though when I first found out she left, I did initially think the CEO had something to do with it. However, Carlito assured me that it wasn't possible. We thoroughly checked those buses before they pulled out. One of us would have had to see her if she was on it.

My phone goes off in my pocket, and I pull it out. I don't recognize the number, but I answer it anyway.

"Yo," I say into the earpiece.

Crying comes through on the other end. "Baby," I don't pick up on the voice. Before placing it back, I pull the phone away from my ear, glancing down at the screen again.

"Who the fuck is this?"

More sniffles. "Miguel, it's me, your beautiful Angel."

My eyes widen. I haven't heard from Candace since I put her ass on one of those buses. Damn, I sure could use her right now. I tug at my semi hard cock.

"Hey, Beautiful. Are you missing me?"

"Miguel, I want to come home. Please, come get me," She whines.

I laugh. I really could use her tight little cunt, but I'm not going out of my way to get it. Besides, I have no idea where she is.

"Beautiful," I start in a placating tone, but she cuts me off.

"If you come, I'll tell you where she is."

Everything around me freezes. I turn my back to my brother and the handful of security guards.

"Where who is?" I don't mean for my words to come out so harsh, but I can't help it.

"Shiloh. I know where she is?"

"Where, Candace? Where is she?" For the first time since Sweets left, I'm starting to feel hopeful. My body tingles all over at the thought of getting my hands on her.

"She's here with me," Candace says. "And she's been touched, Miguel. A lot." The last part is growled as if she wants me to punish Shiloh.

Trust me, I will. But there is someone else I need to deal with first. I hang up the phone and turn back around to face my brother. I knew Carlito was soft for Shiloh. It filled me with joy to know my brother wanted my girl but couldn't have her. However, I never thought he would betray me in this way.

The moment my gaze lands on him, he knows what I've discovered. He starts to back up, his hands held up in surrender.

"I can explain," He pleads. "She begged me to help her."

I smile. "Don't worry, little brother. Before it's over, you will show me just how she begged."

CHAPTER THIRTY-ONE

Times Up

Shiloh

Three days after my fight with Candace, things were finally settling down again.

I hadn't seen her since that day. Frankie and Carter are also MIA. No one has mentioned them until today.

A soldier knocked on my door and said that Dr. Strong wanted to see me. Even though I dread going to see the psycho doctor, I'm pretty sure this is what the meeting is about.

I follow behind the soldier as he takes me on a new route. I don't think I've ever been on this side of the compound before. We stop in front of a room marked private. The soldier opens the door allowing me in first. I enter and immediately scan the room.

The soldiers here are dressing in heavy combat gear as if they are about to stop a riot or start one. A table sits in the middle of the room; stacked on top of it are trays of what looks like bullets.

Some of the soldiers are busy loading large assault rifles with the bullets. If I didn't know any better, I would say they were about to go to war. But with who?

"Ahh, there you are," Dr. Strong says walking over to me. He looks even more frazzled than he did the last time I talked to him. Not to mention, I think there is a splatter of blood on his white lab coat.

His pupils are dilated and the bags under his eyes are more prominent. He looks like a drug addict. And I should know, I lived with one.

He stands right in front of me, his dark gaze looking me up and down. When his eyes land on my stomach I instinctively place my arms over it.

Oh god, does he know? Has he figured it out?

"You've been naughty," he says, looking back to my face. He pinches my chin, turning my head back and forth. When he finally lets me go, I step away from him. I want as much distance from this man as I can get.

"I've stayed out of trouble. I haven't caused any problems." Which is a lie, but I wasn't going to admit to anything.

I don't see his hand because it comes from my right, but I feel it when it flies across my face. Pain radiates from my jaw; the blow knocks me to the ground. What the hell was that for?

He squats down by my face. I clutch my cheek as I look up at him.

"You brought them here. If they try to take my Morgan, I will put a bullet right in your pretty little head."

"What are you talking about?"

I don't understand this guy's obsession with Morgan. He's mentioned her twice in my presence so far. This man is bat shit crazy. I don't care what kind of scientist he's supposed to be.

He makes a tsking sound with his teeth. "You're a stow away, and your time is up." He grabs my arm and hauls me back to my feet. I yank away from him, and he lets me go with a chuckle.

"I volunteered to be here." I argue.

"But did you have permission to leave?" I spin around to face the door and the man that spoke.

My entire body feels like a bucket of ice has been dumped on it. For the life of me, I can't move or run even though my brain is yelling at me to go.

Benjamin Parks is here standing in the doorway. His presence can only mean one thing, Miguel has found me.

"You've caused quite the stir, Sweets." The use of that name causes me to shiver. The power it has over me is still intact.

I turn away from Benjamin, looking for somewhere to run. However, it's no luck. I'm in a room filled with the enemy, and the only way out is behind the man that is here to take me back to my tormentor.

"You've come just in time," Strong says. "We're about to clean house." He turns back to the soldiers and their heavy artillery.

"What are you talking about, Ryder?" Benjamin asks as he steps further into the room. The way his eyes scan the scene before him he's just as confused as I am.

"The research has been canceled. We have direct orders to terminate," Strong says with a grin. He's lying. It doesn't take much to determine that.

Nervousness crawls up my skin. What is he talking about? Terminate who?

"Does Scott know about this?" Benjamin asks. He's too busy looking around the room that he misses the hateful glare Strong gives him.

"You are forgetting this is my research. I choose when it's done."

Benjamin's attention falls back on Strong, and his eyes narrow. "Where is, Asim?"

Dr. Strong tosses his head back and laughs, and it is the most terrifying sound I've ever heard. It's part hysteria and madness combined.

"He resigned about fifteen minutes ago."

I'm getting a bad feeling about this. Seeing all the weapons and the bullets makes me think back to Frankie the night of my attack. He boasted about having special ammunition. Could this be what he was talking about? Everything inside of me tells me I need to let Sigma know what's going on.

Before I can pass a message to my boys, something sharp sticks me in the neck. I turn to my blind side to find a large man holding a syringe. I immediately start to feel woozy.

"What did you give me?" I ask.

His only reply is a smile. I stumble back, my legs buckle, and I nearly fall to the ground.

"Whoa," The big guy with the needle grabs me before I fall. He lifts me easily and place me over his shoulder.

I fight to communicate with Sigma, but my thoughts are slow.

"You should get out while you can, Parks." Strong says even though I can't see him, I know it's him that's speaking.

Big guy turns, giving me the perfect view of the room. Strong stares at me as I'm being carried out. The grin on his face is unsettling.

"Uvonu, what's wrong?" Just the sound of his voice in my head has me calming immediately.

I try to reach out to him, but my thoughts still remain fuzzy.

"Danger...Guns," The two words are the only concrete thing I can think of.

"Where's the danger? Where are you?" he pleads through our boys.

My body sways against the large man's back. I feel myself slipping away to unconsciousness. Oblivion runs her fingers down my spine, luring me to close my eyes.

We stop for a moment—sunlight beams in through the windows warming the side of my face. We are at the top level of the compound and apparently heading outside. Once I get out of this building, I know that I'll be lost to Sigma forever. However, my focus isn't on my well-being or the real monster I'll be seeing soon. It's on protecting the man that I love.

Against the wall is the red square box marked fire alarm. It takes all of my strength to make my hands move, but I do. As soon as I get a handle on the black lever, the big guy starts to walk again. With as strong a grip as I can manage, I pull the alarm. The noise comes instantly.

"What the hell?" big guy says. He spins around, and my head swims from the motion. "She pulled the fucking fire alarm." He says turning back to Benjamin.

"This place is a sinking ship. Let's get out of here," Benjamin shouts over the noise.

Those are the last words I hear before I pass out.

CHAPTER THIRTY-TWO

Breakout

Sigma

The moment I felt her heart rate spike I became alert. My arm stops in mid-swing. The punching bag forgotten. I wait to see if she reaches out to me, but she doesn't.

"Hey, you okay?" Reynolds asks at my side.

I nod before going back to my punching bag. Reynolds steps back in line with my other guards surrounding me. Moments later, a wave of panic hits me, that has me clutching my heart as if it's hers.

This time, I don't wait for her to reach out to me. *"Uvonu, what's wrong?"*

Silence greets me from her end. I do not like this feeling. Unease comes over me. Even when she was in danger with the other breeder, she replied to me.

Suddenly, her voice comes across my thoughts, but it is slurred and jumbled. *"Danger... guns,"* she says.

I send out another message hoping she would explain. When nothing comes back, I open the commander link.

"Something is wrong," I say, making my way over to the wall. I place my hand palm down up against the flat surface. Scanning through every camera system, I spot Dr. Strong heading toward Alpha with armed guards. Before I can notify him, an alarm goes off, startling everyone.

I turn to Reynolds, who looks confused.

"That's the fire alarm," he says.

I open the commander link quickly. *"We're under attack,"* I announce.

"Where's Strong?" Alpha asks.

"On the way to you with a lot of fire power. Something is wrong."

I focus on searching the cameras for Shiloh. It takes a while, but finally one of, the outside cameras spot her. She's being tossed in the back of a black car. Her kidnappers quickly get in before the car pulls away. My angry roar bounces off the walls.

"What's going on?" one of my guards asks. His gun comes up, pointing at me.

"Relax," Reynolds says, holding a hand up toward the other two. "Everyone calm down, there's nothing to be worried about."

I'm afraid, this time, Reynolds is wrong. I snatch the gun from the closes guard before backhanding him across the room. He slams into the concrete wall and slowly slides down. The other guard fire his weapon. I easily dodge the dart, then fire the gun in my hand—the tranquilizer lands directly in the middle of his neck. The guard goes down instantly.

As much medicine they have to put in the darts to knock us out, the human is most likely dead.

I turn to face a terrified Reynolds and storm toward him. He shuts his eyes flinching away from me.

"Take off your shirt," I demand.

Reynolds eyes pop open, and he stares at me with his mouth wide open. "Fucking hell, you can talk?"

"Yes. Now, do as I say if you want to live past this day."

It takes him a moment, but he quickly yanks his weapon from over his shoulder and drops it to the ground. He then quickly unbuttons his shirt and pulls it off, leaving him in his white t-shirt.

Turning away from him, I head to the door. "Stay with me and do as I say."

Reynolds follows me out. We come up on a few more soldiers who seem to be confused. One turns their weapon on me, and before he can fire, I snatch it out of his hands and bend the metal around his neck like a rope. Tightening the gun, I strangle the soldier until he falls at my feet.

"You guys really were playing us, weren't you?" Reynolds asks as he stares over the dead body.

I don't reply. Instead, I go to the nearest wall and place my hands against it. I find the codes to all the cell doors and unlock them, releasing my brethren. We start off again, heading in the direction of the tunnels.

Pain suddenly flares in my chest. My knees buckle, and I collapse to the ground. Reynolds comes up at my side.

"Sigma, what's going on?"

I don't answer him, the searing pain I feel keeps me from responding. My private link comes to life, and Alpha's weak voice comes through. *"Bullets. That's the weapon. He's used the Melcumun from Albatraum to make bullets."*

For the first time, alarm hits me. I was supposed to be discovering what Strong's secret weapon was, but I got sidetracked by Shiloh. Melcumun is a type of metal in the crust of Albatraum. When our planet exploded, and pieces of it fell to earth, the precious metal was stored inside the rock. Strong is using our own planet as a weapon.

Like the others, I feel it the moment Alpha slips away. Even from here, I hear his Uvonu's pained scream.

"We will kill them all," Beta growls into the main link. *"It is time."*

The war chant starts filling the hallways. Reynolds looks around terrified. Getting back to my feet, I go straight for my role in the breakout.

"Come," I demand to Reynolds.

We start off down the hallways—two soldiers round the corner in front of us. One fires off a tranquilizer that I dodge. I'm on him in two strides. Wrapping my hand around his neck, I lift him off the ground and slam him into the nearest flat surface killing him instantly.

Reynolds is fighting the other soldier behind me. He finally lands a punch to the guy's face that has the man stumbling to the wall. The man recovers and charges for Reynolds again; I fire one of the tranquilizers into the man's cheek, causing him to hit the floor instantly.

Reynolds turns to me, out of breath. "Thanks," he says.

I toss him the gun and he catches it. He will need the weapon more than I will.

"Let's go." I say.

"Are we heading to the breeding unit to get Shiloh?"

I round another corner and run into a reincarnate fighting a handful of soldiers. He looks up at me and tosses his head to the side, letting me know he has everything under control. I keep going with Reynolds on my heels.

"No," I finally say answering him.

It was never my job to go to the breeders. We all have our roles in this breakout. Mine is to get to the control room.

"Shiloh is gone. Someone has taken her," I explain, and the reminder causes my anger to rise in me once again.

"Wait, what?" he runs forward and steps in front of me causing me to stop.

"She was taken shortly after pulling the fire alarm."

"Well shouldn't we go after her? I thought she was your girl or something?"

"She is my soulmate. My reason for living," I argue. I do not like him labeling her as something so simple as my girl. "As soon as I and my brothers are free of this place, I will go after her."

He nods his head. "Alright, I'll go with you."

"No. You will go home to your family and be safe," I explain to him.

Although I trusted this human, I cannot allow him to follow me once we leave here. It will not be safe. The less he knows about our whereabouts, the less chance he has to reveal it.

We rush off again. I'm halfway to the control room when his presence rears back to life. It happens only seconds before his angry roar is heard throughout the compound. Reynolds and I both stop.

"He sounds pissed," Reynolds says.

"You have no idea," I tell him before I'm off again.

An explosion has the ground beneath us rumbling.

"What the hell was that?" Reynolds asks.

I smile. "Alpha has just broken out of his impenetrable cell."

Reynolds' eyes widen. I believe he is finally realizing how little control they actually had here.

We make it to the control room, and I yank the metal door off the hinges.

"Oh God. They're here, sir. They're here." The soldier speaking over the walkie-talkie shouts.

The other three fire off their tranquilizer guns. Reynolds takes out one, and I snatch one up by the neck, easily breaking it. The other soldier drops the gun he was holding and lifts his hands up. I ignore him. Grabbing the one with the walkie-talkie, I rip the device from his hand and then use it to knock him out. He lets out one gurgled yelp before falling silent.

I turn to the other soldier, and the scent of urine fills the room. The wet spot on the front of his pants draws mine and Reynolds' attention.

"Eww. Dude, get out," Reynolds tells him.

The soldier trips over his feet in his rush to get away. He jumps back up and sprints out the door.

"What are we doing in here?" Reynolds asks coming up beside me.

I ignore his question. Going over to the computer system, I place my hand against the unit on the wall with all the mainframes and begin to scroll through the information. This system is on a different connection than the one I use on the regular. I could not access this one from the wall as I could the main connection.

I search out every piece of Strong's research and delete the information. I then go through the computer and find all the breeder's information, even going as far back to a place called Vita Labs. I absorb everything I can before wiping the system clean.

It's too late to block the call for help that was already sent out to a nearby military base. We will have to deal with them.

The last thing I do is delete the tracking information of all the airplanes outside. I have to get to Shiloh as fast as possible. I will need a plane for that, and I cannot risk it being tracked.

Finishing up my job, I turn to face Reynolds. "Let's go," I say.

Suddenly, a soldier in full combat gear storms into the room. Before I can react, he fires his weapon, the bullet hitting me directly in the head. Searing hot pain erupts in my brain. My body falls back onto the mainframe and then slowly slides to the floor.

The last thing I see before darkness takes me over is Reynolds fighting the soldier.

Everything goes black and silent around me. And though I can't move, I know that I'm not dead.

Memories start to flood my mind—all of it coming back with clear accuracy. I stop at one particular memory. It's the one I saw that day Alpha was trying to find my secret.

He's standing in his throne room in his true form. The massive rectangular room was brightly lit from the large glass windows that ran the length of the room. The white stone walls with their gold accents were a constant throughout the castle.

"My King, you're not listening to me. The Cresilians have been hopping from planet to planet, destroying everything in their paths. We cannot take Khol's threat lightly."

"And as I told you, Historian, I do not fear them. Khol will not chase my people from our home."

Though my title is Historian, I've been friends with Tovian since we were born. His mother and mine were childhood friends. When my parents died, I was raised in the same home as him. Although I may not be his brother like Pathos and Vinmeer, we are close. Which is why I do not understand his doubt in me now.

I shake my head at his stubbornness. "Put aside your ego, old friend. We cannot win against them."

"Speak for yourself, Vulto," Omega says, stepping into my line of sight. His pale green skin in stark contrast to his fire red hair. His horns curving forward and then upward. The warrior lines on his face etched in silver run from his jaws up to his brow bone.

"We have fought the Cresilians shapeshifters in many battles and have always come out victorious. There is not an army in the next twelve solar systems that can defeat us. Our warriors are limitless."

I turn to glare at Omega. "You are speaking as one that knows and abides by the rules of battle. I'm telling you that Khol has no morals. How do you think he defeated the Qaxals?"

"Wait," Beta says garnering my attention. His dark blue skin marked with his crafter symbols. "Cresilians defeated the Qaxals?"

Built for battle and more difficult to kill than us, the Qaxals are a notorious opponent. It took us three years to finally defeat them in the celestial war.

"Yes," I tell them.

Beta looks over to Alpha, and they share a private conversation. Hopefully, Beta is talking since to our King.

"We all know the Qaxals were softening in their power after we defeated them. This changes nothing." Gamma, shrugs. His skin is the exact same color as his brothers, but his hair is a lighter red.

"I am telling you there is no lengths Khol and his army of Cresilian warriors wouldn't go through to defeat his opponents. If you go to war with them, we will face annihilation."

Alpha scoffs and turns away from me. I knew this conversation would not go over well. Our young king has much to prove. His father was the greatest King Albatraum has had in many solar rotations.

When the time came to pass the mantle onto Tovian, many didn't think he could carry the crown, especially when he was not the original eldest. Pathos, his older brother died in a surprise attack while away from Albatraum. I understand his desire to prove himself, but this is not the time.

"What is Khol's demand?" Omega asks turning to me.

"He wants ten thousand of our fertile women to be handed over to him."

It goes without saying the Cresilians are suffering greatly. An unknown virus ripped through their planet killing off their females; they have been trying to rebuild their population but are unable to find female host capable of carrying their young and surviving their peculiar mating process.

The others around me scoff.

"That's insane," Gamma argues. I agreed with him totally. I have no plans of turning over any of our women to them. Despite what the others think, I do not want to submit to the Cresilians. I do, however, think we need to evacuate.

"We are not handing them any of our females," Alpha reassures us.

"If you will not evacuate the entire planet, at least allow the women and children to leave," I plead.

Alpha turns back to me, his glowing silver eyes narrowing. *"Is that what this is about? You're worried about your precious Uvonu?"*

Immediately, my thoughts go to my mate along with my son. Although Zephyr is no longer a child and is now starting his apprenticeship with the healers, he is still my concern.

"If you will not heed my warning about the Cresilians, please at least allow the woman and children to seek shelter on Vangonia. I've already reached out to Dumas, and he says he will welcome them."

"You did what?" Alpha shouts.

"They needed somewhere safe to go. War is no place for women and children."

Again, Alpha gives me his back as he paces in front of us.

"My knowledge of the galaxies and the species that inhabit the many planets has never steered you wrong, Tovian. Do not lose your faith in my counsel now."

He looks back at me over his shoulder, and I can tell his restraint is wavering. For as long as he and I have been friends, I have never failed him in my knowledge. He knows this.

"King, trust yourself. When we win this war, your people will no longer question your ability as our leader. You will make your father proud."

I close my eyes at Omega's words. He has just tipped the scale and changed the course of our history. This is all Alpha has wanted since the crown has been placed on his head. Tovian's desire to please his people blinds him.

"We will stay," Alpha declares. "If I send off the women and children, my people will think I do not have faith in our warriors. It will make them doubt us."

Shaking my head, my eyes pop open to glare at him. "You will regret this decision."

"Get out, Vulto. If you cannot trust in me, I am dismissing you of your title," He snarls.

I turn and leave the white and gold throne room. It will be the last time I was in the room. Alpha did eventually decide to evacuate our women and children. However, it was too late.

The ship carrying my Uvonu was shot out of the sky the day the Cresilians invaded Albatraum. Thankfully, Zephyr stayed behind to fight with me.

My memories fade, and the noise around me comes back. It all makes sense now. Alpha has been blocking my memories on purpose.

I was the only one out of the five of us that lost their mate in the war. The others had not mated yet. He didn't want me to remember all that I lost for his arrogance.

The connection between us comes to life even though I am blocking it.

"Now you know," his voice sounds hallow, and shame fills the link.

"You kept it from me," I roar.

"*Yes,*" he admits easily. "*I allowed my desire to fulfill my father's shoes ruin my people. I should've listened to you.*"

My anger is palpable as it vibrates through me. I lost everything because of him. None of them know what the emptiness of losing a soulmate feels like.

"*I do not care for your apologies now. You have betrayed me for the last time.*"

"*Vulto,*" he pleads. "*What would you have done if it were you that caused your oldest friend to lose so much?*"

"*I would have owned up to my mistakes,*" I yell. "*I would have never violated your trust by taking your memories. Do you know what made your father the great King that he was?*" I don't give him time to reply. "*It is because he understood that even Kings are not without flaws. Your desire to be great has blinded you. You had no right to take my memories.*"

"*Everything lost was given back to you,*" Alpha's words are a whisper in my head.

It true. I lost Lunno back in the old world, but I have Shiloh here. Although nothing will take the place of my first mate, the way I feel for my human is more than anything I've experienced in this world and the old. I believe it has something to do with this new form and all its emotions.

"*That may be true, but it does not exonerate you.*"

The link is silent, yet he is still connected. I do not care that his sorrow is lapping at my thoughts like waves. Nor do I care for his guilt. His actions were selfish and manipulative. He does not get to erase his errors from our minds. A true king owns up to his faults and admits his wrongs, not cower behind lies.

"*You are right,*" he says, apparently, he was listening to my thoughts. The main link opens. "*I have a confession to make. I need to tell you all this before you continue to fight in my name. I took your memories of the great war because I was ashamed of the role I played in it. My pride aided in the war that caused us to lose our home. An old friend explained to me that even great Kings has flaws.*"

The fog on my memories lifts even more, and I can clearly see all the actions that lead up to the final battle. The links begins to vibrate with ire. But then, something else happens. Not only am I seeing my memories, but I witness Alpha's as well.

I'm there the day his father announce he will be King now that his oldest is gone. I witness the elders of Albatraum berate and belittle Alpha. They said that he would fail because he was not the natural born leader. I witness, through Alpha's memories, as his father stands up for him, assuring them that he is worthy of the crown. I see it all as if the memory is mine.

The connection ends and my mind clears.

"I know you are all angry with me," he goes on to say in the main link. *"I can never forgive myself for the war. I live with the guilt every day. If you desire to abandon this mission and free yourselves, you are free to go."*

There is a lot of commotion through the link. So many voice their anger at his actions to hide the memory, but eventually the noise dies down.

"Though your actions were selfish, I understand your reason. You have led us well here, so I will still follow you," Gamma says.

Soon, every reincarnate share the same sentiment as Gamma.

"Thank you," he says in the main link. He then comes back to our private conversation. *"I know I have no right to ask this of you, but I need you, old friend. I need your help to save my Uvonu."*

He's right; he has no right to ask me. Especially when it was because of his selfishness that I lost my first Uvonu. However, he has been right about one thing all this time; I need to let the pass go. Receiving another Uvonu after losing one is not common on Albatraum. Finding Shiloh is truly a rare and special gift. One that I will cherish.

"I will help you save your mate. But after that, my ties to you are done."

I disconnect the link between Alpha and myself. Sitting up, I find Reynolds still battling the soldier with the gun. Placing a hand to my forehead, the hole slowly closes. Finally, the bullet is pushed out, and it lands in my palm. I toss it to the ground and stand.

Reynolds takes a punch to the face and lands against the far wall. Before the soldier can lift his gun and fire again, I grab the weapon and beat his head in with it. He falls to my feet, and I toss the gun on top of him.

"Shit man, I thought you were dead?" Reynolds says walking up to me while clutching a hand to his jaw.

"No. Not yet," I take off out the door, and he follows behind me. I have one more mission, to find Alpha and help him find his Uvonu. Then we will part ways forever.

Reynolds and I leave the compound heading toward one of the airplane hangars. I pull up short when I run into Zee. The moment I'm in his presence again, I sense the essence of my son inside him. It explains why the name came so easily to me. I guess it's also why Alpha encouraged our friendship.

Grabbing Zee, I pull him into me in what the human's call a hug. My research shows that this is how human males show love to their sons. Zee stiffens, but eventually hugs me back.

"This is nice, Mr. Sigma."

I think about telling Zee the truth. Letting him know he is the reincarnate of my first born, but I change my mind. Now is not the time. I pull away from the hug and pat his arm.

"Mr. Sigma, I cannot find Shiloh," he says, shoulders slump.

I smile at his concern for her. I wonder if he sensed his brothers inside her.

"I know. She was taken. Do not fret; I will get her back." I say before he panics.

"I need you to take Reynolds to the escape tunnels." The tunnels were Beta's secret project. It will be our route out of this prison. It stretches miles underneath the ground and away from this compound.

I used my abilities to procure temporary shelter on the other side of the tunnel until we figured out where to go. Once we are safe enough away, the bomb Beta built will destroy any evidence of our escape.

Zee looks past me to the soldier. *"And then what?"*

"You will go with him and wait for me on the other side."

"But I want to help." His brow pinches with determination.

Pride fills my chest. It is the same thing he said to me the day we were attacked on Albatraum. *"Not this time,"* I tell him. *"Go with Reynolds. I will need you when it's time to save my Uvonu."*

I knew that telling him he could help me save Shiloh would get him moving. He turns to Reynolds and with a tilt of his head, tells the soldier to follow him.

"This is where we part," I tell Reynolds.

"Thank you," he says looking away from me. "For what it's worth, I'm sorry for all the shit you guys went through."

I do not tell him that his government will pay us back handsomely for our troubles. My research tells me it is called Reparations.

Reynolds runs off behind Zee, and I turn to look for Alpha and the others.

After checking for every one's whereabouts on the camera, I meet up with Alpha, Beta, Omega, and Gamma outside the compound.

"He's trying to load Morgan on a plane," I say out loud. I checked the cameras before meeting up with them. "Tarmac C."

"Thank you," Alpha says. I tilt my head down in acknowledgement. Our battle is not over, but I will help his mate.

He takes off running, and we follow him. When we approach the scene, Strong has Morgan by the face, and he smashes his lips to hers. Raging fury fills me as I watch her tiny fist beat at his chest. It doesn't matter if she is my mate or not, the thought of the mad doctor forcing himself on her pisses me off.

Alpha grabs the doctor by the neck and rips him away from her. Strong falls to the ground. Morgan almost tumbles with him, but Alpha wraps her in his arms, standing her up right.

"Alpha," she whispers his name lovingly. I can't help but imagine how it will be when Shiloh and I are reunited.

Alpha pulls away from his kiss with his mate. "Are you alright?" he asks.

Before she could answer, Strong is back up right. "Get away from her. Get away from my Morgan."

Beta and I look at each other before turning to Strong again.

"Why does he believe Morgan belongs to him?" Gamma asks.

I run through the newly acquired information I recently downloaded and find the answer I'm searching for.

"He's been injecting himself with the toxin he gave us." I reply in the link.

"Then he has to be dealt with," Alpha says, then replies out loud to Strong. "Your time is done, Strong."

Dr. Strong laughs. "You think I am the only person you have to worry about? Right now, a fully equipped army is on their way to take as many of you bastards down as they can."

"The longer we let this man speak, the less time we have to get away," Beta says through the link. He moves around the back of Strong. The doctor hasn't noticed because he's still threatening us.

"I say we take him with us, he doesn't deserve a quick death," Gamma says coming up on his left side.

"He will only slow us down," Omega adds taking up the right side.

"You don't deserve freedom. You are monsters. All of you." Dr. Strong continues to shout. "I created you in a lab. I gave you everything. They," He points his finger at nothing, and I roll my eyes in my head. Has the man still not realized he had nothing to do with our recreation?

"They will take it all away from you," He growls. "Especially her."

"He's right," Alpha says through the link as he turns to face his Uvonu. *"They will take all of our mates if they find them."*

He doesn't have to worry about that. I made sure none of the breeders will be traceable. Before I can tell him this, he breaks the connection to us.

When his mate answers, I know why. He's speaking to her through the link with his son.

Alpha grabs her face between his hands and whispers, "I love you. And nothing but death will keep me away from you. Both of you. You must trust me. I have to finish here first."

I admire his strength to let her go. I cannot say I could have done the same thing if this was Shiloh. The ache in my chest that I've been ignoring starts to grow stronger. I need her back with me. The pain will only get worse the longer we are apart.

"Yyyyyyyyyou will come for us? You ppppppppromise?" Morgan stutters out to him.

Alpha smiles before kissing her again. He finally lets her go but places his hand to her stomach. He turns her toward the airplane where Asim and Donvan have been waiting.

"Hold up," Gamma says through the link. *"Are we letting them go?"*

"Apparently we are," Beta grumbles.

"They are helping his mate escape," I explain. *"Although it only requires one person to fly a plane."*

They laugh through the connection even though I wasn't making a joke.

Asim grabs Morgan's hand to help her up on the plane.

"Nooooo," Dr. Strong yells "If I can't have you, no one can."

Dr. Strong aims his gun at Morgan. He fires the weapon, but Alpha shoves his arm up and then bends it backwards breaking the bone in half. Strong screams and falls to his knees.

"Get on the plane, Morgan," Alpha tells his mate.

"I love you," she cries.

He looks over his shoulder at her and nods.

"So," Gamma asks looking around at all of us. *"Who gets the honor of disposing of the scientist?"*

"He is mine," Alpha says coldly.

Morgan's plane starts to taxi out of the hangar.

Strong peers up at Alpha as he approaches. "If you'd have given her the chance, she would have chosen me over you." he says weakly.

"I guess we will never know," Alpha snarls. He then raises his foot and brings it down on Strong's head, smattering his brains against the tarmac.

Alpha turns around to watch Morgan's plane lift into the sky.

"I have to go now," I say to the link.

Gamma, Beta, and Omega turn to look at me.

"Where are you going," Beta asks.

"My mate is in danger. I must get to her to save my sons."

"Wait, what," Gamma asks. *"You've planted your seedling and didn't tell us?"* His eyes narrow at me as he waits for an explanation I will not give.

None of their sadness weighs down the link as much as Alpha's. When I planted Zephyr, Tovian was the first one I told. He and I celebrated all night with drink and laughter. Not this time.

Omega shakes his head. *"I feel like I don't even know you anymore, Sig."*

That is a true statement I do not care to argue with. As I turn to leave an explosion on the other side of the compound has all of our attention.

"Back up is here," Omega says out loud.

"Let's clear this place out, then we can go and save your mate," Alpha says turning to me.

He opens our private link. *"I will not fail you this time, old friend."*

I nod at him and race toward the jeeps filled with soldiers. It's time to end this.

CHAPTER THIRTY-THREE

Hell

Shiloh

I come to suddenly, sitting up in my seat. Scanning my surroundings, I recognize I'm on a plane. From the size and the number of seats, it must be a private jet.

Benjamin is sitting across from me, looking down at his phone. The big guy that carried me out of the compound is beside me. A stewardess stops beside Benjamin and asks if he wants a drink. He shakes his head before looking up at me.

"You're in a lot of trouble," he says with a smile, placing his phone in his lap. "Imagine my surprise when your psycho boyfriend called me with all his threats demanding I bring you to him. Part of me started to deny him." He shrugs. "I don't usually deal with scum like Miguel Estrava."

I scoff as I adjust myself in my seat better. "People like you are funny."

Benjamin quirks a brow. "How so?"

"You think you're so much better than Miguel because you're a CEO. When actually, you're both despicable, worthless bags of flesh. Just because you commit your crime in a fancy suit with a title and he does his in sneakers doesn't make you better than him."

The smug smile on his face falls, and he sneers at me.

"Watch your mouth, girl."

I laugh. "Is that supposed to be a threat, Mr. CEO?"

Rolling my eyes, I look out the window and notice we are descending. "I'm supposed to be afraid of you. Even with your title and all your money, the moment Miguel pulled your chain, you ran off to do his bidding. You aren't even worth my concern."

His hand flies across my face smacking me so hard my forehead bumps against the window beside me.

"Fucking slut. You are used ass that isn't worth the trouble that I spent to come get you."

I rub the ache out of my cheek as I look at him and smile. "I promise if it's the last thing I do. You will regret that."

He looks at me only a few seconds longer before his attention turns to something over my head.

"Ah, you're done." He smiles. "Take your seat. We will be landing soon."

I turn my head to see who he's talking to. I spot Candace, and I'm out of my seat before the big guard or Benjamin can stop me. Fisting her shoulder-length hair, I yank her head back and punch her in the face. She screams as she tries to pry my hands off. I wail on her face harder. I don't stop until big guy yanks me away from her. He shoves me down in my seat.

"If you get our ass back up, I'm giving you another shot," The bodyguard warns.

No telling what was in that shot, or if it's even safe for my babies. I can't risk him giving it to me again. I relax back in my seat; everything here on out will involve me trying to keep my boys safe. Sigma will come for me. I don't know how or when, but I believe with all my heart that he will come.

The jet finally makes a bumpy landing. I'm sweating and my body is shaking because I know what's waiting for me when I get off this plane. Before I left, I would have said Miguel would never hit me. I'm not so sure about that now.

Candace is out of her seat immediately once the plane stops moving. "He's here. Oh my god, Miguel is here," She shouts while bouncing up and down on her toes, clapping her hands. The desire to shove this bitch off the plane eats at me. The door to the jet opens, and the guard yanks me up from the seat and shoves me toward the exit.

As soon as the stewardess gives the okay, Candace races down the stairs toward Miguel. I'm right behind her walking at a lot slower pace.

"Miguel, baby," she screams with her arms out eager to hug him. The moment she gets up on him, he shoves her away with his hand in her face.

Candace hits the pavement with a hard smack. She cries out, but he's not paying her any attention. His eyes are on me.

"Come to me, Sweets," he demands.

"Miguel, baby, what are you doing? Why are you treating me this way?" Candace whines.

She looks over to me and then back to him. She's blinded by her love for Miguel. He has really messed her up in the head. If she were sane, she would be able to look at him and tell that he's not in his right mind right now. Maybe then, she would keep her mouth shut. But she doesn't.

"I can't believe it," She yells jumping to her feet. "You don't love me. You've been using me all this time. It's always been about her."

"Candace," I try to call her name to make her be quiet.

"No, Shiloh," she shouts. "You were right. He doesn't fucking love any of us."

I don't see the gun, but I hear it once it's fired. The shot knocks her head back and she collapses to the ground. A bullet hole is in the center of her forehead.

When I look up from her corpse, his dark eyes are on me, and the gun is thankfully down at his side.

"Come here," his demand is growled through clenched teeth.

My feet will not move to carry me closer to him, no matter how hard I try. Benjamin walks up beside me, yanks my arm, and marches me over to Miguel.

"We're done after this. Don't call me again," Benjamin says.

The first sign that Miguel has lost his grip on reality is that he doesn't say anything to Benjamin Parks for touching me or talking to him the way that he is. Instead, his eyes stay on me—the burning fury behind the brown irises causing my skin to crawl.

"Let's go," he says then turns around. I follow without being told twice.

Miguel crawls in the back seat, and I get in beside him. The car pulls away before I can shut the door good. He grabs me by my hair and yanks my head back against the seat. I cry out from the pain at my scalp. He wraps his other hand around my throat and squeeze cutting off my air supply.

"I should blow your fucking brains out," he snarls down in my face.

"Please," I croak as I reach up to his hand, trying to pry his fist out of my hair. The grip is so tight it has my eyes watering up.

"Please what, Sweets? What could you possibly ask of me?"

I open my mouth, not sure of what I would reply, but it doesn't matter because he kisses me. His tongue goes into my mouth with so much anger and aggression his teeth knock into mine. I'm nearly choking from his tongue being forced down my throat. He bites down on my lip, and I cry out once again. He pulls back, letting me go while sitting back in his seat.

"Take my cock out."

Oh shit, this is about to go bad. My heart pounds so violently against my chest that if feels like one of those old-time cartoon characters. I know back at the compound I was willing to give a little blow job to survive. However, right now, the thought of touching any man besides Sigma makes me nauseas. Yet, telling Miguel no could possibly leave me just as dead as Candace.

"Now," he barks.

I jump at the sudden demand. When I don't move fast enough, he grabs my hair in that tight grip and shoves my face down to the erection that's straining against his pants. I try to pull away, but he won't let me up. He goes to undo his pants, and I have only one option.

"I'm pregnant," I shout the words.

He goes completely still. My admittance can either mean my sudden death, or it may buy me time to get out of this car. He releases my hair, and I quickly move as far away from him as I can get. My back is pressed to the door while I face him.

He stares at me and if he were anyone else, I would have sympathy for him right now. He looks like a man that has just had his heart broken. Only I know that Miguel doesn't actually have a heart.

"You let someone else get you pregnant?" His question comes out as softly as a whisper.

"I had no choice. It was the research," I'm back in survival mode. If I tell Miguel that I got pregnant by the man I love, I won't be getting out of this car. He has to think these babies are just some science experiment, and I have no real attachment to them.

He looks away from me for a moment before turning back.

"You will never carry a baby inside you that I did not give you."

I gasp. "What are you going to do?".

The smile that lifts his lips isn't sweet or kind. It is filled with malicious intent. "Handle it."

Oh god. I send a message to my boys, hoping they will pass it to their father. I don't know the range of their gift, but I'm hoping it will work.

"He's going to kill our babies, Sigma. I don't know how to stop him."

His reply is instant, and it fills me with something I haven't had in years, hope. *"I'm coming, Uvonu. I'm coming."*

**

The ride back to the mansion is short. Miguel grabs me by the shirt and yanks me out of the car. I don't fight him too much. I have to keep my energy. Once we walk inside, I immediately notice how quiet it is. This mansion is usually packed with staff and his girls. Yet, no one is in the hallways.

He shoves me onto the tile floor face first. My outstretched arms are the only thing that keeps me from busting my face open on the ground.

I turn over to see him, not wanting to give him my back. He's pacing back and forth in front of me.

"Miguel, where is everyone? Where is Carlito?"

If anyone could help calm Miguel down, it would be his brother. An angry Miguel is a dangerous Miguel, and right now, he is livid.

He turns to me and laughs; it sounds like the hysterical and crazy one Strong did earlier today.

"She wants my brother," Miguel says. He looks over to the bodyguard with him. "Go fetch Carlito for me."

The security guard grimaces but turns and heads out of the foyer. I immediately get a bad feeling.

"I gave you everything, Sweets. You are the only woman I've ever loved. Yet you played me for a fool."

I'm shaking my head before he can finish speaking. "That isn't true. I love you."

"Stop lying," he shouts, and spittle flies from his mouth.

He calms, running his hand through his hair. "You never loved me the way that I loved you. I see it now."

This is not the time to argue with him about the truth that he never loved me. You don't cage something you love. You don't hold them hostage. I know what love fills like. I've experienced the truest form of it these last five months. What Miguel feels for me is not love.

The security guard comes back in, but he's pushing a giant blue barrel on rollers. My stomach churns at the stench that follows.

"You wanted Carlito, here he is," Miguel points to the barrel with blood dripping off the side. I gag, nearly bringing up my breakfast.

"How could you?" I cry.

I didn't feel the same way Carlito did for me, but he was my friend. Knowing his brother killed him breaks my heart. I never wanted this for Carlito.

Miguel storms over to me and grabs my hair once again, lifting me to my feet.

"No, you are the reason for this. You used his infatuation with you against him. You will apologize for taking his life." He drags me to the barrel. I fight to break free of his grip.

The moment I get close enough to that container to look inside, I scream. I can't make out what part is what. Only bits and pieces are left of my friend.

Miguel shoves my face toward the container, and the smell has my eyes watering. "Tell him you're sorry," Miguel shouts at me. He shoves me closer to the contents as if he's trying to make me bob for apples. "Tell him you are the reason he's dead."

I can't say anything because I'm crying and gagging too bad.

Finally, he yanks me back and shoves his tongue down my throat. I beat my fist at his chest as he tongues me down over his butchered brother's remains.

He lets me go, and I fall back onto the floor.

"Tomorrow, I'll get rid of that fucking parasite inside of you. Then we're getting married. That way, if you ever try to run again, I'll have every legal right to bring you back."

With those words, he steps over me, heading into his office. His new bodyguard follows. The others stand around watching as I break apart on the foyer floor.

**

Later that night, I'm sitting on the chair near the fireplace in my room. My knees are tucked under my chin as I gaze off at nothing. I showered earlier and have been hiding in here since I got back. I'm scared.

There has always been a fine line of fear while being with Miguel, but this is different. Especially when I learned all the women have been killed. Part of me knew and understood that while I was away being free, people were dying. But I didn't expect this.

I place my hand over my belly and rub. "I'm not going to let him hurt you," I promise the boys. Even though I'm not sure, I can keep that promise. "We're going to stay safe until daddy comes."

"Daddy is here," his voice comes alive in my head.

I cover my mouth with my hand to trap the gasp. Tears fill my eyes.

"Siggy," I say his name out loud.

"I'm here. And I'm coming to take back what is mine."

Gunshots go off outside. I jump up and rush to the window. My room faces the back of the house. The bodyguards that circle the property are running toward the front of the mansion.

Suddenly, my bedroom door swings open. I spin around praying that it will be my creature standing there. However, it's Miguel, and he looks even more pissed off.

"Who the fuck do you have coming into my home," he shouts as he storms over to me.

I back into the window with nowhere to go. Miguel wraps his hand around my neck and squeeze. I claw at his grip, trying to get him to release me. When that doesn't work, I go to old reliable; I knee him in the balls. He groans and cups his dick before falling to his knees.

I don't stop to see if he's down for long. I take off running for the door. He tries to grab me, but I dodge his hands. Rushing out of the room, I take the stairs two at a time.

Miguel's heavy footsteps are closing in behind me. I'm halfway down the stairs when he tugs at my shirt. I yank from him, causing him to lose his grip. I then go tumbling down the stairs. When I come to a stop at the bottom, pain radiates from my hip and elbow.

The front door burst open, and three of Miguel's security guards rush in with their guns.

"What the fuck are those things?" One of the men shouts.

"I shot one of them, and he just kept coming," another guy cries out.

Laughter erupts from me. It's loud and coated in hysteria. With everything I've been dealing with today, it makes sense that I've lost my mind.

Miguel finally reaches the bottom of the stairs. He looks down at me, where I'm still sprawled out on the ground.

"What the hell is going on?"

"He came for me," I admit proudly.

Just then, the front door slams open, and in walks Sigma and Zee. His gaze immediately finds me.

The security team starts shooting. Zee easily swats the man closest to him like an annoying fly. The guy goes flying into a wall. Sigma grabs the other two men by the neck, lifts them off the ground, and then slams their heads together like two uncooked eggs. He tosses them to the floor when he's done.

Miguel grabs me off the ground and presses a gun to my head. Sigma takes a step toward us, and Miguel moves us back.

"Stay right where you are, you got damn giant," he yells. "You might can survive a bullet, but she can't."

This brings Zee and Sigma to a stop.

Miguel laughs. "You thought you were just going to come up in here and take what belongs to me?"

Sigma snarls at him baring his teeth. Miguel taps the side of my head with the barrel of the gun.

"Don't get jumpy, mother fucker," He taunts as he drags me toward the back door.

I realize what he's trying to do. Miguel always bragged about having this house custom made. He has it equipped for every type of scenario—one of them being if he needs to flee the house suddenly. There are trap doors all around this place that, once they are activated, no one else can get in.

"He's going to try to run with me," I send the message to him through the boys.

"Relax, Uvonu. He will never get you out of this house," Sigma replies but never takes his eyes off of Miguel.

Sigma and Zee follow as Miguel pulls me out of the foyer into the living room.

"Let me tell you what I'm going to do," Miguel taunts. "I'm going to take my Sweets out of here, and you're going to stay the fuck away from us."

"That will not happen," Sigma says calmly. "I will never stop looking for her. I will chase you down until you have nowhere else to go. There will be no place you can hide that I can't find you. You will die from exhaustion, looking over your shoulder before I will ever give up on her."

My god, I love this man. I believe whole heartedly that he would always come for me. No matter where I went, he would follow.

I think Miguel knows it too because he stops moving. His arm tightens around my chest, and he huffs out a breath. The gun drops to my shoulder. He then places a kiss at the back of my head.

"I told you forever, Shiloh," He whispers in my ear.

He lifts the gun back to my temple. I already know what he's planning. I've always known this would be my only way out. I'd just hoped that I would get my happily ever after. I guess that's what I get for hoping.

The gun fires, and I flinch, waiting for the pain or darkness, but nothing comes. Turning to look over my shoulder, Miguel is being held up by his arm; the gun is pointing toward the ceiling.

His grip on me loosens and I step away, turning to see who is holding him. It's the big one they call Alpha. He glares down at Miguel as if he caught a rodent in a trap. I step away from him. Even though I know he isn't the bad guy, he still scares the shit out of me.

I'm grabbed from behind and turned around. I come face to stomach with my creature. He lifts me up and I wrap my legs around his waist and my arms at his neck, kissing him as if my life depended on it. When he pulls away, I place my forehead to his, taking in his scent.

"You kept your promise," I whisper.

"Of course, I did. I would never abandon you."

I love this man.

"What do you want to do with him?" The deep sound of Alpha's voice takes me by surprise. Sigma lowers me to the floor, and I turn just as Alpha drops Miguel to the floor. He takes the gun from him and tosses it on the ground. It slides right at my feet.

Three more super soldiers are with Alpha. One dark-skinned with golden eyes, one pale and the other tan. From what I remember of Sigma's stories, they're Beta, Omega, and Gamma.

Sigma moves me behind him before he steps closer to Miguel. I grab his arm. He looks down at me, his brow pinched.

"Let me," I pass to him.

He nods and steps back.

Grabbing the gun off the floor I aim it at Miguel. He starts to laugh as he gets up on his knees.

"Are you going to shoot me now, Sweets?" He asks.

I walk right up to him placing the gun at the center of his forehead. I was seventeen years old when this psycho found me. I wasn't even fully a woman yet. He tried to strip everything from me. Tonight, I'm claiming it back.

His dark brown eyes stare up at me. "You can't do it," He taunts. "Despite what you're telling him, you and I both know you still lo—" The gunshot cuts off his words.

His body falls to the ground, and the hole in his head spills blood. I toss the gun beside him. I vanquished my capture, and for the first time, I finally feel free.

Turning back to Sigma, I wrap my arms around his waist, burying my face in his stomach.

"It is done now," Alpha says.

Looking back over my shoulder at him, I shake my head. "No, it's not."

"What do you mean?" Sigma asks.

Gazing up at him, I reply. "I know you deleted all my records from the compound."

"I deleted all the females' records," He adds.

"Yes, but I know there is at least one person who knows I was there. In fact, he probably knows every woman who was at the compound."

Sigma looks over my head and has one of those silent conversations.

"Who is this person?" Alpha asks.

I turn to him, not as frightened anymore. "Benjamin Parks. CEO of Vita Labs."

Sigma and Alpha look to each other as if the name sparks a memory. Sigma walks over to the wall and places his hand against it for a few seconds. He turns back to Alpha and the others and nod.

The dark skinned one smiles. "I guess we will be paying this CEO a visit."

I made a promise to Benjamin on that jet, I intend to keep it.

Sleeper Cell

Sigma

"Zee, again," Thorir calls out to his big brother. His short chubby legs rush to catch up to him.

Zephyr took the news of his relationship with me better than I could have thought. He was proud to be the reincarnate of my son. We have grown closer since the day he helped me rescue Shiloh. He was even there the night his baby brothers were born.

It's been nearly two years since we escaped the compound. I found this plot of land for us, and Morgan purchased it using some of her inheritance. After I took my cut from the human government, Morgan has not had to spend any more money. We used my money to build our homes and recreate a community. It isn't Albatraum, but we are happy.

Vali laughs, and Zee picks him up tossing him over his head. The twins are getting bigger every day. Soon, I will be planting another seedling in my Uvonu. I have given her time to recover from the twins.

I watch my boys from inside of my workspace. On Albatraum I was used to my tower of solitude, preferring to work alone. Even after I mated, I'd often go to my tower for peace. But here, I enjoy being close to my family. I often open up my door and work alongside my Uvonu.

Shiloh found her calling in this new life. She grows plants and herbs that she uses to mix up skin and hair care. I guess her time at the compound taught her to appreciate her skin and hair. Many days while she mixes her ingredients and tries new fragrances, I sit at my computer searching for answers.

The connection between Alpha and I open. It took some persuasion for me to come back here to live with the others. Shiloh wanted to raise the boys around the other offspring. She did not want them to grow up in the human world feeling different. I will give my mate anything she asks for. Although I agreed to come to stay at the community with everyone, Alpha and I still struggle with our friendship. I follow his leadership, but the trust is broken.

"Any news?" he asks immediately.

"None yet."

When I was searching the database the day we broke out, I came across a vague mention of another compound. I 've been trying to locate the information again, but I haven't been able to find it. The human government has done well to keep the information hidden.

"I have a bad feeling about this. Something still feels amiss," He admits to me.

"Have you mentioned your feelings to the others?" I ask him.

"Yes. I told you. No more secrets, remember."

I will admit, he has done a lot better at being forth coming and honest. He has shown us that he is worthy of his title. Not that I ever doubted him. I always knew that Tovian was worthy of the crown, he just had to figure that out.

Leaning back in my chair, I stare out the window as Shiloh joins Zee and the twins in the back yard. Her hair falls past her shoulders, and the white thin dress she wears blows in the wind. She is stunning.

"I will keep searching, and hopefully I will soon ease your fears." I tell Alpha.

He sighs. *"Thank you, old friend. Now go be with your family."* He says before disconnecting.

Standing from my chair, I walk out of my office that is behind my house. The twins spot me and immediately run toward me. I lift them both up, and place kisses on top of their curly heads before placing them back down. I walk over to my Uvonu, and she smiles up at me.

"I missed you today," she says as I wrap my arms around her waist pulling her toward me. She lifts on her tiptoes in order to give me a kiss.

"How did your delivery go?"

"Really well. Fatima ordered a case of my moisturizer and Morgan is loving the deep conditioner."

I smile, and she returns it. "You know what your smile does to me, right?" she whispers.

I knew exactly what my smile did to her. I lift her up, carrying her like a bride toward our home.

"No, but I want you to show me. Besides, I think it is time we add to our younglings."

She tosses her head back and laughs as I step into the house.

"Oh really? Well, I think you need to spend a little time convincing me?" the teasing note to her tone tells me she's being playful. Not that I had a problem convincing her to accept my seedling.

"I guess I'm babysitting?" Zee says through our link.

I laugh as I reply, *"That's what being a big brother is all about."*

I shut down the connection to everyone, then spend hours bringing my mate pleasure through the sexual intercourse.

**

Stryker

Somewhere Across The Country...

Time begins to blur. I don't know how long I've been here. I'm stuck in a small cell that only has a toilet and an uncomfortable bed. I take my meals and use the bathroom all in the same place. The only time they take me out of this room is to go to the chair. I hate the chair. Pain comes from the chair.

They want me to forget something. Something they say isn't good for me. Whenever I try to think of it when I'm strapped to the chair, it hurts. No matter how hard I attempt to hang on to the memory, it slips from my hands like pebbles of sand.

It's a place they want me to forget. No, not a place, a name. Her name. The moment I remember it's a name, a memory appears. It's the only one I have left. They have dug out all the others. This memory of her use to be so accurate I could recall every detail of her face, but now it's blurry. I can no longer make out anything. Only her voice. I think it wouldn't matter how many times they took me to that chair I could never forget her voice.

Like honey poured out of cup, it drips in a low sultry rasp. Even now as the voice simply calls out my name, I can feel the love it has for me and I for her. I don't recall her name or how she looks, but her voice will never be forgotten.

I tuck the memory away in that deep place. The place I keep the other memories that I hide from the chair. The chair doesn't want my recent memories—the ones with the sharp edges. Like the time my dad and I went on that fishing trip to Michigan. Or the memory of baking cookies with my mom. The chair never comes for those memories.

Just the one of her and the one of the other world. A world with grass so green it glows and dance in the wind like a worm on a hook—

the soil made of crystals that reflect like glass. Rivers of beautiful amethyst water tunnels through the streets and the white stone castle that sits on a hill.

Those memories go back much further than the one of her. They are imbedded much deeper than hers.

Squeaking from the door opening catches my attention. I force both memories away as I continue to lie down on my cot. My cell is deep beneath the earth so there are no windows. Yet, I can still keep track of time, and I know this is not when I usually have visitors. Shutting my eyes, I even out my breathing to imitate sleep.

"No word on the females from the C site yet?" Dr. Craven asks. She runs this facility they have me trapped in. I have yet to see her face, but I know her voice.

"No. Not yet. Strong did a shitty job backing up all his files. We lost all the women in his breeding facility." This voice belongs to a man. It is new to me.

"I told you from the beginning Ryder Strong was absolutely crazy," Dr. Craven says as her footsteps draw nearer to my cell.

"Yes, you did. I'm glad I followed your advice on making him think he was the only one creating super soldiers."

Craven laughs. "Strong was a psycho narcissist. He needed to believe he was special."

"I have to hand it to him though. Those soldiers he made were fantastic." the male voice says in awe.

"Hmm. My soldiers are capable of the same; they just don't know it. And it's best that way. Plus, my soldiers have been successfully integrated into society unlike the animals Strong created," From the tone of Cravens' voice, I can tell she's angry. I think the male has offended her in some way.

"What do you think made the difference?" the man asks.

A chuckle from her. "It's simple really. But I wouldn't expect a man to know. While Strong was so busy trying to create outstanding soldiers, he forgot the most common thing in creating humans. They need love. That's why each of my soldiers are given memories of loving parents at the time of creation. It's those memories of love and being loved that makes us human. It's why my creations are so accepted in society."

"And you're sure that when we need them, they will be up for the challenge?"

She chuckles. "Don't worry, Steward Scott. Every one of my sleeper cells are fully equipped and trained by professionals. They can run circles around Ryder's beasts."

"It isn't Ryder's beasts you are up against anymore."

"Oh, that's right, they all died." There is a pause in the conversation and the footsteps. "How is Mason doing?"

"Dr. Hammond has one of the most successfully ran compounds. Not one incident report since he created his soldiers. However, the man gives me the creeps."

Craven harrumphs. "I haven't seen Mason since we got a piece of that meteor five years ago. He was quite polite and shy from what I remember."

"Well, he's changed," the footsteps pick up again. This time they are so close I know they will be coming near my cell soon.

"So," The male, Scott, she called him says. "Why did you bring me down here?"

Their steps stop at my cell bars. I don't open my eyes to look at them, instead I continue to pretend I'm sleep.

"This is Logan Stryker. He was my first successful creation. After him, much like I learned after studying Strong's notes about his subject 0041, the others came."

"Why is he locked up?"

She sighs. "He's going through a little memory modification. It seems Stryker got a little sidetracked and we are helping him get back on course."

"I see. And why am I here?"

"Do you remember the soldier of the DNA you brought me?"

"Yes. It was from Strong's best soldier. He called him Alpha. Were you able to duplicate the strand—"

"No." Craven says, cutting him off quickly. "I told you, their DNA is entirely too complicated and complex to clone. Which is why the only option Strong had was to breed them. However, I brought you here because studying the DNA and comparing it to my soldier's, I noticed some similarities. Your soldier's DNA and this soldier's DNA share 65 % of the same genetic variants."

"What are you saying, Nancy?"

Craven huffs. "I'm saying, Strong's Alpha and my Stryker are brothers."

ACKNOWLEDGMENTS

This one is truly for the readers. You guys spoke, and I listened. Thank you for riding with me for so long. I appreciate all your support. You guys keep me going.

To the crew, I couldn't have done it without you. Thanks for the love and laughs.

To my husband, who is my protector and my cheerleader, thank you for everything. And last, but never least, to my three babies. All I do, I do for you.

ABOUT THE AUTHOR

Tiya Rayne is an avid reader and writer. She has an unhealthy relationship with coffee and is known to hide numerous bags of jellybeans around the house. When she is not reading or writing—which is rare—she's trying to master this thing called parenting. She is married to her high school sweetheart, and they live in North Carolina with their three—subjectively wonderful—children. Tiya also writes Young Adult Paranormal under the pen name KC Connor.

THANK YOU

Wait, there is more to come! You can stay updated with my latest releases, learn more about me, the author, and be a part of contests by subscribing to my newsletter at
www.TiyaRayne.com
If you enjoyed Sigma, I'd love to hear your thoughts and please feel free to leave a review. And when you do, please let me know by emailing me at TiyaRayne@gmail.com or leave a comment on Facebook
https://www.facebook.com/AuthorTiyaRayne/ or Instagram @AuthorTiyaRayne

Until the next time.
Bye!